BEDBUGS

CAN YOU SEE THEM?

LEE ANDREW TAYLOR

CONTENTS

In 1947, after news spread about a possible alien find in Roswell, New Mexico, USA, a UFO fell from the sky, plummeting deep into the soil of a small town in the UK.

Five people died that night...

PROLOGUE

*"Night, night, sleep tight, and don't let the
bedbugs bite."*

I still remember that saying from when I was a young
boy; the words drilled through me, making me think
only of unpleasant things. I would tuck my fingers and
toes inside the bed covers at night just in case the bedbugs
showed up to nibble at them. Plus, lift the covers over my
head to hide so they would leave me alone. I didn't know
what the saying meant, but the words freaked me out.

It's amazing what parents say to stop their children from
climbing out of bed during the night.

It worked on me, but my parents never seemed frightened
by the saying, and that got to me.

If they didn't sleep tight then surely the deadly bedbugs
would get them?

I was young, and not wise enough to work it out, but now
I'm older and much wiser.

The reason why I'm remembering the past, and

remembering the old saying is because of the deaths of five people from my neighbourhood. They were killed in the summer of *1947*, the year of the so-called Roswell, alien landing.

My grandfather was eight years old then, but I still remember the story he told me back when I was a youngster. It was a story about one night that left behind brutally slaughtered bodies. He said the police couldn't explain the murders and so to this day are still noted down as being unexplainable, unsolved crimes.

Those thoughts have been buried within the tombs of my mind for such a long time, so why are they suddenly rising to haunt me?

The year is *2020*, and I am a thirty-year-old Police Chief Inspector.

There's been a wave of gruesome murders in my district, with the victims being hideously butchered like the unsolved ones back in *1947*.

It's something I've never witnessed before.

Their deaths are causing concern and are hard to solve.

But why am I thinking about my childhood? And those awful deaths?

The answer is simple and could be staring me in the face without me knowing. What did happen to those unfortunate ones in *1947*?

I need to go back to the beginning, back to when my grandfather was young, but I can't go back in time. Still, I need to find a way to solve the mystery behind those murders and the ones from today.

I sit holding my head, thinking about the deaths from the past and the ones from the present, but what do they have to do with the bedbugs saying? What if that saying was real?

Someone, somewhere had to come up with it, so why did they?

Do the Bedbugs truly exist?

CHAPTER ONE

JANUARY 2020: ONE HOUR AFTER LEMONSVILLE COUNTY IS ROCKED BY A SMALL EARTH TREMOR

"Is it bedtime, Mummy?" little Tommy said, as his eyelids flickered from pure tiredness.

"Yes, it is, sleepyhead. You look exhausted."

Wendy knew she shouldn't have kept her son up after *7:00 pm*, but today was a special day. It was Tommy Junior's birthday and he was six years old.

"Come on, let's get you to bed before you fall asleep on the sofa."

"Where's Daddy?"

"Daddy had to work tonight. He'll check on you when he comes in. I'll make sure of it."

"Do you think he heard that tremor?"

"Probably. But it was only a tiny one. They are so rare here, so don't let it worry you..."

Tommy yawned; the sound acting like an alarm clock to Wendy to show he was ready to sleep. She smiled as she removed the birthday hat from his head, wiping away cake stains from his Spider-man pyjamas before lifting him off the sofa.

"...Wow, you are heavy this evening," she said laughing.

"That's because I had two pieces of cake."

Wendy laughed again as she carried Tommy towards the stairs, turning on the upstairs light, but her arms ached once reaching the landing. She felt Tommy's head dig into her chest, sensing he was almost asleep as she entered his bedroom, but he gulped after looking across the hall at the bathroom. It worried him to visit that room after going to bed because the darkness would strangle his mind into thinking scary things, so he got down to use the toilet.

A few months ago it was the shadows flashing across the bedroom wall that scared him, with most nights keeping his parents awake by screaming that an evil being was inside his room. It took a while before Tommy's father could convince him that all was okay, but even now, as Wendy watched him leave the bathroom, her thoughts were split on whether or not there would be another frightening challenge for them to solve.

Tommy got into bed to hug his favourite teddy bear, his eyes closing as soon as his head hit the pillow. Wendy smiled as she leaned over to kiss him goodnight, but Tommy burst into life again, not wanting her to leave without narrating a story.

"Okay, I'll tell you a quick one, but then you need to sleep."

"I will." Tommy yawned again before saying, "Tell me the story about the girl with the porridge."

Wendy sighed after thinking back to how many times she'd told him the tale, but Tommy still struggled to name the title.

She walked over to a bookcase, switching on the Spider-man lamp resting on top to light up Tommy's face before removing the book and sitting on the edge of the bed. She opened it and began to read, but Tommy's eyelids shut before she ended the second page.

She closed the book and kissed him on the forehead before returning it to walk back to the door.

"Night, night, sleep tight, and don't let the bedbugs bite," she whispered.

She hadn't said those words before when taking Tommy to bed but still remembered them from when she was a child. She smiled whilst watching him drift off into the land of nod, her mind going back to a time when she was young when her mother said the same saying. She remembered being around the same age as Tommy, picturing her mother calmly saying the words to her, but as she walked out the door, the words left an essence of mystery and worry. To Wendy's mother, the *'bedbugs'* sounded just like any other bedtime saying, but to Wendy, it sounded like scary bugs biting you if you never slept well.

She hoped Tommy wasn't frightened by the words but had a feeling he never heard them.

She looked over at him again before closing the door, her footsteps heard as she walked downstairs and turned off the light.

———

An eerie, dark shadow of a thousand tiny insects emerged from underneath Tommy's wardrobe; a compact shape like an army of ants gliding in unison along the carpet, staying out of the light. It watched him dangle a hand over the side of the bed; his fingers swaying to attract its attention to close in, but it stopped inches away before one of the insects leapt up to smash the bulb inside the lamp. Tommy never woke, even though the room was dark, but he did stir after a few bugs jumped on his hand to make him itch, stabbing needle-like pricks into him to force his eyes to shoot open from the pain. He tried to move, but couldn't, his voice silent upon failing to scream. He stared at the ceiling wondering what the dark was doing to him, thinking it was just a strange dream, a crazy nightmare. But the pain brought him back to reality.

The insects clung to his skin like staples on a magnet, biting deep to release tiny streams of blood as his eyes took photos of pain and torment. He could feel every bite as pleading tears slid onto the pillow, but his desperation to catch a glimpse came to nothing as his fingers tore from the knuckles to land in a pool of blood on the carpet. The bugs stripped the skin from his hand like piranhas attacking their prey, the agony leaving Tommy almost swallowing his tongue.

He felt bugs touch his face, crawling over his mouth to slip between his lips; his eyes bulging in fear as they jumped off his teeth to slide down his tongue. He tried again to scream but the silent words made him feel like a television programme on mute.

The insects violently bit into his body organs, shredding them with razor-sharp teeth to disembowel him quickly before moving on to attack his abdomen wall. They ripped through fatty tissue with ease until small holes appeared on his stomach, blood trickling out to produce a red-coloured painting.

The bugs appeared out of the holes, forming into the shadow again before scurrying over the newly decorated bedsheets to glide along the carpet. They sensed a vibration coming from downstairs, so slipped underneath the bedroom door to reach the landing.

———

Wendy sighed as she tidied the living room, picking up wrapping paper, cups and plates used at the party before tiredly sitting down to watch TV. She listened out for Tommy, smiling because he hadn't woken up, turning off the lampstand to slowly close her eyes as the ghostly shadow crawled along the wall leading down the stairs. It split in two, with one part entering the kitchen as the other closed in; the sound of Wendy's breathing acting like a calling card for the insects to quickly find her. They nestled on the arm of the sofa, close to her feet, but didn't attack. They just waited for the other group to arrive from the kitchen before linking up again to form a human shape.

But someone whistling disturbed them, causing them to vanish.

Wendy woke to the sound of her husband entering the living room, unaware of how close to death she was. She rubbed her eyes as *Tommy Senior* turned on the main light, noticing him drained of energy as he collapsed into a chair opposite. She smiled, happy to see him home.

"Hi, love, did little Tommy go to bed okay?" he asked, glad to be finally sitting down.

"Yes. He stayed up for an extra hour," Wendy replied, rubbing her eyes again. "He thinks he's a big boy now."

"Wow!"

"I told him you'll check on him when you came home."

"No worries. I'll do it now." Tommy slowly got up and left the room, but popped his head back inside to say, "I'd love a cup of coffee."

"Okay." Wendy smiled again as he left.

Tommy Senior switched on the upstairs light before walking up the stairs to near his son's room, listening out for noise and grinning at the silence. He gripped the handle, opening the door a few inches to allow a thin beam of light to shoot across little Tommy's face.

"Are you asleep? It's Daddy," he whispered.

He stared at his son, spotting his eyes open, thinking he was still awake.

"...Hey, son, I'm back from work..."

He became annoyed, thinking he was being wound up after no words arrived back, his tiredness causing him to lose patience. He huffed as he opened the door wider, the light from the landing now covering a quarter of the room.

"...Speak to me. Stop messing about..."

Tommy Senior stared at the lamp. He was pleased that his son had finally slept with the light off but was still confused as to why he wasn't blinking and wasn't speaking.

"...Wow! You must be a big boy now if you don't need a light on anymore," he said, hoping this time to receive a reply.

He waited for a response, a blink, something that would soothe his growing annoyance, but still, nothing arrived.

He entered the room, becoming worried as he neared the edge of the bed, but the sound of something crunching beneath his feet startled him into bending down to search the floor. He stared hard into the darkness still occupying that part of the room, sweeping a hand across the carpet to be covered with a sticky liquid that made him cringe; scowling towards the bed as he wiped it against his trousers.

"...Bloody hell, son, I hope you haven't wet on the floor."

He swept the carpet again until touching something that made him shiver; the feeling unlike any of his son's toys. He picked it up, his eyes bulging as he drew it closer to his face, almost puking after seeing a finger in his palm. He staggered backwards to crush more glass from the broken bulb, shocked as he rushed back to the door to smother the light switch with a bloodstained hand. He switched it on to see the red-stained bed covers, crashing down against the door as Wendy shouted, "Your drinks ready. What's taking you so long?..."

She walked the stairs to find him on his knees; the finger still in his hand.

"...Hey, what's wrong?" she asked.

Tommy stared at the digit as sweat poured down his face; the moment leaving Wendy to think he was about to have a coronary. She panicked, following his vision until seeing what he was holding; shivering as she closed in to hear him cry.

"...What have you done to yourself?" she said; her eyes filling with tears.

She counted Tommy's digits after the finger dropped to the floor; her mouth quivering after realising it wasn't his before slumping down beside him.

"...Jesus, what have you done?!" she screamed.

She shook as she forced herself to look inside the bedroom, her stance weak after rising from the floor to push Tommy away. She slowly entered the room, crying hard after staring at her son's face, his lifeless eyes killing her on the inside. She screamed again after seeing more of his digits on the carpet before the sight of the blood-soaked bed covers hiding his tortured body caused her to choke. She glared at her husband's broken shell, angry for having to be the strong one. She felt faint as she reached the end of the bed, but the sight of her son's feet with missing toes forced her to leave the room.

"...*AAAAAAAAARGHH*! No, not my boy, please, NO!" she shouted, slapping her husband's face.

Tommy Senior hugged her tight as the crying continued, his body almost collapsing as he scanned the room. He let go of her and entered, leaving Wendy to watch him like a hawk as he walked back to the bed. His knees buckled after spotting the wetness from his son's tears on the pillow, gulping from the pain of knowing that young Tommy cried whilst being butchered to death. He glared at Wendy, but the emotion passed quickly after realising she wouldn't let their son come to harm without a fight.

But why didn't she hear our son scream for help?

He pulled the covers away, squirming after seeing his son's ribcage; his legs weakening even more before disappearing behind the bed to puke on the carpet. Wendy almost did the same after seeing him reappear looking white as a ghost, his eyes trance-like as he became lost in his morbid world. He froze, leaving Wendy the only hope of raising the alarm.

She retreated quickly down the stairs, close to falling until pressing a hand against the wall to stop, blinking fast to wipe tears away as she reached the phone. But the horror from the bedroom echoed inside her mind to slow down the call. Wendy was emotionally drained as she held the phone to dial the number, her hand trembling at the sound of someone speaking on the other end. But she was in no fit state to talk as more words penetrated her eardrums.

"Hello, this is Marion. You've reached the Lemonsville County Police Station. How may I help you this evening?..."

Wendy desperately tried speaking, but still couldn't do it.

"...Hello, can I help you? Is anybody there?"

Wendy needed to stop the emotional train of thoughts, but they kept on coming.

Marion spoke again after hearing a whimper; her soft tone now relaxing Wendy enough to speak.

"My son is dead."

CHAPTER TWO

arek Chikowski, a twenty-four-year-old police constable who originated from Poland, drove a rundown police car along the snow-drenched roads. Beside him was his partner, *Nini Chan*. A pretty, petite, Chinese woman in her early thirties. She had graduated from the police academy with Marek after accepting a position to come to the UK five years ago; a decision her parents made after her country was in ruins from the war of *2015*. Her family had been lucky, but Nini knew they wanted her to have a better future after watching them rebuild their house again.

Global warming was the main reason for the war in Asia, becoming worse and worse as each year passed. The Chinese government pleaded with nearby countries to help, but the extreme conditions had most of them scared, so, instead of trying to solve the problem they ended up bombing the most troubled. The bombing ceased after they also faced extinction, leaving billions of people to become millions overnight.

———

The police car sped towards the house, sliding from side to side as the siren blared. Nini slapped Marek for his reckless driving, but he just winked at her as he entered the road the caller lived on.

"I bet you never imagined working in the same town as me after our wonderful time at the academy," Marek said, smirking.

"I wouldn't go as far as saying it was wonderful. More like annoying," Nini replied, bouncing around in her seat.

"You loved it really." Marek waited for a reply but Nini just shook her head. "Whatever then...And anyway, that quake probably spooked the caller. You wait. When we get there it will be a false alarm."

"Hopefully."

People twitched their curtains as the flashing blue light lit up their living rooms, with most feeling annoyed or confused that a car was speeding through town.

Lumps of ice and snow were crushed from the edge of the road as Marek pulled to a stop outside the house; the siren off as he stared awkwardly at Nini zipping up her padded jacket before sighing as he watched her put on gloves.

"Are you ready now?" he said, looking out across the deserted street.

"Yes, I'm ready," she replied, placing on a Cossack-style hat. "Looks like January's weather isn't easing off."

"Nope."

"If I wanted snow, I would've stayed in my own country."

Marek nudged her. "No, you wouldn't..."

Nini laughed as she exited the car, her pace slow to avoid slipping. But, after seeing Marek's legs almost part on the icy pavement, she laughed again. She moved over to help him but his annoying stare stopped her.

"...Leave it. I'm fine."

"It's not my fault you slipped," Nini said, turning to close in on the house.

Marek huffed as he reached her. "It looks like we've been called out to a hoax," he said after seeing no activity.

"You may be right." Nini looked through the front window, noticing a light was on between the gap in the curtains. "I can't see anyone, but we'd better do our job just in case."

Marek watched her near the door before straying to see residents shiver on doorsteps trying to catch a glimpse of what was happening. He ushered them back inside but knew it would take more effort to persuade them.

"If no one answers soon then I'm off," he said after Nini knocked loudly on the door.

"You can't do that, Marek. If we leave and someone is dead, like Marion said, then we're in trouble."

Marek lacked patience. He was cold, nervous, and, after seeing Nini look snug with her hat on wished he had brought his own. He flapped away falling snow, feeling guilty for wanting to leave.

"Okay, but if no one comes soon then I'm off around the back to find a way in."

Nini touched his arm, thankful he didn't go back to the car. She knocked on the door again until her ears twitched from the sound of someone opening it, but the vision of a woman wearing smudged makeup left her flabbergasted. Wendy appeared aged, her eyes motionless as she fought with the recent events unfolding inside her troubled and smashed-to-pieces mind.

"Did you call the police, dear?" Nini asked, noticing Wendy stare right through her.

"We received a phone call at around eight-fifteen this

evening," Marek said, flapping more snow away. "It was made from this address. Did you make that call?"

Wendy shook after Marek's question made her feel asphyxiated, her mouth opening to speak silent words. She reached out and grabbed him, causing him to panic; leaving him lost with what to do next.

"My son is dead."

Nini held onto her before she collapsed, helping her back inside the house as a flashback of the *war* caused her to shed a tear. It was memories of the young casualties, with most in pieces on the ground around her feet. She hugged Wendy, feeling the same kind of pain, but Marek could only watch on, feeling useless as he stood by the door.

Wendy stared at the staircase, her mouth quivering like she'd seen a ghost. Nini let go to watch her near it, seeing her point to the top.

"Is he up there?..."

Wendy remained pointing, oblivious towards Nini's question; her tears dripping to leave Marek feeling a sad gulp in his throat.

"...It's okay. You don't have to go up with us." Nini touched Wendy again, but this time she flinched. "We'll find him. You stay here."

Marek shook his head and released his weapon. He was eager for some action, but Nini looked at him confused.

"Better to be safe than sorry," he said, holding the latest in design weaponry.

Nini smiled and agreed, releasing her gun to see Marek move onto the first step. She stared at her weapon, smiling at its slick shape, pleased to be finally carrying the latest version of the handgun, a weapon that could fire an electric current ten times more powerful than a taser. It was a new way of fighting crime.

The police uniform belt had many snazzy gadgets on it, with night vision goggles, gas pellets, and a slim-line torch all included with the gun. The officers had gas masks tucked into the front pocket of their jackets just in case the pellets were needed, but so far no one had used them, and neither had they used the blowtorch mode on the torches.

This was the future for the police force, meaning they could do more without having to call for backup.

They punched in numbers to decode the guns before slowly walking the stairs; Nini nervously behind Marek, expecting someone to jump out at them. She turned to see Wendy still staring, whispering - "Wait there" before following Marek to the top. But the words 'my son is dead' made each step harder to climb.

Marek jumped after the vision of Tommy Senior kneeling by a bedroom door scared him. "Hey, pal, are you hurt? Your hands are bleeding," he said approaching.

Tommy Senior stared at him, his eyes flickering like he was still living in another world. His skin colour was pale and his hair a frosty white. It reminded Marek of the 'Doc' from the movie - Back to the Future. He was close to laughing but Nini punched him in the arm to stop him.

"You can put that away now," she said, glaring at his gun.

Marek grunted as he typed in the code to turn it off, re-holstering the gun to almost pull it back out again after seeing the finger on the floor.

"Jesus Christ! Nini. What happened here?"

He bit his lip; his hand trembling as he picked up the finger; his eyes fixed on the bedroom doorway until looking inside. Nini did the same, witnessing the bed of death, bringing a stinging pain to her throat. She gulped hard, thinking it was a ritual killing, a sacrifice to some form of Devil. She waited for Marek to step inside, but he couldn't do it, his feet turning cold like they were made of ice to prevent him from moving. Nini stared at young Tommy's empty eyes, her heart bursting with sadness as Marek seemed lost with what to say.

He glared at Tommy Senior as his mind tried working out what he'd just seen, grabbing him and pulling him off the floor to shove him hard against the door.

"I hope you can hear me, you fuckin' scumbag!" Marek screamed, clenching a fist. "What did you do to your kid?!"

He bounced Tommy off the door again as the words smashed into him, but Tommy remained speechless; the words not affecting him. Marek desperately wanted a reaction so he could hit Tommy, so slammed him against the door again. But Nini jumped in between them.

"Hey, there's no need for the agro. He's out of it," she said, pushing Marek away. "Let's just arrest him if that's what we're going to do."

"Arrest him? I want to punch him for what he did."

Nini pushed Marek again. "We don't know what happened, so let's just take him in." She shook after glancing at the bed again. "I can't stick it up here any longer. It's making me feel dreadful."

Marek agreed with her before glaring at Tommy again.

"I'm going to arrest you. Anything you say will be..."

"Where's the rest?" Nini asked, looking at Marek oddly.

"There's no need for me to say the rest. Look at him. I doubt if he'll be saying anything."

Tommy's face shuddered as he stared into the bedroom, but the touch of Marek's hand on his shoulder made him blink to look away. He turned slowly to follow Nini back down the stairs, his eyes locked on Wendy as she remained in the same spot. It freaked Nini out as she neared her, but she refocused again after snapping her fingers to gain Wendy's attention.

"You need to come with us to the station," Nini said. "We can have a nice chat there."

She pulled gently on Wendy's arm until she followed her towards the door, but Nini knew it would take a while before Wendy looked anyone in the eyes again.

"She'll need to put this on before going outside," Marek said, reaching the bottom of the stairs to lift a coat from a hook in the hallway and tossing it to Nini. "It's freezing out there."

"Wow! You do have a caring side," she replied, placing the coat around Wendy's shoulders.

"Sometimes." Marek grinned, glancing at Tommy. "But he doesn't need one."

Nini watched Tommy slump against a wall, his padded work jacket softening the fall as he almost fainted. She shook her head, keeping an arm around Wendy as she opened the door, but the sight of people gathered in the street shocked her. She noticed most of them wearing extra layers of clothing like they planned to be outside for ages, whilst others held hot flasks and heated pads. She sighed as Marek pushed past her with Tommy; his eyes avoiding the bystanders so as not to answer any questions. He rushed the frail father to the police car, grimacing as the onlookers closed in.

"Hey, if you want to remain out here in the cold then it's your stupid fault, but we have a job to do..."

Nini walked Wendy towards the police car, ushering the people away to reach it. She saw Marek open the door before escorting the parents into the back seat, but their motionless sight convinced the bystanders that all wasn't right. Nini became swamped amongst their bodies, her tiny stature disappearing from Marek's view.

"...Just go home!" he shouted. "Nini, are you okay?"

He saw her appear again as her raised hand gave him an answer, but a tall man broke from the group to near him, closely followed by his wife and son.

"What's going on?" The man said, tapping on the car window. "Why are you arresting Mr and Mrs Tanker?"

"Just let me do my job," Marek replied, feeling agitated as he struggled to cope.

Nini saw Marek's hand close in on his weapon, so quickly shouted towards the father, "Please! Go back into your house," before ushering Marek away to point for him to enter the car. "They're helping us."

"Helping you with what?" the wife asked, pressing her face against the glass.

Nini avoided the question, but the wife knew the answer after seeing tears fall from Wendy's eyes.

"...What's happened to little Tommy?!" she screamed.

Again, Nini refused to answer, so the wife prodded her in the chest.

"Stop doing that or you'll be arrested."

"Arrested, like the Tankers?" the wife asked.

"I've just told you they are helping us. That's all you need to know."

Marek opened the driver's side door, feeling the urge to reach for his gun again. It was all getting too much for him.

"Are we going or what?" he said, nervously touching his gun.

Nini waited for the wife to prod her again, but she burst into tears and hugged her husband.

"You go," Nini said to Marek. "I'll wait here for assistance."

He huffed as the family walked away, but the husband swiftly returned to spit at the car.

"I hope you burn!" he shouted, sneering at the couple in the back seat.

"You sure you don't want me to stay?" Marek asked Nini as he moved the husband away.

"No, I can handle it," she replied, glad to see the husband hug his wife again. "Just get them to the station."

"Okay. No worries. See you soon," Marek said, entering the car.

He turned the key, glancing at the dead boy's parents before driving off to leave Nini covered in slushy snow from the spinning tyres. She shook her head to release some from her hat, feeling annoyed as she saw the husband glare at the Tanker house as he kept his wife close, knowing his anger would spread amongst the others soon if he didn't go home.

"Move along. There's nothing to see here," Nini said, escorting the family away.

"But where's little Tommy?!" the husband shouted.

Nini looked to the ground as the sight from the bedroom flooded her mind again. "Please, it's freezing out."

The husband glared at the house again as his wife pulled on his arm. "She's right. It is freezing," she said, reaching out to grab her son. "Let's go home."

The husband spat in the snow, cursing under his breath as Nini watched him with caution. She sighed, happy he didn't do more before taking his family home.

She waited for them to re-enter their house, the street becoming invisible to people again as doors closed all around her. She shivered, not because of the weather but because the reality now hit her. She knew she had to go back inside the house to wait for the medics, knowing the street would fill again with anxious people once they arrived.

She stared at the open door but fear washed over her as she reached it before entering the house to shut out the outside to well up with tears after the stairs came into view. She wiped them away and walked into the living room, standing by the window to feel nerves race through her, viewing the street to wait for stage two of 'operation child slaying.'

———

Marek parked the car outside the police station, annoyed that the married couple were still silent. He stared at them through the rear-view mirror, shouting for them to get out. But neither moved. He exited, grimacing as he opened a backdoor to wait for the couple to unbuckle, but they did nothing. He cursed, leaning into the car to do it before waving his arm like he was guiding traffic on the road. The couple got out like they were heroin addicts; their movement drained of energy. But Marek's patience was fading fast and he just wanted them inside the building. He held them close as he walked them through the main door; the night staff looking on puzzled as they passed. Some shrugged as Marek entered an empty room; the door shutting as soon as the couple were inside.

"Wait here. I don't want you going anywhere."

He watched them sit at an interview table, their stony stares a reminder that they wouldn't be leaving as he exited the room.

"Who you got in there?" an officer asked, walking down the corridor.

"You'll find out soon enough," Marek replied, glancing down the hall. "Do you know where Dan is?"

"Yeah. He's sorting some files out," the officer said pointing. "You've just missed him."

"Cheers."

The officer peered through the small window of the interview room, looking curious as he nodded and walked away.

Marek swallowed hard as sad thoughts of the recent event reminded him of why he was where he was.

He turned a corner to see *Dan* leave the filing room, staring inside a folder as he walked.

"Hey, chief!" Marek shouted. "I need your help with something."

"Oh, you do, do you." Dan closed in on him. "Has it got anything to do with the phone call Marion took?"

"You are good. You don't miss a thing."

"Nope. That's why I'm the chief and you're not." Dan laughed, slapping Marek on the back.

"I've arrested the parents of the boy who was murdered."

Dan's face dropped as the word 'murdered' stunned him. He wasn't expecting the call to be for real, but Marek wasn't laughing back.

"Where are they now?"

"In the interview room."

Marek hoped Dan could spin a magic web and get the parents talking, but a happy chief wouldn't be so happy once he too witnessed their frozen features.

———

TIME - 10.30 PM

Flashing lights got curtains twitching again as an ambulance pulled up outside the Tanker home. Nini watched from the window to see an unmarked police car stop close by, relieved to have some company. She hadn't left the living room since going back inside the house but knew she could be needed to return upstairs soon. She sighed, watching snowdrops land on the glass to block her vision.

The agonising walk back to the front door rocked her again as the stairs acted like a demon to attract her attention, but Nini closed her eyes and breathed deeply, opening the door to two men carrying briefcases.

Must be forensics, she thought, as the men trampled down falling snow on their way to the house.

Nini performed the best smile she could as two *medics* followed the men inside, but she flinched after seeing people stand on their doorsteps again, knowing it was a sign that trouble could erupt. She closed the door in the hope they would stay away but she somehow feared they wouldn't.

One of the medics sniffed, scrunching his face after the smell reminded him of the morgue.

"Fuck! Doesn't look good."

"It's not." Nini led them towards the stairs but her brow leaked sweat as she reached the bottom. "First room on the left."

"You not coming?" the medic asked.

"No," she replied, moving away to let them overtake her.

No more words followed as the men placed protective clothing over their bodies, hands, and feet before slowly climbing the stairs to reach the landing. But one of them cried out, "Oh my God! What's gone on here?"

Nini heard whispering and someone violently coughing. It was her cue to walk away and re-enter the living room.

CHAPTER THREE

A clock hanging on a wall in the house next door chimed midnight as two Russian brothers, who had been drinking alcohol for the past six hours, poured another vodka. They'd been hiding inside a friend's house for the past year, mostly getting drunk and avoiding the police for being illegal immigrants. Neither went outside, not even for a second.

Cain was the eldest by two years; the decision-maker that led to them escaping another war-torn country to flee to the UK. It was he who was the first to give in to the night; the vodka swallowed as he slammed the glass down on the coffee table. He burped, rising from his seat as his brother, *Abel* watched on.

Cain staggered as he tried to find a natural balance, swaying from left to right like he was on a ship in stormy weather to knock over picture frames laid out on the fireplace. He smiled, burped again and grabbed onto a chair.

"Эй, человек, я - прочь к кровати, я чувствую себя больным," he said, staggering towards the living room door.

"English, speak in English," Abel said, laughing.

"I hate this language." Cain rubbed his eyes. "Why speak it if we're the only people here?"

"Because we need to learn it just in case."

Cain yawned. "Hey, man, I'm off to bed. I feel sick."

"See, it wasn't hard to say," Abel said smiling, rushing down more vodka before adding, "You go. I'll be up soon."

"Yeah. You do that..."

Abel poured another glass, laughing even harder as Cain stumbled.

"...What you laughing at?" Cain asked.

"I don't know...Maybe I've drunk too much. Everything is spinning, and you look funny."

Cain laughed back as the words jumbled inside his head to become the greatest joke in the world.

His legs gave way to leave him falling face-first onto the carpet, his finger rubbing his lip to reveal blood.

Abel tried to help but regrettably was useless, as his attempt to get up caused him to pant like someone who'd just run a marathon. He sighed, sipping more vodka as Cain held his head.

"Hey, are you okay down there?" Abel asked, sighing again.

Cain rubbed his lip a second time, cringing after feeling a lump.

"I'll be fine. I've always wanted fat lips." He slowly got back to his feet, slobbering and burping some more as he wobbled towards the door. "I'm off to bed."

"Okay. I'll catch you up."

Abel smirked as Cain left the room before raising his glass to applaud Cain after hearing him fart whilst talking to himself.

"You okay out there?!" Abel shouted.

But no reply arrived as Cain reached the stairs to hear a *cat* meowing outside the front door.

"Go home!" he shouted at it.

"I am home," Abel replied.

"Not you. I was talking to the cat outside," Cain said, reaching for the hallway light. "We have no bulbs?!" he shouted, flicking the switch on and off.

"Nope...Told you yesterday."

"Okay," Cain replied, holding his ears after the cat screeched.

I hope it doesn't make noise all night.

He turned to walk up the stairs but stalled after more screeches drilled into him; his glare towards the front door lasting only seconds before deciding to ignore the cat and go to bed.

The shadow circled the feline, scaring it to retreat against the door; its claws digging into the wood in a frantic attempt to get inside the house before it was attacked. But the bugs smothered it, bringing it down on the doorstep before slipping inside the letterbox to follow the vibration of Cain's movements as he attempted to climb the stairs.

They watched Cain through the darkness, waiting for him to attempt the first step; his head pounding as he reached for the bannister. He gripped it until his knuckles turned white, his balance steady as he made it onto step one. But, as he stared awkwardly at the top, knew it was going to be like climbing a mountain to reach it.

He stood on steps two, three, and four with ease, but slumped and crashed his knees on step five, letting go of the bannister before banging his head on step nine.

The bugs closely followed as Cain climbed the rest of the stairs, creeping along the wall behind him to hide in the darkness.

He laughed as he reached the top, thinking he was some kind of hero as he staggered to his bedroom before bumping into the door and entering. He kicked it shut and collapsed on his bed, but the room spun to almost make him puke as he stared at shadows on the ceiling performing a puppet show inside his mind; taking a deep breath before closing his eyes.

The bugs crawled up the bed to slide over Cain's body before clinging to his face like a death mask to itch his skin. He spluttered and scratched his face, but his lips were stung. He tried to scream but his mouth was numb, his body now paralysed from a fluid released by the bugs.

Some crawled inside his nostrils, biting the bone until it cracked, his cheeks swelling fast to leave crimson-coloured lumps on his face. His insides shuddered from the fear of knowing where the bugs were heading, feeling them scurry towards his eyeballs before their razor-sharp teeth burrowed through the back of them; the dark juice escaping out the front to look like tears of blood sliding down his face.

The rest attacked his body to dismember him with the precision of a surgeon, leaving body parts resting on the bed like a blood-soaked jigsaw puzzle.

———

Abel finished his drink and lifted from his seat, but his legs struggled to maintain a straight line as he staggered towards the door. He reached it after taking a deep breath before composing himself to enter the hallway, listening out for Cain as he glanced at the stairs. But the sound of something thudding on the floorboards above caused him to trip on the first step.

"Sorry if I woke you, brother," he said, smiling.

He walked the stairs upon expecting Cain to shout at him,

but all was silent as each step became harder than the last. He reached the landing before falling back against a wall to stare at Cain's bedroom door.

"...Sorry..." he said again, placing a finger on his lips upon hearing something drip.

"...Hey! I hope you're not peeing on the floor!" he shouted, feeling confused as he knocked on the door.

He waited for Cain to shout back but the silence surprised him, so turned the handle and opened the door to see the moon through the open curtains in the room. But he froze after seeing blood drip off the side of the bed. He choked after seeing Cain's leg, with the boot still attached resting on the floor, knowing it was the reason behind the loud thud.

"...Cain!" was all he had time to say before bugs flew at him, sticking to him like he was a human flycatcher.

He swiped at them, feeling lost as to why there were so many; his drunken state slowing the process for his mind to convince him he was in trouble. He smiled, thinking it was some kind of a game, but, after glancing at the leg again, his thought quickly changed.

"...Hey, Cain. What is going on?!" he screamed, as bugs raced across his face to sting his mouth.

Abel panicked as his face became numb.

His hands lashed out to try to stop the bugs from biting him, but he was failing fast. He shook at speed to get rid of them but the pain he now felt made him tired. His legs became heavy as he crashed down against the base of the door; his heart pounding as the blood from his wounds excited more bugs to pounce.

One ripped off his right ear lobe as others avoided his tiring attempts to swat them and attacked his body, injecting him again, and again until he cried.

He rose from the floor in a final effort to escape, but his

body began to stiffen as bugs burrowed inside his skin, leaving him hopelessly digging fingernails into his face to try to capture them. But the more he tried, the faster they moved.

He fell like a cut-down tree, smashing his face against a wall as he toppled down the stairs; snapping his neck as he landed at the bottom before the rest of the bugs formed into the shadow again to float like a flying carpet towards him.

CHAPTER FOUR

Nini sat in the kitchen stirring a cup of tea for what seemed like the hundredth time since making it five minutes earlier, as her thoughts drifted to the murdered child upstairs. She believed his soul was floating above him, watching the men inside the room, hoping for a positive outcome to be able to leave. She was brought up that way, to assume that a murdered victim's soul would haunt the place of death until the culprit was found. That's why Tommy Junior's restless spirit wasn't able to go to heaven. It wasn't allowed to.

She heard the men walking about, their focus lacking as they tried to come to terms with what they faced. The occasional "What the fuck?!" "How did this happen?!" and "I feel sick," were the only words to come from them apart from actual vomiting and coughing.

She picked up a magazine off the table and flicked through the pages, hoping the distraction would prevent her from crying.

———

Cliff, a tall, clean-shaven man, with a fading head of hair was in charge of the forensics team. He had driven down from the city to meet up with *Rob*, a twenty-five-year-old newbie.

The medics consisted of *Terry*, a fifty-year-old man with a bushy beard, and *Gordon*, who had long, shoulder-length hair. He wore a bandanna but was now using it to cover his nose and mouth.

Cliff walked around the boy's bedroom, studying everything in sight, but was still confused as to what happened as the others closely watched on.

"Search for fingerprints to see if there was a forced entry, and check the carpet for unknown fibres and footwear prints," he said to Rob.

"And us? Do you need any help before we take the body away?" Terry asked.

Cliff stared at the boy again but looked away quickly after sad thoughts entered his mind.

"Sure. You can help search the carpet," he said, moving over to the bed. "Nini mentioned the parents were arrested but she isn't sure if they did this."

"But did they see who did this?" Gordon asked.

"Nope. That's why we have to be thorough." Cliff grabbed his case. "Now let's get to work."

Rob gulped before opening his own, reaching inside to hand Terry some test tubes.

"I'm sure you know what to do. Just put fibres, liquids, dirt etcetera into these." He then handed Terry a set of tweezers. "And use them."

"Gotcha," Terry replied, smiling as he handed the items to Gordon. "You heard the man."

Rob grabbed a fingerprint brush and some powder. "Do you want me to start with the door?" he asked Cliff.

"Yeah, while the others check the floor," Cliff replied.

"Then move onto the window and the bed frame. I'm going to examine the body."

Terry and Gordon knelt on the floor, but Gordon yelped like someone had just pinched him.

"What?!" Terry shouted, watching Gordon rub his knee.

Gordon picked up a small soldier, cringing as he threw it at a toy box. "Stupid thing. It dug into me."

"Have you finished messing around?" Cliff asked, unamused.

Gordon placed up a hand; his face red with embarrassment after Terry shook his head. He tried to ignore Terry as he searched the carpet but knew he and the others were watching him closely now.

Rob brushed the door on both sides, taking fingerprint samples as they appeared, but Cliff was struggling to examine the body; his breathing becoming erratic the closer he got to achieving it. He eyed the others, happy they hadn't noticed before taking a deep breath and opening his case.

———

Nini neared the end of the magazine, closing it to stare at the cup of tea, now cold, not touched. She groaned as another yelping sound emerged from upstairs as the words: "How many friggin' soldiers does he have?" grabbed her attention.

She stood and stretched her legs, hoping it'll all be over soon before grabbing her phone to dial the police station, happy to hear Marion's voice on the other end.

"Hey, is Dan free?" Nini asked, praying he was so she could receive a progress report.

"Nah. He's with the boy's parents." Marion waited for Nini to say something, but nothing arrived. "Why? Do you want to leave a message?"

Nini slowly walked over to the window to see house lights still on, as curtains constantly twitched. "Just tell him I'm still at the house."

"You sound tired."

Nini nervously laughed. "Tired is one word for it."

She almost dropped the phone after hearing a crash coming from upstairs, followed by the words: "Fuck me! If I kneel on another toy soldier again I'll scream."

"I heard that. What's going on?" Marion asked.

"It's the clean-up crew. Looks like they brought a child with them."

"Oh."

"Will be in touch once I know more about what's going on here."

Nini moved away from the window and disconnected the call, gulping after the one thing she didn't want to think about reappeared in her mind. She dreaded going upstairs but knew it was a possibility if the others didn't bring the body down soon.

———

Terry handed Rob the tubes containing what was found on the floor, as his eyes lit up after seeing the case fill with evidence. But Rob looked beyond Terry, shuddering as he handed him another bag.

"Use this for the fingers over there."

"Best give us two," Terry replied, pointing. "The boy's toes are by the other side of the bed."

"Fuck!"

They looked over at Cliff scanning an ultra-violet light over the bedding and mattress.

"You found anything worthwhile?" Terry asked.

"Still searching," Cliff replied, moving the light over the boy's body. "I think it's going to be a long night."

Terry felt emotional after placing the fingers inside a bag, his heart melting as he closed in on the toes. He thought only of his grandchildren, knowing some were around the same age as the deceased, his mind lost as to why this happened.

Gordon approached Cliff's case, reaching inside to grab a swab stick before swabbing the inside of his mouth.

"What are you doing?" Cliff asked.

"I'm looking for clues to help find the killer," Gordon replied, smiling. "I've seen them do this on TV."

But Cliff glared at him, shrugging his shoulders to say, "So, you think this is a joke?"

"Nope."

"Were you in this room at the time of the murder?"

"No. I was playing pool in the hospital canteen."

"Then why are you swabbing yourself? You dummy."

Terry whacked Gordon on the back. "What's got into you?"

"Sorry," Gordon replied, blushing again. "Tonight's just freakin' me out."

"It's freaking all of us out," Rob said. "Just do something constructive."

Gordon apologized again before returning to the floor.

He lay on his belly before sliding under the bed in an attempt to do something more constructive, but the others laughed at him for getting stuck. They watched the bed shake as Gordon wriggled free; his complexion burning from more embarrassment after returning to his feet. He gulped as the others stared at him like he had a bomb strapped to his chest before sweating when Terry pointed at his leg. He became scared, shivering as he slowly looked down, as a putrid stench wafted beneath his nostrils.

"Shit! It stinks," Gordon said, wiping away a patch of Tommy Senior's sick.

"Not that. What's on your thigh?" Terry asked.

Gordon flinched as he searched his other leg before laughing after pulling a sticky lollipop off his clothing.

"It's just a sweet," he said, sighing. "Probably belonged to the kid." He put it in his mouth. "Still got its flavour. Bonus."

"Why did you do that?!" Cliff barked.

"Sorry, mate, did you fancy a suck?"

Cliff snarled. "No, I don't. But I am concerned that the sweet hidden beneath your teeth could well be contaminated."

Gordon shrieked and spat it out. "Shit! Do you think it's infected with somethin'?"

"I wouldn't know now because you've wiped away all the evidence."

Gordon felt faint after Cliff's words made him choke, his stomach grumbling like it was telling him to get to the bathroom quickly. The others glared at him as he rushed out of the room.

"Why the hell did you bring him here?" Cliff snapped towards Terry. "He's a liability."

"Sorry. He's just shaken up. I will talk to him."

"You do that," Cliff replied, cooling down. "We have a job to do."

"But do you think he's infected?"

Cliff came close to cracking a smile. "No, but let him sweat on it for a while. It'll teach him a lesson to not touch things without asking me first."

"You got it. I'll keep it zipped," Terry replied, smiling.

"And anyway. Unless Kojak came here to kill the boy, I doubt the sweet had anything to do with what happened." Cliff reached inside his case, pulling out swab sticks before adding, "But that's not the point. Your partner should've thought before doing anything."

He turned to swab the inside of Tommy's mouth as Terry and Rob eagerly watched on, but the teeth dropped from the gums as soon as they were touched and the jaw collapsed. It shocked Cliff into backing away as Tommy's ribcage crumbled into tiny pieces.

"Was he attacked with acid?" Rob asked.

"No idea? But we need to find out," Cliff awkwardly replied.

He glared at Gordon as he snuck back into the room, studying him to see if he would act up again. But Gordon quivered after seeing Tommy's eyes sink into his skull.

"Are you okay?" Cliff asked.

"I'm sorry about the sweet. It's just, I need my sugar rush so couldn't resist."

Terry placed an arm around him. "You can be a right arse sometimes, but the sweet had nothing to do with this case."

———

Marek and Dan sat with the boy's parents, feeling frustrated by the lack of success. Dan had fired everything he had at them, every spoken threat and even the charge of murder, but neither was enough to penetrate their emotionless wall. They remained in the same docile state, not looking at the officers.

"Is everything I'm saying sinking in?" Dan asked, leaning over the table to glare at them before kicking his chair away.

But still, there was no eye contact and no sign of weakness from either parent.

"...You're both in serious trouble. You'll be going down for life for doing this to your son." Dan looked over at Marek and shook his head, knowing his plan was failing. "If I don't get them talking soon then this case could linger like a bad smell for weeks or even months."

"Shall I get a doctor in to check them out? They look freaked out to me," Marek said, trying to make Tommy Senior blink.

"Do what you want. I can't do anything with them."

Dan watched the parents closely as Marek left the room, eagerly waiting for a moment of weakness that would change the outlook of the investigation. But deep down he knew they were probably innocent.

They are way too gone to be playing mind games.

———

Marek raced over to Marion, rushing his words as he told her to phone the hospital. She became curious, knowing he was on edge; her hand reaching for the phone as he turned to race away.

"Is everything okay in there?" she asked nosily. "I could bring some tea and biscuits in."

"Everything is good. Just phone the hospital and ask them to send a psychiatric doctor. We need one fast. Dan needs the couple checked out."

"No problem. I'm on it." Marion placed the phone against her ear before saying, "Oh, can you let him know that Nini phoned? The medics and the forensics team are still at the house searching for clues."

"Nice one. Let's hope they find something soon."

Marek was gone again, leaving Marion to make the call.

He stepped back inside the interview room to find Dan staring out the window, his mind baffled as he shut the door.

"Is everything sorted?" Dan asked.

"Marion's on it. She said Nini called. The big boys are still with her."

"Good, good," Dan replied, turning from the window to scratch his head.

"What do we do now?" Marek asked.

"We wait. It won't take long before someone turns up from the hospital."

————

Charles West, a fifty-five-year-old, tall, thin man, arrived at the police station to be greeted by Marion. She smiled at him as he neared, pleased to see a smartly dressed man stand in front of her.

"I'm here to see chief inspector Daniel Boone," he politely said, holding a black, leather case.

"Yes. He's been waiting for you."

She showed him to the interview room, knocking on the door to the sound of Dan saying, "Come in..."

Charles bowed his head to show his appreciation towards Marion, but his tiny spectacles almost fell off his face. Marion giggled, walking away to smile as he opened the door.

"...So, you're the psychiatric consultant?" Dan asked as Charles neared him.

"Yes, I am. Charles West is my name," he replied, snapping a finger in front of Wendy and Tommy. "How long have they been like this?"

"Since I picked them up from their house," Marek replied.

Charles sighed before releasing a small, medical torch from his pocket. He shone it in the eyes of the couple; his face scrunching after neither flinched.

"So, Charles, what's your verdict?" Dan asked.

"It's a tricky one," Charles said, facing him. "I've never

come across a case quite like this in all my experiences with traumatised people."

"What do you mean?"

"Well, it seems to me that both of them have witnessed something of a brutal nature, and, what they saw in that house cannot escape from their inner being because it's been burned into their eyes..."

The way Charles spoke fascinated Dan and Marek; his tone soothing them into believing anything he said. They watched him release a stethoscope from the case; his focus alert as he studied the couple.

"...Did you know your eyes could be used as a camera?" Charles said, placing the stethoscope on Tommy's chest.

Dan almost laughed, thinking he was joking, but Charles never smiled as he listened to Tommy's heartbeat.

"...Your vision acts as a lens, so, when you blink, you take a picture of what you last looked at." Charles checked Wendy's breathing but seemed happy as he returned the stethoscope to the case. "So, on occasions such as this one, the images could stay visible for up to twenty-four hours."

"Occasions? What do you mean by that exactly?" Dan asked.

"What I'm saying is fear or shock. A shocked expression is normally an expression caused by something that has sent fear through your body. Everything that's happening to them at this moment has slowed things down, including time, thereby producing this zombified appearance." Charles snapped his fingers again, but still, no reaction arrived from either parent. "There's my proof right there," he said, turning back to face Dan.

Marek remained quiet as he stood in the background waiting for Dan to take control again. But he wasn't. He was just lost with what Charles was saying.

"...You see how they both have this stare about them?..."

Dan and Marek nodded.

"...They aren't blinking, so aren't producing images." Charles released a notepad from his case, turning to a blank page. "Imagine blinking at a normal rate," he said, writing on the pad.

Marek closed in to stand next to Dan as the moment became too interesting to miss out. He became glued to what Charles was saying, his face happy and surprised like a child on Christmas Day opening presents. Charles had suddenly transformed into a teacher to Marek, his knowledge soaking into him until he understood the parent's condition.

"Go on," he said, hoping for more to come from Charles.

"You are constantly producing pictures, but eventually, the album inside your mind gets filled up."

"Then what happens?" Marek asked.

"Once it's full, the old pictures become lost and new ones take their place." Charles scrunched his lips at him. "Am I making any sense? Are you keeping up?"

"I think I follow you," Marek replied, rubbing his eyes.

"Well, imagine being shocked by something so bad that you became frozen by it. Your eyes aren't blinking that often now so the visions stored inside your head are still very much visible. What I need to do now is to find them and we'll have a breakthrough."

"And you think you can do that?"

"To be quite frank with you, I don't know, but I'll give it a go."

Charles turned back to face the couple as he tried again to produce a flicker of emotion. Dan watched him sit opposite to write words in his notepad, but the parents still didn't budge. It annoyed Dan even more and he cursed under his breath.

"Let's leave him to it," he said, nudging Marek. "Maybe they'll talk if we weren't here…"

Marek agreed, pleased to be leaving the room again.

"…We'll be outside if you need us," Dan said to Charles, opening the door to allow Marek through.

He waited for a response, but Charles just raised a hand.

———

Nini checked her watch to see it was past *three* in the morning before staring at the living room doorway in the hope that the men upstairs would soon be finished. She huffed as the room suddenly became colder; her heart tightening from thoughts of the boy's soul still being inside his bedroom. She zipped up her coat as the urge to leave the house crept up on her, moving towards the door to the sound of someone talking upstairs. She looked at the ceiling as the voice stopped, her hands sweating as she turned on the TV to see a woman in the right-hand corner performing sign language to a movie. She watched the woman wave her hands around as her mind tried to work out why the programmes for the deaf were on early in the morning.

Surely deaf people slept at the same time as non-deaf people?

She turned the TV off as a loud thudding echoed into the living room, the sound of feet constantly drilling into her coming from separate parts of the ceiling. She knew the men were wrapping up for the night, their movement increasing to make her smile.

She saw Rob slowly walk down the stairs; his lungs filling with fresher air as he reached the bottom. He held his briefcase tight as he nodded before Cliff arrived next, Nini noticing just how drained they were as they reached her. She was pleased to see them.

"Is everything sorted?" she asked.

"Pretty much," Rob replied. "The medics are bringing the body down."

"This is the easy part," Cliff said, putting his case down on the floor. "The hardest is seeing what will happen once the body has been removed from the house."

Nini knew he was right, but she was way too tired to think about the prospect of people still watching the activity unfold. She knew there would be some still interested in what was going on, but hoped that the minus degrees temperature would stall them in their attempt to find out more answers.

The sound of the medics moving swiftly to the top of the stairs brought a tear to her eye, the body bag hiding what was left of young Tommy coming into view as it was carried down. Nini bowed her head as they neared, the sadness creeping up on her to make her quiver. But she was thankful that the body was finally leaving the house. She waited for Terry and Gordon to reach the front door before opening it to let them out, as the freezing wind gripped her ears as she placed on her hat. She let the others pass before switching off the lights, the door closing behind her as another chill forced her to stare at the bedroom window.

Cliff turned to her as he followed the others onto the street, but she just waved as the sound of bystanders closed in. She moved quickly through the snow, shaking her head at the people, confused as to why they would risk catching pneumonia.

Most of them turned to go home after witnessing the body bag, the sight causing a few to cry as the medics placed it inside the ambulance. Nini placed on her gloves and watched on, but no one neared the medics. They just stared, knowing who was inside the bag.

She stood next to Cliff as the ambulance drove away, but her smile towards him freaked him out.

"Hey, could you drop us off at the station before heading back?"

Cliff hugged her, knowing she needed one. "No problem. Just climb inside," he said, opening the back door of his car.

CHAPTER FIVE

Hidden beneath the housing estate of Lemonsville County sat a damaged metal-like spacecraft, unnoticed by anyone since it fell from the sky seventy-three years earlier. After the Roswell incident in *1947*, no one seemed prepared for more aliens being on Earth, especially a UFO landing happening in the UK. But one had plummetted at such a speed, crashing through the ground to leave a crater the size of a football field.

It had left the townsfolk thinking about many possibilities, with the most probable one being some kind of earth tremor, but no one assumed it to be the actual outcome. Over the years, after finally forgetting about the crater, the area had been refilled to expand the town. And in *1990*, after the refill had cemented the land again, more houses were built on top.

———

The bugs appeared inside the UFO, scurrying closer to their queen, a large, slug-like creature of around eight feet in length. She had no eyes but sensed their location, smelling the blood still leaking from the body parts delivered after the bugs' recent kill. She had remained dormant all these years, only waking after the latest earth tremor shook the UFO, her strength now gone because her babies from seventy-three years ago never returned with food after murdering the five people. She could only produce two lots of babies in a lifetime without a male, so chose now to do it, the tremor now leaving an opening for her new breed to teleport easily.

She sluggishly moved towards the smell before whip-cracking a lance-like leg from her slimy body to skewer the cat's stomach, a faint 'meowing' sending a signal that it was still alive as it was pulled towards a toothless mouth in the centre of her body. She shrieked with pleasure after swallowing the cat, exciting the bugs to push the rest of the food towards her; her leg stabbing into an arm before sending it towards her mouth. She shrieked again after the rest of the body parts were devoured, sluggishly moving away to cough up a thigh bone before slumping back down.

———

Nini arrived back at the station. She shivered as she removed her hat and gloves before walking towards Dan's office, glad to see him still there.

"Welcome back," he said, waiting for her to tell him about the encounter inside the house. He knew it was going to be emotional.

Nini sat and watched him pour coffee into a cup; her face melting after appreciating the heat flowing through her fingers as he handed it to her.

"How was it?" Dan said, watching her flinch.

"It was nothing like what I'd ever seen before," Nini replied, sipping the coffee. "The poor boy was torn apart."

"Sorry, you had to see that on your first day here."

"It shouldn't have happened on any day," Nini nervously replied. "I don't want to see anything like it again."

Her emotion changed quickly after a reminder of seeing the bodybag caused her to flinch again. And Dan noticed.

"But do you think the parents are the killers?" he asked.

"No!" Nini swiftly replied. "I could tell just by looking at them. They were lost to what had happened."

"Yep. My thoughts exactly," Dan said, pouring another drink. He shook his head before adding, "So who did it then?"

Nini shrugged, sipping the coffee again. "There was no trace of anyone being inside his room. No sign of forced entry, no fingerprints, apart from the family, and no mess." She watched Dan sit opposite. "The room was untouched, chief, but someone had attacked the boy and left no evidence."

Dan rubbed his face as he waited for more to arrive, but Nini was out of words to describe the night. She sunk into her chair, wrapping her hands around the cup to remain warm.

"This is going to be a long night," Dan said, smiling with gratitude. "But you need to go home and get some rest. It's been a tough first day for you."

"I'm worried about the parents. How are they doing?"

"The psychiatric doctor is still here, trying to make a breakthrough. But, if nothing changes soon then I'll have to keep them under surveillance."

"You can't keep them here, chief, they need proper help."

"I know; that's why I think they should go to the hospital." Dan smiled again. "You're good at knowing what I'm thinking." He exited his seat and walked over to his desk, grabbing a folder with the words – Tanker Case – written on the front before adding, "But don't get too good at it or you'll be applying for my job."

"If your job means staying here for long hours then I'm happy with what I've got."

Dan choked on a laugh as he said, "Tonight's turning into a double shift, so it looks like my job is safe."

Nini finished off her drink before sliding the Cossack hat back on her head and leaving her seat. She tapped Dan's arm as she listened to the ice-cold wind blowing against the window; her cheeks puffed after feeling it slip through to touch her. She wasn't looking forward to stepping back outside.

"I'll leave you to it," she said, placing on her gloves. "I hope it's over by the time I return. I wouldn't be able to stomach another shift like this one."

———

The bugs returned to the surface, listening for the slightest of vibrations as they teleported from street to street. They sensed someone was nearby, their speed picking up as the dark shadow easily moved across the cold wind. But, the person closing in found the weather to be a struggle.

Peter Thornton was eighteen years old, a skinny teenager who was returning from a house party. He felt his bones freeze each time the wind touched him; a reminder that he should have stayed where he was until the morning. But his drunken state made him act like a fool. He wanted to impress his friends but was booted out of the house for fighting with the host. Now he was all alone and too drunk to know where he was.

The wind was so strong that it almost turned him around like a human weathervane; his coat held against his chin as he tried mapping out the direction to his home from within his mind. But it wasn't working and he was way off course.

The bugs watched him struggle to walk in a straight line, the shadow keeping out of sight as they circled him. They moved across the snow like they were floating on it; the circle keeping Peter inside as he kept walking. He swayed across the street as the circle tightened, wandering away from the houses to end up at an old abandoned play area. He staggered towards a swing, almost slumping to the ground before gripping onto it, not seeing the bugs close in as he sat down to squash the layer of snow resting on it. He rocked as his jeans became wet, but he didn't seem bothered by it as he choked and spat on the ground; staring at the bugs with a blurred vision to laugh after thinking that the drugs being passed around at the party had sent him on a strange trip. He laughed again and spat at them, but the bugs formed into a shape to hypnotise him.

He moved his eyeballs up and down before staring at it, still not taking it seriously; spitting once more before starting to sing. He pushed the swing back and forth; his croaking voice slurring out words from a song dated back to the eighties to drift towards a house across the street. Peter coughed at the sound of someone shouting at him, turning his head to see an elderly man lean out of a window acting furious for being woken up. But Peter waved in the man's direction before singing the song again.

"Hoy! Keep that fuckin' noise down!" the man bellowed.

Peter stopped singing and rubbed his eyes, the words surprising him as he stared hard.

"...Can you see me, you dumb fuck?" the man said, feeling more annoyed for letting the cold into his home.

"Shut up. You're just jealous because I can sing!" Peter shouted back.

"If you don't stop that awful racket then I'll come down and make you," the man raged at him.

Peter laughed harder and louder than before as the sound of the window slamming caught his attention. He noticed the man was gone, so smiled because he thought he'd won the battle, but, as he attempted to leave the swing, the smile faded. He couldn't move his legs. He tried and tried but they felt like logs stuck in the ground, his movement coming to nothing as he panted for air. He laughed nervously after glancing at his feet to see bugs swarming over his shoes; releasing tears as they crawled up his legs. He tried to shout but could only slobber after being pulled off the swing, his body tightening as he desperately dug his hands into the snow to slow down.

But he was now panicking as the bugs reached his stomach.

Their strength was too strong for him to fight back as he was dragged along the ground. And seconds later he disappeared, leaving behind just a line in the snow.

The elderly man appeared in the distance, gripping his walking stick tight, preventing him from falling over as he neared the swing. He searched for Peter but noticed he was gone.

"You better run, you fucker!" he hollered, rotating to look around. "Don't come back here if you know what's good for you."

He held the stick in the air, grinning like he was Rocky Balboa; the teenager fleeing because he had scared him off. But the stick quickly landed on the ground after he slipped on the ice; his legs wobbling as he turned to walk home.

CHAPTER SIX

The night was over and another day had taken its place as *Jonathan Shallow*, a forty-year-old, bald, athletic sergeant arrived at the station.

He looked around, surprised by the lack of communication, his usual greeting becoming lost in the silence from the other staff. He frowned as he walked into his office, feeling concerned to find notes stuck to his computer screen.

Last night must have been a busy one.

He peeled them off and stared at them, feeling angry after reading one; his mind soaking up the information about what happened last night.

Why wasn't I informed?

He raced from his office to see a constable close in, his heart thudding from thoughts of finding out more information. But the constable ignored him and headed towards another room.

"Hey, Ben!" Jon shouted. "Were you here last night?"

Ben Dover wasn't one of the finest recruits at Lemonsville police station, and, just like his partner, *Neal Down*, were classed as the two idiots of the force. Neal was next to Ben as Jon approached the room, readjusting a pair of spectacles as Ben replied, "No, I've just arrived with Neal."

Jon glanced at Neal in frustration, knowing it would be tough to get anything useful from either of them.

"Have you seen Dan anywhere?"

"Nope," Ben replied.

"Why? What's up?" Neal asked.

Jon looked them up and down after thinking back to the roster sheet of who was on duty last night. He knew they were scheduled on; his face burning with rage because they had probably been sleeping in the supply room when all the horror happened. He glared at them and frowned before turning to walk away.

"If you see him tell him I want a word."

They watched him rush back to his office, shrugging towards each other as they sat down.

"What did we miss?" Ben asked.

"No idea. But he looks mad."

Jon sat at his desk, staring at the notes again, as thoughts of it not being real washed over him. *But it had to be.* He knew the handwriting was Marion's but that didn't mean the two jokers he'd just spoken to wasn't trying to prank him. He rubbed his chin and read the note again about the young boy being murdered, stunned to see the next one mention the parents had been taken to the hospital. He almost collapsed, needing to find Dan urgently before glancing at a third note with the words - 'The printer needs more ink.' He cursed under his breath, throwing the note in the bin before leaving his office again, looking at his watch to see it was now *9:15 am.*

Where's Dan?

He began to worry, thinking something had happened to him, but, Ben arrived to say that Dan was coming in later.

"Why wasn't I informed sooner?"

"No idea. Marion's just told me. Said Dan's mother phoned."

"His mother? What did she say?"

"Something about him working through the night."

"Yeah, I figured that." Jon stared out the window before saying, "I'm off to the hospital. See if I can find out more about what's been going on."

"But Dan's at home."

"Jesus, Ben, you need to get on top of what's been happening. I'm sick of babysitting you and Neal."

Jon stormed past him but stopped after seeing Neal guzzling water from the staffroom drinks machine.

"Why's he doing that?!" he shouted, as Ben closed in.

"He's probably just thirsty," Ben said, smirking at Neal.

"What did you do?!" Jon yelled.

Ben's face exploded into patches of redness before caving to admit to putting hot sauce on Neal's toast. "Sorry. But it was funny."

"You need to snap out of this bullshit behaviour." Jon glared at Ben, but the moment almost caused him to lose focus. "This ends now..."

He watched Ben sneak off to smack Neal on the back after he suddenly began choking; his tongue still burning as Ben offered him a glass of water.

"...I need you both to go to the street where the incident took place," Jon said, walking towards the reception desk. "Just go house to house and gain information. I'll talk to Dan on my way back from the hospital."

"What incident?"

"Bloody hell, Ben, don't you check the computer for updates?"

"Do we have computers?" Ben replied as Neal took the glass.

"Mother fucker! Are you being serious?"

Ben smiled, hoping that Jon would finally do the same after knowing he was being wound up.

"It's cool. I'll find the address," he replied, worried after Jon's expression remained stern. "Speak to you later. We have this."

Jon gulped as he neared Marion, watching her shake her head towards the two fools. She knew they would probably mess it up.

"Just knock on a few doors, and write down anything that sounds like it could be vital. There's been a child killed so I don't want any fuckups," Jon finished, raising a hand before walking out the door.

———

The house on Cassidy Street was now being overrun by other members of the forensic department, so Neal and Ben never entered the house. But they did watch it for a few minutes to get an idea of just how frantic the situation was. They saw people go in and out looking tired and upset whilst noticing the police tape blowing in the breeze, but neither felt comfortable about going inside. They sighed, lowering their heads as they arrived next door, Neal knocking as he waited for someone to answer.

"Hello. Can I help you, officers?" a tiny, old lady said opening the door.

"Did you hear anything unusual last night?" Ben asked.

"Unusual?"

"Yes. Did you hear any loud noises coming from next door?"

The old lady stared long and hard at the house. "No, officer, I don't hear that well these days. And besides, I was in bed for nine."

"Okay. Thanks anyway."

One house down and another dozen or so to go, Ben thought as the lady shut the door.

Neal headed for the house on the other side of the Tanker house, almost bumping into one of the forensics team as he neared. He apologised quickly, not wanting to stay and chat as he reached the front gate. Ben caught him up as he neared the door but Neal stalled from knocking to gawp at the front step.

"What's up with you?" Ben asked, noticing Neal stare hard.

Ben slid his boot over the recent snow to see bloodstains on the concrete step, touching it to shudder as Neal banged on the door. He shrugged upon feeling the need to tell one of the forensics people, but Neal nudged him to say, "Forget about it. It's nothing," before banging on the door again.

Ben stared at claw marks engraved into the door, nervously cringing to work out what it was as Neal stopped knocking.

"...That's enough," Neal said; his patience drifting. "Two houses down. Got to keep moving."

He walked away but slowed down after seeing neighbours appear on the street, watching the forensics team go in and out of the Tanker house. But they suddenly looked over at him to make him panic. He wanted to hide, so ushered Ben closer as they approached.

"What's happening, officers?" a woman cried out. Whilst

another said, "What's going on with the parents? I saw them leave in a police car last night."

"Please get back. We need to do our job," Neal said, struggling to remain calm.

"I have the right to know. I live here, so what's happened?"

Neal couldn't find the words to tell her because he knew next to nothing about what happened last night, so blagged his way through the conversation.

"As far as we know there's been an incident, and we're just asking for help," he said.

"Please! You have to tell us what happened?" The woman pleaded, becoming teary-eyed as she gripped his arm. "I saw the ambulance take a body from the house early this morning," she cried out, pointing towards the Tankers. "The parents were escorted away long before that happened, so what's going on?"

Ben stepped in to help Neal but soon had the hands of many people touching him, trying to gain his attention. He backed off, lost with what to do, as Neal walked the distraught woman back towards the others.

"We don't know much. Honest. That's why we're here," Neal said, noticing more forensics people enter the Tanker house. "Yes, an ambulance took a body away, but I'm not authorised to tell you who it was."

He puffed out his cheeks after the woman burst out crying, almost close to tears himself as the reality of what happened inside the house hit him.

"Not little Tommy. Please say it's not him!" she yelled, placing a hand over her shaking mouth.

"To be honest, I don't know who it was."

The woman wiped her face to leave mascara on her hand. "It had to be him. He was the only other person living there."

She sobbed some more, staring deep towards Neal as she waited for an answer. But he shyly looked away.

———

Jon walked down a corridor inside the hospital, heading towards where Charles West was last seen; catching sight of him looking exhausted as he appeared from a side door. Jon moved swiftly to reach him but the sound of his boots smacking down on the floor startled Charles to turn around.

"Hi...Dan's not arrived at work yet, so I thought I'd visit; see what's going on with the parents," Jon said, watching Charles almost drop the folders he was carrying.

"I'm not surprised you haven't seen him. He was here till gone six this morning."

"Wow!" Jon followed him further along the corridor. "Any progress?" he asked, as Charles neared another door. "Are they talking?"

Charles sighed as he gripped the handle. "Still the same I'm afraid. Whatever happened at their home last night has affected them deeply."

"But did they kill their son?"

"No chance." Charles opened the door before adding, "Somebody else was in the boy's bedroom but they aren't saying who."

"So you think they know who the murderer is?"

"They must know."

Jon's heart sank as Charles entered the room. "Thanks for the update," he said, watching the door close.

———

Chantelle Spencer glanced at the computer screen to see the time had reached *11:00 am*. She was new to the role of being a receptionist at the station so found it difficult to juggle incoming calls and keep the frantic visitors at bay. She sighed, glad of her patient manner as she reached out to answer another call.

"Good morning. How may I help you?" she said, feeling nervous.

She listened to a freaked-out mother going on about her teenage son not returning home last night, the pressure to say the right words after hearing the woman cry causing her to sweat. She told the woman that he had probably stayed at a friend's house, but her words weren't greeted with optimism as the woman became angry.

"…There's nothing we can do right now because he's only been missing a few hours. He'll come home when he's hungry."

"But I've phoned all his friends. No one's seen him since around four this morning. I've even contacted the hospital, but still nothing."

"He's at the age where he can look after himself. I'm sure he's fine," Chantelle said, trying to calm the woman down. She heard the woman frantically breathe so knew the attempt hadn't worked. "Look, if he hasn't returned by five just let us know and someone will search for him…"

But Chantelle's eardrum began to hum after the woman slammed down her phone, the moment leaving Chantelle feeling awful from the guilt of doing something wrong. But she never had time to dwell as the phone rang again to distract her.

———

Dan arrived at the station a few minutes later, yawning like he still needed sleep. He saw Neal and Ben try their best to keep the angry and confused visitors away from Chantelle as she took another call before slipping past unnoticed; shaking his head as he reached his office to collapse into his seat. He listened to the voices, glad to not be caught up in the situation before closing his eyes to imagine being somewhere else. It pleased him to hear the people slowly leave, but words coming from Ben and Neal as they neared made him want to hide under his desk.

"Hey, chief, nice to see you've finally shown up for work," Ben said laughing.

Dan scowled as they strolled into the room. "Neal Down and Ben Dover!" he shouted. "Where have you been?"

"We've been doing house-to-house enquiries," Ben replied; his laughter fading.

"And who ordered it?"

Ben and Neal looked at each other like they feared a disciplinary telling off over something they didn't know they'd done.

"Jon told us to do it," Neal replied, waiting for Dan to lose it.

But Dan breathed deeply as he left his seat before walking around them to make them nervous.

"Okay," he softly said, sitting back down again.

"Anything else you want to add?" Neal asked.

"Not really."

"Cool." Neal smiled at Ben before turning back to Dan. "For a moment there I thought we were in big trouble."

"You are," Dan quickly replied, watching their faces drop. But he gave in and smiled seconds later to say, "Just fill me in on what's been going on today before I fall asleep."

LEE ANDREW TAYLOR

———

The time had moved to *1:00 pm* when Dan next checked his watch; his mind lost after the different scenarios spilt out in front of him about who the killer could be. He read through the statements collected by Neal and Ben; his eyes draining from the stress of finding no witnesses as he mumbled at being annoyed for not getting any closer to catching who killed the boy. He dug elbows into the desk, wrapping palms around his head like some form of a crash helmet before shutting his eyelids to create a picture of the murder from inside his mind; visioning flashbacks from Nini and Marek's explanations.

A boy murdered...No witnesses...And his parents aren't talking, were the three main agonising points torturing him.

He shot up in his seat after a knock on the door spooked him, the sight of Jon entering to say, "Are you okay?" snapping him from his thoughts.

He rubbed his eyes as Jon sat opposite, slowly relaxing his mind before sighing to say, "Not really." As he leaned back in his seat to glance over the statements again. "Did you get anything out of the boy's parents?"

"Sorry, no," Jon replied, holding up Ben's statement to squint at his poor handwriting. "Charles thinks they could be in that state for quite a while."

Dan choked after another sudden attack of tiredness hit him. "Fuck! They're the key to solving this."

He handed Jon the statements written by Nini and Marek, with the words – no forced entry, no sign of a killer, no murder weapon – being circled in red ink.

"What the fuck happened last night?" Jon asked, terrified to know the answer.

"You know what happened. A young boy was murdered."

"But surely there has to be a reason as to why the parents aren't talking? And why there are no witnesses and no evidence to help us?"

Dan rubbed his eyes again before leaving his seat to aim for the door. "We'll find out what happened. It's our job."

CHAPTER SEVEN

The queen slithered along the floor of the UFO; her energy slowly returning after eating more food given to her. She'd grown since last night, her body changing to produce more legs from within her slimy, slug-like shell and her mouth showing signs of teeth. It was like she was being re-born again; the body that terrorised the planet she was originally from now returning.

The bugs formed a circle around her like they expected another order, her shrieking producing a creepy pitch that echoed in the darkness. The sound excited the bugs and they understood it. They formed into the compact shape of the shadow again as a snake-like tongue whipped from the queen's mouth to coil around Peter Thornton's leg. She swallowed it whole, regurgitating pieces of cloth seconds later before slithering off again; her shriek repeating as the bugs vanished.

———

Grant and *Gina Lovell* were the owners of the local store, meeting through an online dating site over twelve years ago before marrying two years later. Gina was the bossy one, with her ideas for the store becoming the only ones over the years, but Grant accepted it. He preferred to keep a low profile when it came to the business so didn't mind her taking over.

They watched the store become full; the trauma of last night's tragedy at the Tanker house being talked about as shoppers browsed the shelves. But no one believed the parents had killed their son. Gina overheard them complain about the lack of progress made by the police in finding out what'd happened, showing worry towards Grant as the shoppers left. He shrugged as he turned to see the old lady who had spoken to Neal and Ben earlier that day, smiling because he hadn't noticed her sneak in past the angry-faced people.

"Okay, Vera, you got everything?" he asked, opening the door for her.

"What? Are you saying I got apple hips?" Vera replied, staring at him confused.

Grant burst into a laughing frenzy after forgetting about Vera's hearing.

"I said, have you got everything!" he shouted.

Vera smiled and nudged him. "Sorry. This new hearing aid is rubbish." She fumbled at the volume control. "Yes, I have all that I need for today."

"Good..."

Grant watched her leave before slipping out another giggle; the door closing as she slowly disappeared down the street. He walked past Gina, noticing her place a hand over her mouth. He knew she was dying to laugh.

"...Shush! She'll hear you."

Gina pulled her hand away. "No, she won't. She's virtually deaf."

Grant smiled and kissed her on the forehead. "I'm off to the storeroom to give it a tidy-up."

The words shocked Gina because Grant usually waited for her to tell him to do it. But he wasn't backing down or cracking a joke as he slowly walked away.

He opened the storeroom door, sniffing deeply to smell the sawdust from the new improvements before pulling a cord to switch on the dimly lit bulb in the centre of the room; staring at a corner as something unusual caught his eye. The darkness still had control over most of that side so couldn't make out what it was. He stared hard until a human-like shape spooked him before nervously reaching for a broom to whisper – "Hello."

He felt stupid for speaking, but the figure didn't move.

A faint sound echoed through his eardrums, worrying him to almost leave the room. He didn't recognise it but knew it was coming from the area he was staring at. But the sound of insects scurrying close by creeped him out to kick a nearby box.

"Fuckin' bugs!" he hollered, reaching for a can of insect spray from a shelf. "I'll find you and I'll kill you."

He laughed as he moved boxes, but the figure caught his eyeline again to increase his nerves.

"Okay, mate. You need to come out of there. This is a food store, not a doss house to hang out in," he said, plucking up the courage to close in. "It's time you went home."

He moved another box to be greeted by a flood of ants, but the spray suffocated them before they could escape as the smell made his eyes water.

"That'll teach you to mess with me," he said, staring at

them curled up on the floor before laughing again as he reached out to grab the silent figure. "What the fuck!"

It was just a hat stand, with coats and a hat still attached.

Grant kicked himself after forgetting that Gina had moved things around; staring towards the door to be reminded of where it used to be.

Fuck me, woman, you had me there.

He stared at the ants again but something pinched his left ankle to leave him cursing.

Damn, those little shits are good.

He tried to walk but fell to the floor within seconds, his ankle now numb and swollen.

"Jesus, what's up with my leg!" he screamed, unable to move his left side.

He desperately tried to regain his balance but the pain was too strong; both legs were now numb as sweat gushed down his face. He stared at the door in the hope of seeing Gina nearby, attempting to shout again to produce a faint muffle as his hands lacked the strength to lift off the floor. He lay on the cold surface, terrified after seeing a dark shadow glide towards him; trembling as it pounced to drag him into the darkness.

Gina neared the doorway, twitching her ears as she waited for Grant to shout again. She thought he was playing with her before so refused to leave the shop floor, but the silence now intrigued her to know what he was up to. She assumed he was smoking, using the storeroom as an excuse to have a quick cigarette; her anger brewing because he wasn't allowed to.

"I've caught you!" she shouted, swinging the door open to find him not there. "Grant!"

She followed the brightness of the room until spotting a pair of legs on the floor; her mouth quivering as tears suddenly streamed down her face. She closed in as fear overtook her, knowing Grant wasn't moving as she checked to see if he was still breathing. But a blast of insects shot out of his mouth to scare her into backing away; crawling over his body like they were protecting their catch.

Gina raced from the room, reaching for her phone whilst glaring at the stockroom door; dialling the emergency number as she tried to make sense of it all. A part of her didn't believe what she'd just seen, but she shuddered, crying hard after visioning the insects again.

She tried keeping herself together as someone answered her call, stuttering her way through reporting Grant's condition until the person took her seriously. She tiredly ended the call and walked back towards the room, but Grant was gone.

Where is he?

She rushed inside, desperately moving boxes in an attempt to blank out thoughts of the insects; her heart racing because Grant was injured. She felt on edge after seeing no sign of him before frantically trashing the room to knock over the hat stand. But the tears kept falling as she exited the room to use the phone again, holding it with a trembling hand before dialling a number.

"Hello, this is Lemonsville County police station. What seems to be the problem?" Marion asked, back on duty behind the receptionist's desk.

"I can't find...my...husband...," Gina mumbled. "He's...gone."

"I'm sure he hasn't," Marion replied as distressed shouts shocked her into holding the phone away from her ear. "Okay! Okay! Is this you, Gina?"

"Yes."

"Marek and Nini have just arrived...Are you still at the store?"

"Yes," Gina whispered.

Marion knew she sounded scared, but still wasn't sure why? Yes, the news about Grant going missing sounded very real but she knew how over the top Gina could be, especially if she'd been drinking.

"Stay there. I'm sending them to you now." Marion quickly replaced the phone before shouting out to a yawning Nini. "I know you'd rather grab yourself a quick pick-me-up cuppa coffee but I need you to go to the Lovells store. Gina reckons Grant's disappeared."

"She hasn't been drinking again, has she?" Marek replied, smirking.

Nini nudged him. "Stop being a complete idiot and let's just do our job," she said, yawning again.

Marion watched them stare each other out before shaking her head after reading notes on the desk linked to the mother of the missing teenager.

"Hey! Stop your stare-off. This could be serious," she said, waiting for them to look at her. "A teenage boy hasn't returned home since last night. And his mother's phoned six times already."

"So why aren't we investigating that?" Marek asked.

"He's a teenager, so is probably just messing around to upset her." Marion looked at the notes again. "She was told to get back in touch if he hadn't come home by five."

"Does Dan know that we're off to see Gina?" Nini asked.

"I've not spoken to him yet. He's in his office if you want to tell him."

Nini knew it was the wisest choice.

She pulled on Marek's arm until he followed her, as Marion shook her head again to the sound of Neal and Ben entering the station; frowning to see them acting like children.

———

Gina stared deeply at a patch of blood on the stockroom floor as tears landed on top to create tiny circles of water. She glanced at the mess she'd recently created, feeling angry with herself for losing it but also extremely upset after finding no trace of Grant ever being there.

"Grant, Grant, where are you?!" she shouted, swiftly turning to the sound of the storeroom door opening.

She held out her arms ready to wrap around him but sighed when Nini and Marek appeared.

"Hi, Gina. What's happened here?" Nini asked, closing in.

Gina tried to speak, but her words sounded more like a gurgle as she pointed at the red stain.

Marek reached into a pocket to produce a small tube before dipping the tip of a cotton bud into the blood. But it made him squirm.

"We need to test it to see if it's Grant's," he said, placing the bud into the tube.

"His blood?!" Gina bellowed. "Don't you believe me?"

She broke down again, close to dropping to her knees as Marek shrugged towards Nini.

"Say something," Nini whispered, shrugging back as she held Gina upright.

"Yes, I believe it to be his blood, but it still needs to be tested," Marek said, hoping Gina would calm down.

He was pleased to see Nini walk her towards the door, smiling because the only sound she made was now just a few sniffles before releasing his torch to shine around the room.

"Hey, Gina. I thought you were a neat freak?" he said, shocked by the clutter. "Your stockroom is a mess."

Nini glared at him as she walked Gina out of the room, but Marek scrunched his lips as the hat stand glowed within the torchlight. He lit up the rest of the floor, searching for more blood; pocketing the tube after no trace was found before turning to leave.

Nini stood by the counter, smiling as Gina's breathing slowed down. "I need something from you to figure this out," she calmly said.

But Gina stared at her as she thought of a way to explain what she saw before being accused of something she didn't do.

"Grant was in the storeroom with these creepy things all over him," she said, cringing.

"Things?" Nini asked, appearing baffled.

"I was here, cleaning up after the recent customers...while Grant entered the storeroom." Gina broke down, crying again as Nini held her hand.

"Go on," Nini softly said.

"I went to check on him...but he was lying on the floor, not moving...Then these weird insects shot out of his mouth."

Marek returned to hear the words, close to laughing as he twisted up his face like some kind of a mad person before spinning a finger at the side of his head. Nini watched him mime the words – 'I think she's a bit loopy' – before shaking her head and ushering him away.

"Where are the insects?" she asked Gina, seeing her shiver like she was about to have a breakdown.

"You're saying that bugs came out of your husband's mouth?" Marek sarcastically asked as he unwrapped a chocolate bar and took a bite. "So, what happened to him?"

Nini huffed. "I hope you're going to pay for that. I can't work with you any longer. One day is enough for me."

"Hey! What's got into you?" Marek asked, taking another bite.

"You! You're an arrogant fool."

Gina released her hand before placing fingers in her ears, backing away to drown out the bickering between the other two as Marek studied her. He wasn't impressed by anything she said.

"Where's Grant now?" he asked, watching Gina mumble to herself.

"I don't know!" she screamed.

Nini hugged her tight as Marek huffed and left the store.

"Listen, Gina. It all sounds a bit weird," Nini said, letting her go. "I need to ask you something, so please don't get mad."

"What do you want to ask me?" Gina nervously wiped her eyes.

"Are you still overdoing it with the booze?"

But Gina lashed out and pushed her. "No, I'm not. Why would you say that?!" She rushed towards the main door to see Marek stare at her. "Who's been telling you? I need to know!" she hollered at Nini.

Nini gulped as she glared at Marek; now feeling disgusted for believing him after he mentioned it back at the station.

Gina's not an alcoholic. He was winding me up.

"Sorry, I shouldn't have said that," she said, feeling small as she watched Gina shiver whilst staring at the storeroom door. "I think we should go to the station. Get out of here for a while…"

Gina said nothing as Nini walked her to the door, but Marek smirked as he opened it from the outside.

"...We'll do everything within our power to find Grant," Nini said, escorting Gina towards the police car.

Marek tutted as he reentered the store, picking up the keys off the counter to lock up as Nini placed Gina inside the car. He saw an ambulance arrive, so pointed at his watch, miming – 'Jesus, they took their time,' as the driver exited.

"It's a false alarm!" Marek shouted before seeing the driver curse under his breath.

CHAPTER EIGHT

Dan felt sorrow towards Gina after seeing Nini and Marek escort her into the station; her head bowed like she was trying to hide. It worried him to think she could end up like the parents of the murdered boy, silent and lost inside a troubled mind.

"Hey, Dan, we've brought Gina in for a chat," Nini said.

"Cheers," he replied, rubbing his chin. "I will find her a quiet room."

He approached Gina, hoping that she'd look him in the eyes, but she just mumbled before slowly following him away from the others. Marion smiled with excitement at the chance of receiving some juicy gossip after watching them enter an interview room, but she stuttered on asking as Nini approached and instead pretended she was busy. That was until Marek laughed.

"Tell me, tell me, tell me!" Marion shouted at him.

But her actions were more like a teenager trying to get her friend to spill the beans on a recent boyfriend rather than being sympathetic towards the troublesome Gina.

"Nothing to tell that you don't know," Nini interrupted, leaning on the reception desk.

Marek laughed again, closing in to gently nudge her.

"Marion, don't listen to her. Check this out...She was waffling on about some crazy bugs jumping out of Grant's mouth."

"No fucking way!" Marion replied, intrigued as she bit into a biscuit.

Nini nudged Marek back, glaring at him with disgust at how easy it was for him to tell Marion about Gina. She was convinced that he had no heart, no emotion, and no feeling or thought about any other person than himself, appearing to be more like a deadly serpent than someone she could trust. She felt like storming into the interview room to ask Dan for a new partner but changed her mind swiftly after sighing at the thought of teaming up with Neal or Ben.

She breathed deeply as Marek continued to entertain Marion.

"True," he replied, ignoring her.

She walked away to fetch a drink, leaving him to carry on childishly laughing with Marion about his visit to the store.

"...That's what she said." Marek laughed, even more, annoying Nini to almost spill her drink.

She attempted to hush him, but he blanked her upon slapping Marion on the arm.

Nini sighed again after now feeling invisible before sipping her drink and cringing at the sound of Marek's hyena-like giggles. She hoped Dan would hear him enough to leave the interview room to reprimand him for being an arsehole, but had a feeling Marek would avoid it. She faked a smile and watched him perform, as her mind drifted back to the Academy.

He hasn't changed, she thought, shaking her head.

"...It made me think that maybe she's on the pop again," Marek blurted towards Marion.

"Hold on!" Nini cried out. "Is she a drunk or not? Because I felt stupid for accusing her before."

"Maybe she is, or maybe she isn't," Marek replied, smirking. "Either way, she's here and he's missing."

Marion looked across at Nini as she closed in, but Nini's ice-cold glare made her gulp. She became red-faced, turning away to do some typing as Marek kept talking. She tried to ignore him but he was like a magician, his words putting her under a spell to keep her nosiness alive.

"You don't seriously believe she's still drinking the vodka do you?"

Marek almost laughed again, shaking his head after feeling smug for messing with Marion's mind.

"Nah! Not this time," he replied, hearing Nini huff at him again before storming off into another room. "This is way too messed up to just be drink talk."

He grinned at Marion, pulling a face to make her laugh.

————

Dan sat opposite Gina, watching her tremble in the chair. She wasn't speaking and it made him nervous. He clasped his fingers together, patiently waiting for a sign of progress, but was taken aback by Gina's constant flinching like someone was touching her.

————

Marion typed up a letter, but the telephone rang again to spook her. She answered it to be hollered at by a woman; her voice heard by Marek. He winked at Marion, feeling thankful it wasn't him who took the call, but the woman's shouting became intense. He waved as he walked away, leaving Marion struggling to calm the woman down, shaking her head as the shouts rang in her ears.

"Okay. Can you please lower your voice and tell me again," Marion said. But the woman stopped talking. "Hello, are you still there?"

Marion waited for a response; panicking after thinking she'd upset the woman with her bluntness. But she relaxed after hearing a cough.

"Yes," the woman softly replied.

Marion recognised her as being the mother of the missing teenager.

She stared at the notes again until a shiver shot down her spine, knowing now that the woman was frantic.

"I'm putting you through to the sergeant," she said, throwing the note with – We will search for him after 5:00 pm – in the bin.

"About time. If something's happened to him..." the woman said as the call was transferred to Jon.

"Hello, can I help you?" he asked, fearing abuse was about to come his way.

"You lot are taking the piss!" the mother raspily hollered. "My boy's been out all night...It's now gone three in the afternoon and there's still no sign of him...He's not answering his phone and his friends still haven't seen him."

Jon looked at the computer to recap the conversation she had with Chantelle earlier, seeing the times of each call and what they were about.

"Okay, Mrs Thornton. You are so right," he said, cringing from the thought of another person being attacked last night. He wasn't a fool; he knew her son wasn't deliberately ignoring her. "I'm sending some officers out to you. Give them as much information as you can on where you think your son might be."

"Okay."

Jon heard her sniffing but had a feeling she was trying to keep the phone at arm's length so he couldn't.

"This is a small town, so I'm sure we'll find him soon."

He ended the call as a sudden rush of water filled his eyes before

racing from his office to the sound of his boots pounding on the ground; reaching the interview room to nervously knock on the door.

"Come in," Dan said, as Jon entered.

"Sorry to disturb you, chief, but can I have a quick word with you outside?"

Dan stood up, smiling at Gina before lightly touching her shoulder.

"I won't be long, so take this time to gather your thoughts. I need you to tell me everything about what you saw, even if it hurts. It will help us find Grant."

Gina reached for his hand, gripping his fingers like she feared him leaving; her face shattered from too much sadness to let go. Dan smiled again before gently removing her grip, seeing tears slide down her face as he pointed towards the door. He walked over to it to be watched as Gina wiped the tears away.

"So, what's up?" he asked Jon, following him out of the room.

Jon's words flowed quickly as news about the missing teenager caused Dan to gulp.

"This can't be just a hoax, chief. The mother is extremely upset."

"Who you got on the case?" Dan asked, squirming at the thought of the goon squad visiting her.

"I'm sending Neal and Ben to her house." Jon sighed after Dan frowned at him. "You think they'll fuck up, don't you."

"When have they ever not?" Dan shrugged. "Whatever is happening in this town needs to stop. Let's just hope they found out where her son is."

Jon nodded as he glanced at Gina drawing an imaginary picture on the table with her finger.

"Is she okay?"

Dan turned to watch her before saying, "I don't think so. Her husband's disappeared and now we have a missing teenager."

"And a dead boy," Jon interrupted.

"Not a great last twenty-four hours," Dan replied, turning to enter the room again. "Let's just pray that this mess gets sorted out soon."

———

Neal drove to the edge of Cassidy Street, pulling up on a kerb as Ben glanced at his watch.

"It's after three-thirty," he said, watching Neal turn off the engine. "I'm starving. We missed dinner."

"Me too. But we'd better not mess this up. Dan will fire us for sure if we ditch this and grab some food."

Ben giggled. "Yeah. Better get this over with first."

They exited the car to feel a cold breeze move swiftly down to their boots; their toes being the target as a glum look was passed between them. Neal stamped hard to try to stay warm but almost slipped as he slowly walked towards the house.

"Shit, Ben, I've forgotten the name of the person we're supposed to visit," he said, sliding his boot through some sludge.

Ben giggled again. "*Angelica*. That's the person's name."

"Why does that name ring a bell?" Neal asked, scrunching his eyebrows.

"Because she's Quasimodo's sister," Ben replied, still laughing.

"Shit! She is?"

Ben slapped Neal on the back before kicking snow at him.

"No, she isn't," he said, gaining on the house. "I'm joking."

He waited for Neal to reach him before nearing the front door, but the sound of someone opening it made them nervous. Mrs Thornton stared at them before collapsing to cry fast tears.

"He's dead, isn't he," she sputtered.

Neal and Ben looked at each other like they were meant to know the answer but had somehow forgotten it.

"Dead! Why would you say that?" Ben asked, hoping someone from the station hadn't phoned to tell her more information.

"Because you're here."

"We're here because we were told to come here. Something about a missing son, not a dead one."

Mrs Thornton felt stupid for not believing that the police were taking her seriously. She stopped crying and led them into her house, excited at the prospect of hearing positive news.

"Let's go into the living room," she said, wiping her face dry.

———

Dan waited for Gina to open up and explain what happened to Grant, but his constant parading up and down the room received no joy.

"Look, Gina, this talk about bugs isn't making any sense to me. I just can't imagine that a pack of wild ants would jump out of Grant's mouth."

"They weren't ants!" she snapped back.

"What were they? Centipedes, cockroaches, spiders, earwigs. What!..."

Gina came close to screaming after Dan mentioned more insects, shaking continuously until he went silent. Her actions worried him, but he was glad she was finally opening up.

"...Hey, it's okay," he said, wrapping an arm around her. "I'm just trying to figure this out so we can find Grant..."

Gina appreciated his kindness, his gentle approach relaxing her.

"...Do you feel better now?" Dan said, smiling.

Gina did, but she also felt embarrassed for having another outburst. She watched Dan reach for a notepad and pencil, knowing he wanted her to use them. She grabbed them as they were pushed in her direction.

"Sorry about that," she said, leaning back in her chair. "They looked like bugs. Just your usual, tiny insect."

"Okay. I believe you." But Dan was still confused. "Just draw what you saw for me. I'll send Marek back to your store."

Gina started to sketch; the drawing intriguing Dan as she finished. He nodded as the pad was handed back to him, ripping off the page before walking towards the door.

"Would you like to stay here while he does that?" he asked.

Gina nodded as fear for Grant's life washed over her

again. She knew that no matter where she was she would still be frantic over where he could be, but right now couldn't face going home.

Dan left the room shouting, 'Marek!" until spotting him coming out of the canteen area, but his mouth and chin were covered with crumbs from the toast he'd just eaten.

"Yes, chief."

"I need you to go back to the store." Dan handed him the drawing, noticing him cringe. "And look for insects similar to this."

Marek stared at Dan as the word '*insects*' caused him to shudder. "Are you being serious? Creepy crawlies give me the willies."

Dan almost laughed as Marek placed the paper into his pocket. "Yes, I am. If you see any, catch them and bring them here."

"Why?" Marek asked. "You do know Gina's probably drunk again and just making it up."

Dan glared at him, hoping that Gina didn't hear; knowing he would be back at square one if she did. He knew she'd been drinking; he could smell it on her, but what could he do? Her husband was missing, with the only clue being insects that may have been coming out of his mouth.

"Just do what I ask," Dan said, reaching for the door handle. "This may be serious."

"Come on, Dan, you don't truly believe there are killer insects out there, do you?"

"It's not about what I believe, it's about what Gina believes."

Marek huffed.

He still didn't think Gina's story was true but was too tired to argue over it, so just held up a hand and walked away, shaking his head at the thought of seeing what she described.

———

Neal and Ben sat watching Mrs Thornton pace up and down inside the living room, panicking to make the wrinkles on her face stand out. She puffed out her cheeks several times towards them after repeating where she thought her son may have been until Ben caught on that she wanted them to write the destinations down.

"Whoops, sorry," he said, opening up his notepad. "I keep forgetting this bit." He smiled at her, but she wasn't impressed. "Is it okay to call you Angelica?"

"Sure. That is my name," she replied, huffing.

"Okay, Angelica, tell us again what your son said to you before leaving home."

"Nothing much. Just that he was off to a friend's party."

"Did you fight before that?"

Angelica stopped pacing and glared at Ben.

"Woooooh! Hold on a minute. Are you suggesting I may have something to do with his disappearance?"

Neal noticed she was close to throwing something at Ben so quickly interrupted. "No! Nothing like that. We're just trying to gain a clearer picture of your son's recent activities."

"Peter. His name's Peter!" Angelica snapped.

Neal felt embarrassed upon checking his pad to find no name for her son, just a few scribbles and a game of *hangman* that he started with Ben earlier that day. He apologised for his lack of sympathy, realising now just how shit an officer he was as he showed Ben the pad; writing '*Peter*' on the next page to the sound of Ben shouting, 'T'.

Neal sighed towards him, shaking his head as Angelica reached into her pocket.

"Most of his closest friends were probably at the party

last night. They're all local," she said, pulling out a list and handing it over to him.

"Okay. We'll get onto it right away." Neal walked towards the door before adding, "We'll be in touch."

Angelica smiled, thinking her son was about to be found, but her smile swiftly disappeared after seeing the clumsy officers almost trip over each other to leave the room.

She walked them back to the front door, opening it to let them out, but a strong breeze gripped them, dragging them away from the house. They braced the weather, zipping up their jackets as they reached the car, but Ben stared down the street like something had him hypnotised.

"What are you doing?" Neal asked, watching him walk in the opposite direction. "The car is here."

"It'll be quicker to walk in this weather. Trust me."

Neal laughed. "Trust you? It's too slippery. We'll just keep falling over."

"Where's your sense of adventure?" Ben asked, sliding down the road to lift ice and slush. "The first house is not far away."

He carried on towards it but was hit on the back by a snowball, his nose twitching after a strange aroma drifted beneath his nostrils.

What's that smell!" He yelled. "Smells like shit!"

Neal looked at his glove to see dog poo attached before glancing at the ground.

"Sorry! I'm bad. Must have rolled dog poop inside the snowball before throwing it at you," he said, bending down to wipe it off his glove.

"I hope it's not on my back?!" Ben yelled. "It's making me feel sick."

Neal shrugged his shoulders before cautiously closing in

to remove it from Ben's back, avoiding eye contact in case he broke into a fit of laughter.

"Look. I know all this police work is boring for you," Ben said as Neal wiped the glove into the snow again. "But we have to be professional right now and find her son."

"Gotcha!..."

Neal glanced over the road at a play area as he reached the corner of the street, his eyes wide with excitement as he steered off course to aim for the same swing Peter Thornton was last seen on.

"...Fancy a go?" he said, jumping on it like he was a child again to almost slide off. "The damn seat is frozen."

Ben kicked up snow in anger after his serious chat with Neal came to nothing, awkwardly watching him swing back and forth in the hope he would be finished within a few seconds. But Neal suddenly began singing the same song Peter did.

"What am I going to do with you?" Ben said, listening to Neal shout out the lyrics. "You're deafening me."

He closed in to stop Neal but was interrupted by a louder voice blasting out words from a house over the road.

"Hoy! I told a little fucker to stop singing that song earlier this morning, and now you're trying to ruin a classic...Just shut the fuck up!"

"Hey, mate!" Ben shouted, spotting the old man leaning out of his window. "You do know that you're talking to highly regarded police officers?"

"I can't see shit from this distance, but I don't give a fuck if you're the police or not. Just stop that racket before I come down there and scare the piss out of you as I did with that other dickhead."

Ben and Neal laughed to send the man's temper up a

level. He sneered at them, but his presence wasn't making them stop.

"Hey, mate, have you got Tourette syndrome?!" Neal hollered.

"Fuck off have I. I'll give you Tourette syndrome if you make me come down there."

Neal jumped off the swing, folding his arms before standing next to Ben, grunting and annoyed to the point of wanting to arrest the old man.

"Come down here and try on this silver bracelet," he said, waving handcuffs to upset the man even more.

"Fuck you! You prick!" the reply came, as the man spat and slammed the window shut.

"Now look what you've gone and done," Ben said, walking away. "Stop acting like a kid and ignore him."

Neal put the cuffs away, laughing even louder as he caught Ben up.

———

Marek gawped at the stockroom floor, scratching his head and feeling lost after checking his watch to find the time had fast hit *4:00 pm*. He shone his torch around the room, nervously wanting it to be over so he could get back to the station.

He walked over to the can of insect spray, picking it up to see dead insects nearby; cringing after touching them to place inside a small, plastic bag, feeling positive they were ants. He tucked the bag inside his jacket pocket before lighting up another part of the room, his attitude towards Gina's story now changing rapidly the more he searched. He sweated, feeling spooked upon slowly leaning over a piece of old furniture, tensing as the hairs on his arms stood up. He thought about the last time he was as nervous and on edge but couldn't remember a single day as the silence inside the room smothered him. He felt fear but had no idea why?

"What the fuck!" he shouted, suddenly jolting back upright. "What's that noise!"

A faint whistling pushed its way through the silence, making him more scared as his sweaty fingers lost their grip on the torch. He heard it bounce off the floor; the light still beaming as he bent down to pick it up. But the noise closed in to leave him blindly guessing what it was.

He trembled even more as he headed for the door, his lips now dry and his complexion pale as he reached it. He touched his weapon, ready to pulverise the noisemaker, but the sound was gone before his gun was released.

"Fuck this shit. I'm outta here!"

CHAPTER NINE

Dan faced his office door as a 'thudding' sound closed in; the blurred image of Marek running past the frosted glass panels as he reached the doorway was the reason why. Dan shouted for him to 'come in' before the knock arrived, expressing deep concern after noticing Marek was a nervous wreck. He watched eagerly as Marek sat in a chair, his head bowed so as not to make eye contact. Dan knew something was wrong.

"What you got for me?" he said, hoping Marek snapped out of the state he was in.

"Don't make me go back there," Marek replied, slowly raising his head. "The fuckin' room creeped me out." He puffed out his cheeks and gripped Dan's desk. "But I did find a few dead bugs."

"That's great, so why are you acting nervous?"

"Because a weird whistling sound spooked me."

Dan giggled under his breath, but Marek's agitation made him stop. "Maybe the bugs were boiling a kettle?"

Dan knew he shouldn't mock Marek, especially when he

knew about his phobia of creepy crawlies, but the moment had given him the ammunition, so he couldn't resist it.

"Not funny, chief. It was freaky."

The phone rang to spook Marek into almost falling off the chair; his heart pounding as he sat back to compose himself. Dan sighed, watching him fidget; waiting for him to finish before answering the phone.

"Hello," he said, passing it from ear to ear.

Marek listened in, but Dan had stopped speaking to just nod or shake his head. It confused Marek, so he tried working out the conversation from Dan's facial expressions. He waited, watching Dan closely; getting nowhere as he leaned forward again.

"What was that all about?" he asked, as Dan replaced the phone.

Dan smiled; his face glowing like someone had drawn back the curtains to let the sunshine in.

"That was Cliff from forensics. He's been working overtime on the murdered boy's case."

Marek's eyes lit up; his nerves drifting away to be replaced with suspense as the waiting hooked him to know more about what Cliff just said. He hoped for some positive news to end the nightmare, but Dan stalled on letting him know.

"What happened? Did he find anything?" Marek asked, watching Dan stand up to stretch his legs.

"Wow! He sure did...According to him, the boy had been brutally eaten..."

Marek coughed into his hand; wiping saliva down his trousers as a sick taste touched his tongue. He waited for Dan to say more, hoping he was joking, but Dan remained stern as he slowly walked around the room.

"...He said the attacker was unlikely to be a person because the bites were very small."

"Hold on. Did a person eat him or not?!" Marek snapped.

Dan gulped, feeling annoyed at the outburst, but he let it slide after thinking how close to shouting he was after he was told. He reached a nearby table, pouring water from a jug into a glass before taking a sip.

"Probably not." He drank some more, shaking to spill some onto the floor. "He's not one-hundred-per cent sure, but whatever did it was more animal-like than human."

"Surely someone would've spotted a crazed animal in the boy's bedroom? This doesn't add up," Marek replied.

"Hey. I'm with you on this. This doesn't add up at all."

"So, what do we do now?"

"I need to call a meeting...Grab all available officers and bring them here."

"No problem...Will do." Marek left his seat and aimed for the door.

Dan closed his eyes to soak up the past few minutes, knowing that soon his room would fill with worried people. He heard them approach, running like sprinters in a race; each staring at the person beside them to figure out who was in trouble.

"Okay. I want you all to listen." Dan looked at the open door, hinting for Nini to close it; waiting for her to do it before nodding. "I've just received a call from the forensic department and it's not good news."

"Not good?" Nini asked, standing next to the others again.

"Not good because the cause of the boy's death is baffling to understand." Dan remained as positive as he could but knew the others were watching him like a hawk. He deliberately stared at Marek before adding, "This conversation isn't for anyone else to hear, and that includes Marion. So no gossiping with her."

Marek smiled, thinking Dan was winding him up, but Dan's stare stayed strong. "Why would I tell her?"

Nini sucked her bottom lip and cringed.

"You want me to answer that?" Dan asked, watching Marek suddenly become dumb to the question. "I know you told her about what happened at the store and that you thought Gina was a pisshead..."

Marek's cheeks burned from embarrassment; his eyes wide upon glaring at Nini.

"...And don't even think about blaming her. She didn't tell me." Dan threw a pencil at Marek to regain his attention. "You should always remember to never spread gossip with a gossiper, as the gossiper will always carry on the gossip to others..."

Jon cracked up with laughter.

"...What you laughing at?" Dan asked.

"Sorry, chief. I was just thinking about how hard it would be to say that after a few beers."

"Are you agreeing with Marek that Gina is an alcoholic?"

"No, chief. Not me."

Why am I working with these clowns? Do they ever take anything seriously? Nini thought, shaking her head.

She was taught from a young age to be professional in everything she did upon remembering her family back home struggling to cope with death during the war.

She sneered at the others - *Why do they joke like the young boy's death was nothing?*

Dan smiled at her, knowing she was finding it tough. But his expression suddenly turned sullen after glaring at Jon winding Marek up over his ease to tell Marion virtually anything.

"Okay! Snap out of the games and listen up," Dan said,

sitting back down. "I've just been told that the boy was eaten by something..."

Nini shuddered, close to tears as she hid behind Jon.

"...Whatever attacked him bit his fingers and toes off and ate his organs," Dan continued, squirming after hearing Nini choke.

Jon grabbed onto her before her knees buckled; her voice trembling as she thanked him. He hugged her as Marek cursed under his breath, annoyed with himself for not finding better clues at the store.

"...This couldn't have been done by the parents, so we need to find out who? Or what did it?" Dan finished, slamming a fist down on his desk.

————

Nini and Marek cautiously patrolled a street as Dan's speech lingered inside their minds. But Marek sensed Nini was thinking about more than just her job, so kept his distance; dreading she would go all girly on him if he intervened.

Nini stared at the night sky, shaking her head after noticing it was a shade darker than usual. She adjusted her Cossack hat after the wind almost blew it off her head before closing in on Marek to use him as a shield to divert the wind and falling snow away. He smiled, glad she wasn't having a nervous breakdown.

They walked towards the local pub, as the brightness inside acted as a lighthouse to gain their attention. But, as Marek opened the door, he found the place practically empty of people.

"We get information then we leave," Nini insisted, shrugging as she followed him inside.

"Yes, boss," Marek replied, smirking as he eyed up the

room. "The news about the boy must be keeping most people at home."

"I don't blame them."

Those who were seated put down their glasses to pay attention before following the officers' movements to make Nini shiver more than she did outside. She looked over at them and smiled until they turned away.

"Hello, officers," said *Dave*, the landlord.

Nini waited for Marek to drill the barman with useful questions, smiling because it was his chance to show her he was stepping up by taking his role seriously. But Marek scrunched his lips and pointed.

"A pint for me and whatever my partner wants."

Nini glared at him, but he ignored her as he pointed again at the drink he wanted.

"We're on duty!" she hollered, hearing chairs scrape on the wooden floor as people got excited. "We have a job to do."

"I'm tired. I need to recharge."

"You won't recharge on alcohol," Nini said, attempting to pull him away from the bar. "Dan will fire you."

But Marek pointed again until Dave took him seriously; feeling Nini's breath before seeing the disgust on her face.

"Just leave it," he said, watching Dave pour the drink. "After the day I've had, I don't give a flying fuck if Dan takes my badge...I'm having a pint." He calmed down, taking a deep breath before saying, "What are you having?"

"This is a joke, right? You're not serious about this? You're pranking me because it's my first week."

Marek smiled at Dave as the pint was placed on the bar before picking it up to take a huge swig. "Thanks."

"Come on, Marek, get your head together," Nini begged.

"Look. We need this, so let's just take a few minutes to unwind before going back out in the freezin' shit cold."

Nini wasn't blind or stupid, she knew this was Marek's way of coping. She had seen this attitude back at the academy after someone close to Marek died; watching him build a brick wall to defend himself so no one could witness emotion. The wrong choices he was now making were too familiar, so she played along.

I'll have a soft drink," she said, nodding at Dave.

Marek nudged her, pointing at the alcoholic drinks to make her change her mind. But Nini wasn't budging.

"Any particular flavour?" Dave asked.

"Surprise me."

"Wooah! girl. Did I hear a touch of sarcasm in your voice?"

Nini smiled at Marek, letting her guard down as a sweaty-faced woman ran into the pub repeatedly screaming that her daughter had disappeared. Nini rushed over to her, gripping her arms as she sat her down; now back to glaring at Marek as he took another swig of beer.

"Where was she last?" Nini asked; her words acting like a starter pistol to make the woman leave her seat.

But Nini grabbed her before she could race back outside.

"She was just with me!" the woman shouted, as beads of sweat dripped from her brow. "She ran ahead as we were returning home, turning the corner. But when I got there she was gone."

Marek placed the pint glass back on the bar; his head returning to the game as he said, "She's probably just hiding, but I'll check."

He raced towards the door, stepping outside for a second before returning to ask where the daughter was last seen; watching the mother produce a photo.

"On this corner, by the pub," she replied, close to collapsing. "Please! You have to find her."

Marek nodded; grabbing the photo before racing off again.

———

Gina nervously stood outside her store, staring inside like she expected Grant to be there. She had left the police station a while back but had walked the streets until her feet couldn't walk anymore. Now, she was home, back at the place where the horror began.

She smiled briefly after remembering the conversation with Vera; her silly earring aid bringing a giggle to remind Gina of the last time she'd spoken to Grant. She fumbled with the key; her heart beating too fast as she placed it inside the lock; opening the door to stare at the storeroom.

She edged backwards, close to running away; feeling hurt that Grant had left her alone; her head spinning after the reality of what happened crashed back inside her mind. She slowly entered the store, shutting the door as she awkwardly neared the counter; plucking up the courage to reach the storeroom. But she suddenly SCREAMED!!!

And Jon heard her as he patrolled the street nearby.

He reached for his gun and rushed into the store, finding her trembling and crying into her hands; not asking why upon following where she was pointing. He saw part of a human skull, with most of the flesh eaten away. He entered the storeroom to see a foot lying close by, almost gagging as he suddenly shivered.

"Are you okay?" he asked; composing himself before realising he'd chosen the wrong words.

Gina grabbed the wall, sinking to her knees as Jon slammed the storeroom door shut. He reached for his radio before moving her away to sob into his chest, listening to her breathe deep and fast to puff like someone having a panic attack.

"Who was that?!" he shouted.

"It's Grant," Gina whispered.

———

Marek was left breathless after searching high and low for the missing girl; running up and down the street outside the pub many times to no avail before heading down another one to stare at a distraught man standing in the middle of the road.

"Are you okay, sir?" he asked, closing in to see the pain on the man's face.

But the man looked right through him.

Marek gripped his gun after seeing a kitchen knife in the man's hand; backing away as it was raised.

"...Whooh! Put that down!" Marek blasted. But his words just bounced off the man. "I said, put that knife down now!"

Marek released his gun, feeling nervous as he saw the man grimace. But, as he pointed it, the man suddenly sunk to his knees.

"My daughter's gone missing!" he cried, dropping the knife in the snow.

"I know. I have a photo of her," Marek said, holding it in the air. He approached the man with caution, keeping his gun on safety. "I'm looking for her now."

"No! That's not her!" the man screamed. "Why would you think that's my daughter?"

Marek's jaw dropped like he'd just been given the biggest shock ever; feeling lost and confused, unable to answer. He watched the man become agitated, fearing he would reach for the knife; concern drilling through him as his finger neared the safety switch.

"Because your wife is in the pub," Marek spluttered. "I've just seen her. She's in pieces." He tapped the photo. "She's worried about this little girl."

"That's not my little girl," the man whispered, staring at the photo until a tear slid down his cheek. "And my wife isn't in the pub."

Marek shivered after a woman shouted in the distance.

He watched her rush out of a house; her voice shrilling as she aimed towards him.

"Our daughter's vanished! What are you going to do about it?!" she screamed, prodding him in the chest.

Marek panicked.

His finger became twitchy, close to making the gun live after seeing the man get to his feet, but relaxed after the man pulled the woman away to hug her.

"Let's get this straight," Marek said, staring hard at the photo again. "You're the parents of a missing girl, but not the girl in this photo?"

"Yes!" the man shouted.

"How old is your daughter?" Marek asked.

"She's twelve...She's only twelve!" the man cried out.

Marek re-holstered his gun, grabbing his radio to say, "Nini, come in," whilst rushing over to kick the knife away.

He smiled, pleased with the quick response, Nini's words acting like a wand to stop the parents in their tracks.

"Nini. Ask the woman you're with how old her daughter is?"

"Why do you want to know her age?" Nini replied.

"Because another young girl's gone missing."

Marek struggled to cope with the situation. He had no clue what to do next and the parents felt it. He glanced at them, faking a smile as he waited for Nini to reply; fearing the street could erupt into a frenzy of frightened individuals at any time.

"Marek," Nini said. "Her daughter is twelve."

"The same age as the other girl." Marek gulped after the mother burst into tears again. "I'm with the parents of the other girl. We need to find them."

He replaced his radio and picked up the knife, closing in on the parents to see them in shock; needing now to get them out of the cold.

"Let's get you both back inside," he said, escorting them back to their house. "I need a photo of your daughter to help in the search."

———

Dan put the phone down for the third time in only a few minutes, rubbing his face after his awkward call to the hospital. He needed to convince them that it wasn't a false alarm this time at the Lovells store after glancing at the notes he'd recently written. He had told Jon to stay with Gina for as long as he was needed whilst hoping Nini and Marek got the information on the missing girls. He wanted to know if there was a connection between them and if they were trying to prank their parents.

He hoped they were, but knew it was unlikely after adding up how many people had been reported missing since last night. He sighed, fearing Lemonsville could soon end up being labelled a health hazard of a town if the crimes carried on for another day.

He left his office; his face drained of energy as he walked over to Marion. "Have you had any more strange calls recently?

"Not since the teenage boy's mother. Why?" she asked.

"Because I have," Dan said, slumping his arms out on her desk. "There's either someone playing a wicked joke today or we have a serious problem of missing people…"

Marion remained quiet, allowing Dan the time to think.

She watched him struggle to find something to say, knowing whatever was happening was taking him out of his depth.

"…Take my calls. I need to do some investigating of my own," Dan said, walking away.

CHAPTER TEN

The clock hanging from a wall inside the police station read *7:00 pm* when Marion opened the doors to allow a pack of journalists to enter. But Dan was slow to filter out of his office to greet them. He had organised a meeting but now wished he hadn't after staring at mobile phones closing in on his face. He sighed, feeling pressure within a minute; his tiredness growing to make him angry. He held out his hands to swipe the phones away but the journalists' persistence wasn't fading.

"Tell us what's been happening with the investigation?!" one of them shouted.

"We've been working flat out since finding the murdered boy this morning," Dan rushed from his mouth, catching his breath before sitting at the reception desk.

"But hasn't there been another murder since then?" the journalist slyly asked.

Dan felt the eyes of every reporter attacking his skin, flinching from the thought of how quickly the information got out.

"Yes," he said, fidgeting as the journalists smothered him again. "Both murders are being looked into."

"Do you have any leads?" another reporter asked, pushing his way to the front.

"I won't be giving out any names until we've done our investigation…"

Dan knew the reporters were hitching to attack him with more questions about the day's events, so got in first, spilling the beans on everything he knew, including the recent disappearance of the local girls.

"…I want you to listen!" he snapped; watching the journalists concentrate on him as they pushed their devices closer. "I need everyone to stay inside until we, the police, find out what's going on. This is baffling for all of us."

"What do you think will happen tonight?" cried out an old, fat woman from the Daily Review.

But Dan just stared at her and grimaced after thinking of the right words to say. He didn't want the locals panicking to the point of chaos but knew he'd said too much already to prevent it. He rose from his seat as the woman repeated the words before moving towards the centre of the room to take a deep breath.

"You want to know what will happen tonight?"

"Yes," the woman replied, keeping her phone close.

"What do you think will happen? My staff and I will be investigating it…That's what will happen."

The woman nodded before smiling as she stepped back to allow a teenage apprentice from the Bugle Newspaper to near Dan.

"Do you think there'll be more disappearances?" the teenager nervously asked.

"I honestly don't know." Dan wanted to say more but knew there wasn't more he could've said to make the situation any better. "My officers are prepared for anything and everything, so, if whoever's doing this wants a fight then they'll get one...We'll zap them if they try anything else."

Dan watched the journalists retreat to allow him more room to move, with the teenager closely following to put his phone away before heading towards the main door. He nodded towards Marion, feeling pleased with what he'd said; smiling as she opened the door to let everyone out.

"Thank God that's over," she said, sighing as she shut the door.

————

Neal and Ben re-entered the station to find the reception area empty of people; looking around like they'd missed out on something.

"I thought Dan was holding a meeting?" Neal asked.

"Looks like it's already finished."

They walked towards Dan's office, pushing each other like bored little boys.

"I know you're out there!" Dan hollered, hearing them close in. "I hope you're not fuckin' about?..."

He braced himself as thoughts of them messing up again tapped at his brain, waiting impatiently as they slowly opened the door to smile at him. He hated it when they were like this, too professional in their approach. But, he had a feeling their false smiles meant they'd been up to something he wasn't going to like.

"...Where have you been?" he asked, as the door was closed.

They burst out laughing to surprise him, annoying him to want to grab the bin to throw at them.

"...Hey! I'm bein' fuckin' serious!" Dan yelled; his tonsils shaking like someone was using them as a punchbag. "I've been looking for you for ages."

He shook his head as he watched them soak up his words like they do every day until relaxing to smile. He couldn't stay angry with them for long. They were like a breath of fresh air, a family pet to him, but sometimes he needed to shout to release the stress they put him through. If he wasn't shouting at them then one of the others was. Even the cleaner was known to do it.

"We've been out investigating again," replied Ben.

"Oh yeah. Any luck?" Dan asked, crossing his fingers.

"Nope," Neal said, smirking.

"Pass me your notepads. I want to see for myself..."

Dan skimmed through the pages of Neal's pad, closing his eyes like he hoped something would disappear from a page when he reopened them. But the half-completed game of 'hangman' was still seen next to the notes from today.

"Fuck me, Neal!" he yelled, throwing the pad at him. "Hangman?"

"I told him not to do it, chief," Ben said, giggling. "But he didn't listen."

"Stop lying...You asked if the letter 'T' was in it back at the mother's house," Neal replied.

"And was it?"

"Just shut the fuck up," Dan said, almost falling into his seat. "Don't you two have an off switch?"

He sighed as he waited for another wisecrack, but all they did was shrug at him before Ben said, "Sorry, chief...There was one weird moment though."

"And what was that?"

"Some old bloke gave us grief."

"Why?" Dan asked, scrunching his lips.

"Because I was singing," Neal interrupted; his face

quivering as he fought the need to laugh again. "I swear, that's all...He flipped out, shouting something about having a go at someone for singing the same song. But I think he was a bit senile."

"And who was this someone?!" Dan fumed, cringing from the thought that he was right about the pair messing up. "Go back to the old bloke and find out."

"Why?" asked Ben.

"Because it could be a fuckin' clue on the missing youth. You flippin' dimwit."

Neal and Ben darted out of the office, bumping into Jon, Nini and Marek before racing off down the corridor; neither looking back to see Jon's glare.

"Hey, chief, what's up with the goonies?" he said, entering the room. "Did they forget something?"

"Don't talk to me about those clowns," Dan replied, still fuming.

He watched the others settle inside the room, his breathing slowing before collapsing into his seat to listen to Nini describe the final moments with the missing girls' parents.

"Did you tell them we will find their daughters?" Dan said, sighing before staring at the ceiling.

"I gave them hope, chief."

"Hope is better than them being dead."

Jon's heart tightened after Nini's news brought a tear to his eye. He gritted his teeth as thoughts of his daughter being in the same situation entered his mind, the news hitting him hard to cause a lapse of focus as Dan noticed. He leaned back in his chair before making eye contact, smiling at Jon to see he was alert again as Marek and Nini bickered once more.

"Okay, that's enough!" Dan snapped, leaning forward

again as Nini moved away from Marek. "You all need to be ready now the news has spread."

"What's the plan?" Nini asked.

"I've got Chantelle coming back in. She's manning the phones whilst we find out what's going on."

"She won't like that," Jon said. "It's her Yoga class tonight."

"She looks like Yoda," Marek interrupted.

"Not Yoda, Yoga," Nini said, nudging him.

Dan cursed under his breath, ready to step in again to remind them who was in charge, but the phone on his desk rang, shutting everyone up to glare at it.

"Hold on," Dan said, answering it to shout, "Why don't you go and fuck yourself!"

"Dan, are you okay?" Nini asked, concerned after seeing him slam down the phone.

"No, I'm not," he replied. "Some idiot just asked if he could order a cheese, tomato, tuna, bacon, egg and beans pizza." Dan sighed, shaking his head as the others giggled. "Do I look like I work for a fuckin' pizza joint?"

"Phone them back and ask if they want pepperoni added?" Marek said, still giggling.

But Dan didn't find it funny.

"Okay. Let's get back to business. The fun's over," he said, glancing out the window.

He knew the darkness could make it harder for them to find the culprit to leave everyone vulnerable, especially if their energy got drained. But right now his main concern was Nini.

Is her mind damaged after her ordeal at the boy's house?

He wanted to wrap her up in cotton wool and say how sorry he was for not welcoming her with an easier first day, but her second had been just as horrific and he knew it. He saw Jon's fighting spirit and Marek's pumped-up attitude so knew they were up for the challenge, but he wasn't so sure of Nini.

"...Make sure to keep your guns on stun only. I want whoever is out there captured alive," Dan sternly said, reaching into a cabinet to fetch his weapon. "Nini and Marek, you patrol the outskirts of town."

"And where will you be?" Nini asked, nodding.

"I'll be with Jon, knocking on a few doors."

Dan walked out of his office, closely followed by the others; each passing Chantelle to see her enthusiastically smiling as another call came in.

———

The queen slowly moved along the floor of the UFO as her old skin dropped off to be eaten by the bugs. Her eyes appeared as dark as a shark's as wings protruded from her back, moulding her slug-like shape into a menacing creature. She shrieked as her legs grew longer; her body thinning to reveal muscle instead of fat. She was transforming back into the hunter she was before crashing to earth, hungry, needing more of the food she'd recently tasted. She slapped out a tongue, excited to be soon hunting the new type of prey; rising to almost reach the upper shell of the UFO.

She chattered towards the bugs, shrieking as they formed into the shadow again; watching them vanish before closing her eyes.

———

Ben and Neal arrived at the housing complex where the old man lived but became hesitant as they closed in on his front door.

"You do it," Neal whispered.

"Why are you whispering?"

"Because this guy is scary."

"Now you're scared of him? You should've thought about this when you were teasin' him in the park."

Ben huffed, pushing Neal out of the way to knock on the door, but the sound of it being unlocked caused him to shiver.

"Who the fucks out there?!" the old man shouted, opening the door slightly to partially reveal his face.

Ben freaked out after seeing an eye glare at him, cowering behind Neal to push him closer to the door.

"You talk to him," Ben whispered. "It was you who sang and pissed him off."

Neal nervously stared at the door, watching it open wider to reveal the old man scowling at him.

"Are you going to talk or what?" he said, looking Neal up and down. "Just don't be selling anything. I don't want no shit."

"We're the officers you spoke to earlier," Neal spluttered, backing away as the old man grunted at him. "Do you remember us?"

"Remember you! Fuckin' remember you!" the old man yelled, prodding a finger into Neal's chest. "I remember the din of some law fuck tryin' to sing."

"Yeah! That was me," Neal replied, excited that the man remembered him. "Did you like it? Such a catchy tune."

Ben shook his head, feeling thankful that it wasn't him talking to the old man before cringing as Neal was prodded again. He heard Neal whimper so stepped in to drag him away, leaving the old man annoyed as he tried to catch his breath.

"It was the worst song ever," he replied, breathing deeply. "If you've come here for applause then forget it. I'm busy."

"No!" Ben quickly said. "We're here to talk to you about something."

"Where's the other fucker?!" The old man coughed, squinting as he tried to see past the officers.

"Who's that?" Neal asked.

"Stop taking the piss." The old man moved the officers to one side. "The worm who was singing in the early hours."

"That's why we're here," Ben said, hoping the man would back down. "We need to ask you about the person you spoke to."

"Ask me? But he works with you, doesn't he?"

"Is it okay for us to talk inside?" Ben nervously asked after watching a few nosey neighbours appear on their doorstep.

The old man stared, reluctant to answer, but, after moving up close to see Ben's I.D badge, backed off and lowered his guard.

"It's a bit messy inside," he said, scratching his head. "Just don't fuck with me or I'll punch the shit out of ya'..."

He watched the officers pass by, spooking them with a grin before suddenly swinging his fists like a deranged lunatic.

"...Float like a butterfly, sting like a bee!" he cried out, swiping the air.

"Hey, calm down, Cassius," Neal said, dodging the latest swing before it hit him.

The old man ferociously coughed again after a sharp pain shot through his body, forcing him to drop his hands to place them on his lower back. He felt stupid for not having his walking stick, cringing as he closed the door to follow the officers towards the living room.

"In you go," he said, reaching out to grab the stick. "The snake won't bite you."

Neal and Ben shivered; their eyes scanning the room in fear that a snake would pounce.

"Show us where it is," Neal said, nervously searching behind him.

The old man laughed. "Fuck me! And you call yourself the police." He laughed again, walking towards an armchair to sit down before adding, "There is no snake. I was winding you up...Now relax."

Ben sighed, feeling less worried as he took in the sights of what was inside the room; seeing stacks of newspapers piled up in a corner and ornaments that looked over fifty years old placed beautifully inside a glass cabinet. He admired them, feeling excited before checking the walls to see paintings similar to those of the great artists; stopping on one that looked identical to the 'Mona Lisa' by Leonardo Da Vinci.

"Bloody hell. Is that?" he asked; his eyes glued onto the painting.

The old man sneaked up behind him, ushering him away before covering the painting with a towel.

"Is that what?" the reply came, as he grunted.

"It looks like that famous painting of the moaning lady."

"Yeah. It looks like the Mona Lisa," Neal said, watching on with interest.

"The Mona Lisa! The fuckin' Mona Lisa you say," the old man blurted out, choking from another laughing fit. "How could someone like me afford a priceless painting like that?"

Neal and Ben shrugged their shoulders and smiled.

"But it looks very much like it," Ben replied, checking out the rest of the room.

"Ha! Ha! Ha! Stop it." The old man slowly sat down again, rearranging a cushion to place behind his back before adding, "No, no, no, that's a painting I did many years ago."

He glanced at Ben, feeling nervous; faking a smile until Ben nodded and looked away. But Neal inspected the other paintings to freak him out.

"You're very talented...Fair play to ya'," Neal said, nodding.

Ben walked over to the papers, tripping on the carpet to crash into them before finding his feet to pick up the ones fallen on the floor. He held up a hand to apologise, feeling the old man's angry breath as he placed some back on the pile. But one paper, with an article on the front page relating to the Mona Lisa, grabbed his attention. He read the page, engrossed in a story about the painting being stolen from a London museum before checking the date to find it was *1990*; turning to see the old man fidget in his seat like a naughty child.

"Isn't that a coincidence," Ben said, smiling; holding up the paper like he was selling it on a street corner.

"What's that then?" Neal asked.

"The Mona Lisa was stolen thirty years ago and here we have a perfect replica." Ben walked towards the old man to see beads of sweat form on his brow. "Maybe you should sell your painting to the museum. It's a bloody good likeness."

"Yeah, maybe," the old man replied before bursting into another coughing fit.

"And you need to get that cough looked at," Neal said, grinning.

Ben sat opposite the old man, worrying him to the point of accepting defeat. He held his hands out like he expected to be handcuffed, but Ben just shook one and smiled.

"Listen. We've been here for a while but we still don't

know your name," Ben asked, as Neal glanced through the papers.

"Mick. Just call me Mick."

"Mick, you don't need to be worried." Ben scrunched his eyebrows. "Those paintings are excellent." He let go of Mick's hand, pointing at the 'Mona Lisa'. "I read that one of the robbers was described as a Michael Evans, which was weird." He stared hard until Mick looked away. "And he was never caught..."

Mick breathed heavily from the thought of more police banging down his door to arrest him, nervously waiting to be marched out of his house. But Ben just exited his seat to laugh out loud.

"...It's strange that you have similar names."

Mick looked oddly at him; his breathing calming down again after realising he was dealing with a couple of stupid morons.

"That is strange," he replied, sitting upright. He felt angry and annoyed again but remained calm, hoping the officers would soon leave. "So, this person I shouted at. He wasn't one of you?"

"Damn! I forgot why we were here," Ben replied, tapping his head. "Nope, he wasn't...Why would you think it was a policeman?"

"Because it was very early in the morning...Only you lot are stupid enough to walk on the freezing streets then."

Neal chuckled as he placed a paper onto a new pile.

"Why are you laughing?" Ben asked.

"He's got a point," Neal replied, placing another two papers on top. "We're usually the only ones on the street late at night."

Ben sighed, fearing he had reached a dead end. He walked

towards the door, ready to leave, but Mick's grunts stopped him.

"Whoever he was, he sang the same annoying song...I shouted and he gave me some lip."

"Then what did you do?" Ben asked.

"I went outside to shut him up."

"And was he there?" Neal butted in.

"Was he fuck! The little bugger ran off..."

Ben nodded, taking in what Mick said before clicking his fingers to let Neal know it was time to go.

"...You're not going to write my statement down?" Mick questioned, slowly exiting his seat.

"Damn! I forgot," Ben replied, watching Neal catch him up. "But don't you worry, I have it stored in my memory."

Mick puffed out his cheeks, fearing the worst once the officers returned to the station. He just hoped they didn't forget.

He saw them near the door so smiled slyly when Ben touched the handle, but his smile faded after Neal pointed at the paintings.

"The matchstick men one," he said, staring at Mick closely. "You did a great job with that also."

Mick said nothing as he ushered them towards the door, but Neal suddenly raced back to the newspapers to place one under his arm.

"Is it okay if I take this?"

Mick gulped, glancing at the paper before smiling and nodding after noticing it wasn't the one with the robbery in.

He opened the door and watched the officers leave.

CHAPTER ELEVEN

Dan and Jon sluggishly patrolled the street, glad that the snow had stopped falling as the extra layers of clothing protected them from the quickly decreasing temperature. They turned into another road, lighting it up with their torches, but the silence sent shivers down their spine.

"It's fuckin' freezin'!" cried Jon.

Dan nudged him. "Stop moaning...We're not going to find the killer if we remain at the station all night."

"I know." Jon folded his arms. "What's the plan?"

"We need to find a link between where the murders and the missing girls took place...There has to be a connection."

Jon rotated in a circle to flip up snow and slush, ignoring Dan as he rubbed his eyes to stare into the darkness. He moved his torch from side to side, squinting to leave Dan bemused before squinting again to refocus.

"We know what the connection is," Jon said, sighing.

"I know, but we need to work out why it happened in those areas?"

Dan produced a small map from beneath his padded

jacket, showing Jon markings and names with a red line connecting them all.

"What's that?" Jon asked, knowing full well what it was as he tried acting more interested.

Dan smiled as he pushed the map closer. "These are the areas to where there's been a reporting of some kind." He waited for a reply but Jon was too busy concentrating. "Do you notice anything?"

"Yeah!" Jon raced from his mouth. "They're close together."

"Exactly!" Dan shouted, scanning the street to route out the distance between each crime. "The boy was murdered here," he said, pointing at the spot on the map. "The Lovells store is here, and the missing girls were here."

Jon saw concern grow on Dan's face, knowing his brain was working quickly to try to come up with an answer.

"But what about that area?" he asked, pointing at a spot Dan never mentioned.

"That's where the teenager may have disappeared from after speaking to the old man."

"Old man?" Jon asked, feeling lost.

Dan remembered, that although he'd mentioned the oddball officers annoying him when the meeting took place, he hadn't said why they had pissed him off so badly?

"Sorry. I forgot to tell you." Dan pointed at the map again. "The old man that lives here..."

He explained what Neal and Ben told him, leaving out the not-so-important bits to move on to the altercation between the old man and the missing teenager until Jon got up to speed.

"...I'm pretty sure it's him the old man saw," Dan said, putting the map away. "So I sent Neal and Ben to his house to question him."

"Do you think whoever's doing this is still here?"

"Maybe," Dan replied, slapping his hands against his thighs to keep warm. "There's only one way to find out."

Jon suddenly jolted, turning around quickly to stare at something behind him.

"What you looking at?" Dan asked, worried.

"I'm not sure," Jon replied, shaking his head. "But I think I just saw a black shadow moving along the road."

"A black shadow! Like a ghost?"

"I've no idea." Jon puffed out his cheeks and blinked before shaking thoughts of the darkness playing tricks on him from his mind. "It was there then it vanished."

"Spooky!"

They walked towards the end of the street, hearing a dog bark excitedly in the distance.

"Now that's goin' to wake up the neighbourhood," Jon said, annoyed at how frequent the barking was.

Dan nodded in agreement as the dog's tone changed to a squeal.

"...Maybe the killer is back?" Jon questioned, concerned now the dog had stopped making a noise.

"Nah...It's probably just had a nightmare."

"A nightmare?" Jon scrunched his nose. "Do dogs have nightmares?"

"Ha! Ha! Ha! I've no idea."

———

The bugs hopped off a German Shepard to leave it staggering from the fluid entering its body. It whimpered until its face froze, its legs buckling to send it crashing to the kitchen floor as the bugs hopped back on to shear its fur with ease.

They chattered, regrouping after hearing a vibration close

by before racing inside the dog's mouth to leave it shaking as a sleepy-eyed woman entered the room.

"Basil," she said, walking past the dog basket to reach the fridge.

She opened it to pour orange juice into a glass, allowing the light from the fridge to brighten up the dog like a Christmas tree, but not once did she turn to see it still shaking violently in its basket. She whistled as she shut the fridge door, walking back through the darkness to exit the room.

"...I'm glad you've stopped that howling," she said, yawning.

She took a swig of juice and reached the stairs before walking back up to enter her bedroom; switching on the bedside lamp and placing down the glass. But her husband wasn't in bed.

"Derek! Are you in the bathroom?..."

She called out to him a few more times, feeling frustrated after receiving no answer; giving in to lift the bedcovers to see bloodstains on her husband's side of the bed. She panicked, racing from the room to find the bathroom door open.

"...Derek!" she yelled. "Are you in there?"

She entered to find it empty.

———

Dan and Jon closed in on the woman's house after hearing more shouts, racing to bang on the front door as a shuddering scream shook them. They looked at each other and braced themselves before Dan produced a hefty kick to smash the door open; entering to see the woman almost fall down the stairs in an attempt to reach him.

"My husband's vanished. He's vanished!" she hollered, shaking nervously.

Jon hugged her as Dan rushed upstairs, gripping his gun as he reached the bedroom to see the bloodstains on the sheets.

He searched under the bed, feeling baffled that no drops of blood were seen; cursing as he opened a wardrobe to find no clues before slamming it shut to race towards the next room. He scratched his head after seeing no sign of the husband as he listened to Jon try to keep the woman calm.

Jon escorted her towards the kitchen before turning on the light to see fur on the floor, as the dog's mangled body and half-eaten organs sent the woman into a fit of hysteria.

"Oh, my God! What's happened to Basil!" she shouted, crying into Jon's chest.

"What the Fu..." Dan said, gulping as he reached the room to see Jon take the woman outside.

Dan unclipped night-vision goggles from his trouser belt before shaking his head and placing them on; turning off the kitchen light to loud cries coming from the woman that freaked him out to almost fire his gun. He relaxed, seeing the images of the two people outside before slowly entering the next room. But a cold eeriness shook his bones. He gripped the gun tighter and raced back towards the stairs, looking up as the sound of '*thudding*' closed in before staring hard until seeing a human head bounce off each step to land by his feet.

"...Fuck me!" he shouted, almost jumping out of his skin.

He came close to retching after a vision of the head belonging to the husband shook him before a creepy whistling coming from the top of the stairs grabbed his attention. He stared upwards again but froze after witnessing a dark shadow glide up a wall.

What the hell is that?

He lifted the goggles and rubbed his eyes before replacing them to find the shadow had gone; his blood now boiling from a mixture of anger, adrenaline and fear as he climbed the stairs to search the wall. He shuddered from the thought of someone jumping out at him, but more screams coming from the hysterical woman forced him to return downstairs. He raced into the kitchen, ignoring the carcass on the floor, reaching outside to see Jon's energy drain in a flash. But the woman's recent explosion of crying left him confused. He watched Jon hug her before following his vision, feeling horrified to see body parts scattered on the ground.

"What happened!" Dan shouted, removing the goggles.

"They fell from the sky," Jon shyly replied, pointing at a leg.

"The husband?" Dan said, choking after almost treading on a hand.

Jon nodded.

They saw the woman stagger off and lean against a tree, crumbling to the ground within a second to violently vomit.

"But there's no head," Jon said.

"I've just seen it roll down the stairs," Dan whispered, checking to see if the woman was listening. "Take her to the hospital."

"What are you going to do?"

"I'm going to find the bastard who did this."

"Where are you going to look?"

"In this house." Dan gripped Jon's shoulder. "I saw something at the top of the stairs, but it disappeared before I could find out what it was."

"And you want to go back inside alone to look for it? That's crazy!"

"I'll get Nini and Marek to help." Dan looked over at the woman again. "Just make sure she's okay."

He watched Jon approach her, pleased to see him help her towards a nearby bench, but his ears twitched from the sound of more whistling to leave him convinced that what he saw was still inside the house. He turned and glared at it, wanting to run back in to zap anything that moved but knew it was stupid and a possible suicidal thing to do. Whatever he saw, whatever he thought he saw, he didn't want to see it again without backup.

He reached for his radio as a haunting image of the shadow raced inside his mind, giving Jon another glance before contacting Marek.

"Hey, is everything okay where you are?"

"Yep. Why?" Marek replied, tapping Nini on the arm to mime – 'Something's wrong?'

"I need your help," Dan said, hearing faint whimpering from the woman as Jon escorted her away from the house. "I'm in Tower Street, number twelve. It's near Cassidy Street... Get here pronto."

Dan was gone, leaving Marek to stare at Nini.

"What's wrong?" she asked, worried by his expression.

"It may be nothing, but the chief needs us..."

Nini was off, racing towards town before Marek could finish his sentence, her journey taking her past the old abandoned railway station, an area covered with train carriages and overgrown greenery. It was on the edge of town, about a ten minutes walk, but the area wasn't mentioned on Dan's list of places to search. Nini had pleaded with Marek to check it out after having a strange premonition, a feeling of something clawing at her brain that made her anxious. But neither had spotted anything unusual.

She stopped running to crouch in pain, rubbing her temples like she'd just experienced a migraine attack, cringing from the sound of Marek shouting - "What's up?!"

"I don't know," she replied, staring at one of the carriages. "But something's buggin' me about that."

"You're not using your mumbo-jumbo, Chinese spiritual bollocks on me again, are you?"

Nini glared at him, forcing him to back down. "It's not bollocks!"

"Whatever!" Marek snapped, smirking to annoy her as he walked past.

———

They looked shattered as they arrived at the edge of Tower Street, breathing heavily as they checked the numbers on the houses. They saw Dan appear frantic at the edge of the pavement, so raced towards him to stare into his saddened eyes. But Nini pushed Marek as they neared the house to stop him from treading on a mutilated arm.

"What the hell's that!" he shouted, feeling grateful for her quick thinking.

"The answer behind why I needed you here so badly," Dan replied, sighing. "The head is inside the house."

Marek kicked the arm into a bush to infuriate Nini, as more thoughts of him still being the uncaring arse wipe she met at the academy crashed into her mind.

"Why did you do that?" she said, staring at him as she neared Dan.

"It was in my way," Marek replied, pulling a face.

Dan stood by the entrance to the house, hesitant on going inside; his hand nervously pointing towards the kitchen to spook the squabbling duo.

"I saw something inside there," he said, breathing deeply.

"Something?" Marek asked, cautiously stepping back a few feet.

Dan glared at the house, thinking back to what he saw; his eyes soaking it all in.

"I saw a dark thing...It was there one second but the next wasn't..."

Nini and Marek shrugged their shoulders, finding the words tough to believe. But Dan repeated them until they did before he slowly walked back inside.

"...Oh yeah," he said, placing on his goggles and gripping his gun tight. "There's also a dead dog in here...What's left of it..."

Nini cringed as she waited for Marek to follow Dan before grabbing her weapon and doing the same.

"...Put your goggles on," Dan demanded. "We need to split up."

He raced through the kitchen as Nini stared hard at the dog. But her goggles steamed up to make her dizzy. She took them off and wiped them to feel a nudge from Dan before turning to see him pointing at the living room. She knew he wanted her to go inside. She did, but the sound of his boots connecting on the stairs caused her heart to flutter nervously.

Marek gawped at the pet, prodding it with his boot before staring at the human head in the hallway.

What the fuck is going on!

———

Dan re-entered the victim's bedroom, hoping to find something more useful when searching again. He knew that time was against him as the chances of arresting someone dwindled by the minute, but he needed to remain positive to get through another night. His head pounded from stress, making him feel ill as thoughts of another day ending with more heartache sent shudders through his body. He looked at the bloodstains on the covers again, grimacing because he needed this to end before turning sharply as more whistling brought a sudden outbreak of sweat to drip off his brow.

"Where the fuck are you!" he yelled, leaving the room.

He knew, that if nothing was found soon then the morning would bring with it another problem, an avalanche of unwanted people from out of town trying to take over. People that were bigger than him and his team, people from the larger tabloids, and people who would make him feel smaller than anything he could imagine. He raced into another room, feeling exhausted as his goggles filled with tears.

Nini exited the living room to find Marek holding a half-eaten kidney, scratching his face with bloody fingers to make him look like a Native Indian getting ready for war. He bent down to place the kidney on the floor before moving other body parts, putting them inside the jigsaw-like mess.

"What are you doing?" she asked, closing in to take off her goggles.

"What does your Chinese spiritual bollocks have to say about this?" Marek asked, staring at her. "This is weird...How can someone do this to a dog and dismantle a human without being seen?"

"Marek. I don't want to hear it!" Nini shouted. "I can't stand this."

He hugged her, allowing her to cool down before wiping his bloodstained hands down the back of her jacket.

"Just wondering why the wife wasn't touched," he said, sniggering as he let go.

Nini snapped out of her panicked state after hearing Dan walking down the stairs; her focus back to show him she was ready to carry on as his footsteps closed in. She breathed deep and fast, flinching after the kitchen light was switched on.

"Why have you got blood all over your back?" Dan asked, standing in the doorway to reclip the goggles on his belt. "You'll have to pay for the dry cleaning."

Nini glared at Marek, feeling annoyed at how easy it was for him to pretend she wasn't there. She turned around to face Dan, ready to tell him the truth, but Marek spoke first to leave her cursing under her breath.

"What did you find up there, chief?" he asked, putting his goggles away.

"Nothing! I found nothing up there!" Dan shouted, kicking a bin. "I can't deal with any more of this shit tonight." He walked over to the door and calmed down. "Nini, I need you to stay here until the medics take the body, or what's left of it away."

"And me?" Marek asked.

"You can come with me back to the station."

CHAPTER TWELVE

Dan remained fuming as he and Marek entered the police station, leaving Neal and Ben bewildered.

"He looks pissed off," Neal said, watching Dan storm off towards his office before seeing Marek approach a drinks machine.

"Yeah. It's been a rough night," Marek replied, jumping from the sound of a can dropping.

Neal and Ben looked at each other and smiled as Marek picked up the can. But he suddenly stared at something Ben was holding.

"What you got there?" he asked, opening the can of pop to take a sip.

"Oh...I'm just reading a paper that Neal retrieved from the old man's house."

Marek laughed. "I didn't know you could read."

Ben smiled.

Marek took another sip and sat in a chair, appreciating the softness of the padding to leave him relaxed.

"Talking about the old man," he said. "Dan told me he was a witness or something."

"That guy's a mental case," Neal said, laughing as he sat next to Marek.

"But he is a great artist...Don't forget to mention that," Ben replied, looking up from the paper.

Marek seemed lost and unsure of anything coming from the other two being believable or not, but they were entertaining and that was good enough. He tried to focus but their words went over his head.

"Yeah, he's an awesome artist," Neal replied, facing Marek. "You should've seen some of the paintings he had. They looked well real...They were sick, man."

Marek nearly laughed again after hearing the excitement in Neal's voice, but the sound of Ben flipping pages over grabbed his attention.

"What's so interesting about that?" Marek asked.

Ben stopped reading before looking up to see him study the paper.

"For one, it's dated back to nineteen-forty-seven. That's like loads of years ago. Plus, there's some interestin' stuff in it."

"Name one thing interesting in that so-called paper you got?"

Ben closed it to leave Marek gulping after seeing the front page. Whatever was on it had him hooked.

He snatched it to leave Ben confused before racing towards Dan's office.

"Hoy!" Ben shouted as Marek disappeared from view.

———

Dan looked up from his computer to see Marek close in, hoping for some positive news as his office door was knocked.

"Come in."

"Check this out," Marek said, entering the room to throw the paper onto the desk.

Dan stared at it, mystified as to why it was important.

"What's this?"

"Read the front page..."

Dan did.

"...Could be something," Marek finished saying.

The headline read – THE HUNT IS ON FOR THE KILLER OF FIVE LOCALS...

Dan skimmed down the story but stopped after two lines, slowing his reading to find it interesting.

"...What do you think?" Marek asked, knowing Dan was intrigued.

"Wow! Where did you get this?"

"Neal got it from the old man's house...It's interesting, don't you think?"

"It could be a link," Dan said, reading some more. "According to this, the deaths were all of a similar style, with each person being ripped to shreds and parts of their anatomy taken." Dan scratched his head and read some more. "This happened seventy-three years ago, but the killer wasn't caught."

"Do you think it's related to what's happening now?"

"I don't know, Marek, but I think a visit to the library is in order...I need to check it out to see if the killer was eventually found."

"And if not?" Marek asked, unconvinced. "Do you think the killer is back?"

"How can the killer be back after all this time?" Dan replied, laughing nervously. "Serious! How can someone kill again after seventy-odd years away?"

"I don't know, but this report could still be a clue."

"I know you're trying to help, but think about it. Do you

honestly believe that we have an ancient killer on the loose?" Dan questioned, watching Marek sigh as he sat in a chair opposite. "You do know they would've either died or got caught by now."

"I know...Sorry for wasting your time."

"Never think you're wasting my time...Anything is possible with this case, but that can't be the answer."

"You're right. It must be a copycat killer of some kind," Marek said.

Dan nodded as he turned the pages of the paper to stop at another headline - FLYING DISC FOUND NEAR ROSWELL, NEW MEXICO...

And below it was a photo of a ranch with debris scattered nearby.

He read the story, finding it was aimed at a possible sighting of a fallen UFO.

"Jeez! I remember hearing about this," he said, leaning back in his seat. "My grandfather mentioned something about the so-called alien find near Roswell...I think they changed the story to a weather balloon crashing down in the end."

He pushed the paper over to Marek, keeping the page open to see his eyes widen with excitement.

"Yes! It was huge talk back in Poland," Marek said, glancing away from the paper. "Weren't pictures taken of an alien on an operating table back in the seventies?"

"I think so...It was before our time, so let's not think about it now." Dan closed the paper and rose from his seat. "Aliens! As if." He laughed and walked towards the door, signalling for Marek to follow him. "I want you to check old archives in the police database and look for violent criminals that could and would do this type of crime."

"Sure thing," Marek replied, reaching the door. "Then what?"

"Then look for criminals with priors for copycat style acts of violence, but no one over the age of fifty." Dan opened the door to allow Marek through before leaving the room to walk him down the corridor. "Whoever's doing this can sneak in and out without being noticed, not even leaving fingerprints...This is a pro, but I seriously doubt if they're an old one."

Marek nodded before entering a room to sit at his desk as Dan aimed for the daft duo.

"Neal!" he hollered, closing in. "Tell me more about the old man's house."

"Have I done something wrong again, chief?"

"Not this time. But you may have done something useful."

Neal babbled on as he described the ornaments and paintings from inside the house, feeling proud as he mentioned the talented artist he'd spoken to, but Dan yawned and placed up a hand.

"Slow down," he said. "Just tell me about the newspapers?"

"What do you want to know?"

"How many? And how far back do they go?"

"Jeez! Chief, there were loads there. Hundreds I reckon, but I'm not sure how far back they go."

"It's okay," Dan said, shaking his head. "Just go back there and search through them again. Bring back the ones linked to the murders on the front page of the paper you have here."

"Is this a joke?" Neal asked. "Because I don't think the owner will be too happy to see me again tonight."

"Are you a cop or a little mouse?"

"A cop," Neal replied. "But he's a touch crazy."

"If he asks why you are returning so late just tell him to paint a portrait of you. That's if he's such a master at it."

Neal frowned.

He felt shocked at how brutal Dan's verdict about the old man was but figured he was stressed.

"We'll get the papers," Ben piped up to say, tugging on Neal's arm.

———

Dan sat in his car staring at the entrance to the library, checking his watch to see it had just turned *9:30 pm*. He fidgeted, scanning the street for a sign that someone would arrive to let him in until feeling convinced it was too late. He bit his nails, losing patience, close to driving off as thoughts of the murders from *1947* made him quiver. He closed his eyes, reminiscing the story from the paper, but a car horn blaring made him jump. He stared ahead as headlights almost blinded him, crossing his arms over his face as a car pulled up. He sighed, feeling relieved after seeing a woman, whose face was partially hidden beneath the fur-trimmed hood of a thick winter coat exit the car, the wind blowing the fur reminding him that he also needed to brace against the cold.

He opened his car door, exited and stretched, noticing the woman watching him take a step towards the library.

"Sorry about this," he said, closing in. "I know you're very busy and probably got loads to do tonight, but this is serious...I need access to some of your files."

The woman reached the main door, pleased to be sheltered from the wind; removing the hood to reveal her beauty as her bronze skin and dark eyes stopped Dan in his tracks.

"Is there something wrong?" she asked, noticing him blush as she opened the door.

Dan became excited by her cool South American accent, the words bouncing off him, making his knees weak as she allowed him inside.

"...Yes, I am a busy woman, so hope this doesn't take long...I need to be home for my sons," she said, shutting the door.

"I'll do my best," Dan replied, unzipping his jacket. "I noticed you have an accent. Where are you from? Argentina?"

"Brazil...But come here around ten years ago...Why all the questions? Do you want to see identification?" she said, scowling at him.

"Wooah! Calm down! I was only being polite." Dan held up his hands, feeling confused as to why she was stressing so badly.

"Sorry, just tired...I'm worried about my boys because of the loose killer."

"You mean killer on the loose," Dan replied, smirking."

"Ha! Yes! Sorry. My English is still sometimes poor."

"It's okay. You're doing well. I understand you."

Dan was led down a corridor until entering a large room full of books, walking past the Sci-Fi section to see an alien bug poster on the wall before stopping at the horror one to pick up a novel about killer rats.

"Looks like a cool story," he said, smiling as he read the blurb before putting it back.

"Yes, the S.T.A.R.S. project is very popular. I like the author."

Dan smiled again as he followed her down another corridor, closely watching her take off her coat to reveal an hourglass body. But this time he didn't blush.

"Do you have a name?" he asked, acting like a lovesick teenager.

"We all have names Mr policeman...But you can call me Sabrina or Miss Fernandes."

"Okay, Sabrina. Can you show me where the files are?"

"Did you think I was taking you on a tour?"

"No."

"We are heading there now, so follow me."

Sabrina scowled again like she did when Dan first entered the library, moving swiftly to extend her distance to leave him catching up.

"I'm looking for archives from the year nineteen-forty-seven," Dan rushed from his mouth as Sabrina kept up the pace. "Do you have records dated back that far?"

Sabrina stopped and smiled at him. "Mr policeman, we have records dated back to Noah's Ark. Do you want to see them?"

Dan almost laughed. "Just call me Dan," he said, smiling. "Very funny, but forty-seven will be fine."

"Okay, Dan, follow me." Sabrina led him to a room labelled staff only. "Here you will find what you need."

She unlocked the door and led him inside, turning on the light to reveal wall-to-wall filing cabinets before smirking as he sighed.

"But which one do I need?" Dan asked, feeling the pressure as he slowly walked over to them.

"Get closer. You will see the years...Look for nineteen-forty to nineteen-fifty...Good luck." Sabrina turned to walk away. "I will lock up in ten minutes."

"You will what!" Dan panicked.

He counted the cabinets, frantically searching for the one he needed, finding it to hear Sabrina giggle as she left the room.

She's a strange one, he thought, slowing down to open it.

But he saw nothing resembling old papers, tapes, or even discs relating to nineteen-forty-seven; just a memory stick inside a folder. He picked it up and stared at it as thoughts of it collecting ten years of data sent negativity through his mind. He knew the library was downsizing its paperwork to help the planet but didn't know it had already begun. He just hoped it had what he needed.

He sat down and switched on a computer, waiting for it to boot up before wiping his eyes and inserting the stick; moving the mouse to click on the removable drive to see folders representing each year. He found the one he needed, so scrolled down the months until opening the right one, searching through important events until finding a section aimed at Lemonsville County. But Dan knew he couldn't get drawn into just staring at the town's history. He needed to find the report on the murders.

"Is everything okay?" Sabrina asked, holding a mug of hot coffee. "I thought you may want this."

Her sudden appearance spooked Dan, making him nervous the closer she got.

"Where did you pop up from?" he said, watching her place down the mug. "You're like a sexy ninja."

"Am I?" she replied, laughing. "Just wanted you to come on me."

Dan spat his first sip of coffee over the screen before blushing again as he cleaned it off with his sleeve.

"I think you meant to say you wanted to come and see me or something like that."

"No! Did I say some filthy whore words?" Sabrina apologetically asked. "I see you have redness on your face, so maybe I say it wrong?"

"Believe me, I've heard worse."

Dan smiled until Sabrina relaxed; her head nodding as he took another sip.

"I see you kept it inside your mouth this time."

Dan giggled as he hovered the mouse over links involving the town, but Sabrina noticed he was struggling to find what he needed.

"You seem lost," she said, standing behind him. "Here, let me help you find what you need."

Dan smiled as she placed a hand over his to guide the mouse until stopping to click on a page explaining the deaths.

"How did you know what I was looking for?"

"I didn't, but I'm a Brazilian woman, so knew you needed my help for something..."

Dan almost laughed again, thinking she was making it up, but Sabrina looked deeply into his eyes to almost hypnotise him.

"I can see sadness like many deaths not explained...You are here to find answers."

"If I can," Dan replied, checking the computer screen again.

"There's been a lot of terrified people in here today, concerned about the young boy...His death led me to this page."

"So you know about what happened here in nineteen-forty-seven?"

"No," Sabrina softly replied. "I don't know what happened back then, but I do pick up things...We, librarians, don't just replace books all day."

Dan was mesmerised by her voice. It soothed him, making him feel relaxed.

"Did you pick up anything that could help me with his case?"

"I've no idea, Dan, but I've studied this town's history, so knew you were looking for a tragedy like this."

"You're very good," Dan said, taking another sip. "But is your research as good as your coffee-making skills?"

"I hope so," Sabrina replied, watching him sip the drink again. "Is it?"

"Not bad...Marks out of two. I'd give you one." Dan laughed hard, close to dropping the mug; knowing his crudeness had gone too far.

Sabrina squirmed, feeling confused as Dan returned to the screen to look at news reports about the *1947* deaths; her mind digging deep to work out what he meant. But then it dawned on her.

"You would give me one." Sabrina pulled a face, staring at Dan to make him feel uneasy. "It was very funny," she said, slapping him on the arm. "You would give me one means you would fuck me. Yes?!..."

Dan suddenly sweated as he tried to ignore her, but Sabrina laughed to make him feel less awkward.

"...Naughty, naughty, mister policeman," she said, waving a finger as she walked away. "You are a naughty man."

Dan smirked as she left the room again before slapping himself in the face.

What am I doing? She may be pretty but I have a job to do. I need to focus.

———

Marek looked away from staring at the computer screen, breathing deeply to hear something '*smack*' against the window. He exited his seat and walked over to it, seeing trees blow rapidly as debris whirled in the air; sighing as more flew against the glass.

I hate this weather, he thought, checking his watch to see the time reach *10:00 pm*.

He brushed a hand across his face before snapping back into work mode, returning to the computer to stare at a photo of an elderly man on-screen; sitting back down to read a report about an incident taking place in *2010*. It was a violent crime, committed in a nearby town by the man. He had seriously beaten a young couple half to death, only stopping because someone walked past and disturbed him.

Marek stared at the image again, feeling curious to know more about him.

But is he a potential suspect?

He knew Dan specifically asked for no leads over the age of fifty, but he couldn't let it go without doing more investigating. At the time of the incident, the man would have been around seventy; way older than the person he was meant to look for, but Marek still wrote the information down. He scrolled to the next page to see that the town was only twenty miles away before reading a paragraph describing the man as being very strong. But it was the next piece of information that hooked him. The man had injected the couple with a numbing drug before beating them.

He can't be the killer, but it's the only lead I have.

Marek printed off the photo and pinned it to a notice board before stretching his joints to hear bones crack, the sound reminding him of a Bruce Lee movie to make him smile. But the question of who the old man was? tapped at his brain. He left the room, determined to find an answer; noticing how quiet the station was.

"Sorry, mate," he said, after racing into the staff room to find Jon waking up on the sofa. "I didn't know you were back."

"Yeah, been back a few minutes," Jon replied, sitting upright.

"You fancy a cuppa?" Marek asked, switching on the kettle.

"Love one." Jon rubbed a hand across his drained face, yawning to bring water to his eyes before getting up to hand Marek a cup. "What happened in the house after I left?"

"Nini and I arrived to find a dead dog and someone's head at the bottom of the stairs."

"Yeah, was awful...How did Nini take it?"

"She's tough...She'll probably act like it's nothing but inside she'll feel like crap."

"Yep." Jon walked over to the sink, turning on a tap to splash water on his face. "So, have you got any leads?"

"I may have a suspect."

"That's great news."

"But is it though," Marek replied, cringing at the thought of telling Jon who he had in mind. "He's very old."

"How old?"

"A lot older than the age range Dan told me to check for."

"Then forget about it...We need serious suspects."

Marek reached for the kettle after hearing it turn off, pouring hot water into cups before adding sugar and coffee.

"But I have a strange feeling about this guy," he said, adding milk to the drinks.

"You've been spending too much time with that partner of yours," Jon said, laughing into his hand. "Soon you'll be joining one of her classes to see if you can solve crimes with your mind."

Marek picked up a teabag and threw it at him. "Who told you about her weird premonitions?"

"It's all in her file, mate...She's a true believer all right."

"Okay, but just hear me out." Marek handed Jon the cup

of coffee before replacing the milk in the fridge. "The guy I'm looking into did a horrific crime down in Lockscroft, so I want to head down there to check it out."

"It's a bit late for that, don't you think?" Jon said, looking at his watch.

"There's no time to think, Jon, people have been murdered and kidnapped...If we stop to think about it then more deaths could happen. I'm not waiting around for that."

"Okay. Drink up. I'll go with you."

———

Dan searched through more articles relating to the crime from *July 1947* before writing notes on his pad.

But why just one night?

He read the article again before skipping to the next day, noticing a report about a massive manhunt taking place involving the locals. They'd helped the police check houses, streets, parks, and wooded areas, but, after going through Lemonsville with a fine-tooth comb found no evidence. The town became infested with government officials, who moved the search to other towns until finally, the whole of the UK was under investigation.

Dan searched for more information but came to a dead-end as the words no clues, no witnesses, and no suspects tormented his mind. He scrolled down the years, close to giving up, but, as he reached *1995,* saw an article stating what he suspected. The headline reading:

Hunt Is Over

'After 48 years of trying to solve the case of the five victims murdered in 1947, the local authorities have closed the case file, admitting defeat in their quest to bring the killer to justice.'

But who was the mysterious killer?

Dan turned to see Sabrina close in, knowing why she was there.

"Have you found what you came here for?"

"Yes, thanks," he replied, feeling sleepy. "I have what I need for now."

"Good, because I need to get home to my boys."

Dan closed everything down and removed the stick, smiling at Sabrina as he placed it back inside the cabinet.

"I'm all yours," he said, following her out of the room.

"You wish you were all mine."

Dan was left confused by her flirty nature, the way she bounced his words back to him with an added touch of sex appeal secretly turning him on. He was glad of it because it stopped him from thinking about sad stuff for a while.

Sabrina led him back out of the library, not saying another word to drive him crazy. He watched her lock up again, wanting to speak but was now too nervous to, so just smiled at her as she walked back to her car. Dan walked back to his but kept turning in the hope she would do the same, his heart melting to see her glance at him.

He waved as she drove away.

CHAPTER THIRTEEN

Ben raced through the newspapers, desperately searching for ones related to the incident from *1947* as Mick glared at him; his patience almost evaporating after only a few seconds.

"I thought you got what you needed when you were here before?" he said, biting his tongue so as not to swear.

Ben smiled at him before placing a newspaper into a new pile. "We did, but the chief needs us to look for something else."

Mick feared they were closing in on him, seeing him for the fraudster he was. He knew he couldn't keep up with the lies about the paintings. *The officers were stupid, but not that stupid.*

"Something that's in my papers?"

"Yeah, but don't sweat it, man. We won't be long."

Neal stared closely at the paintings again before touching the Mona Lisa.

"Not being funny, Mick, but you could make a killin' by selling this...Why don't you paint one of me while Ben checks out your papers."

Mick laughed, hoping he was joking. "Come on. It's past my bedtime. I need to sleep."

"Neal, you are meant to be helping me," Ben interrupted, adding another paper to his pile.

Neal smiled before moving away from the paintings to tap Mick on the shoulder.

"Oh well…Maybe another time then."

Mick sighed, cringing from the thought of seeing these clowns again after tonight, hoping there was never going to be another time as he sat in his chair.

"Oh! That paper we took from you," Ben said, counting the ones in his pile.

"Yes. What of it?" Mick nervously replied.

"I need to find out more about the story on the front page."

Mick seemed mystified after forgetting what the main headline was, his face scrunching from fearful thoughts of having a bad memory once Neal reminded him. He shook, cowering in his seat, his breathing getting faster and faster to leave him panicking. But the officers watched on, surprised to see him in such a state.

"You've come back here to mess up my papers," Mick raced from his mouth, clutching his chest. "And rant on about murders from a long time ago. And that's it?"

"Yeah, that's it," Ben replied. "Do you know anything about it?"

Mick slowed down his breathing and exited the chair before reaching for his stick to help ease the pain shooting down his legs.

"You don't need more of those to know what happened," he said before angrily snatching a paper from Ben's hand to throw onto the sofa. "I'll tell you what happened."

Neal and Ben watched him as excitement glowed on

their faces. They were ready for him to tell them the story, but Mick felt like he was on a stage and it made him nervous. He stared at the officers before pulling many faces, sucking up air to hold inside his mouth to leave them worried for his health. They saw Mick's cheeks bulge like he'd just eaten a small ball until suddenly he breathed, pointing his finger.

"Pull it," he said, smirking.

Neal and Ben looked at each other, feeling confused. But Mick's smirking left them intrigued.

Neal nodded and smiled before pulling on the finger, but was soon gasping for air after Mick farted.

"What the!" Neal coughed, holding his nose to the sound of Mick laughing like a crazed hyena.

"Why did you do that?" Ben asked, spitting out the foul taste.

"Lighten up guys. Seriously! You need to chill out a bit."

"Do you know anything about the paper or not?!" Ben shouted.

"I would've been very young back then, so I can't help you."

Ben cursed under his breath before grabbing the paper from the sofa and placing it with the others.

"And you have no recollection of what happened as you got older?"

"What's with the questions, man?" Mick backed away after thinking they were setting him up, asking him decoy questions to force a mistake. "I moved away from here years ago. When I was young...Not long after those murders." He breathed deeply and glared at Ben. "I only came back here a few years ago."

Ben looked him up and down and nodded before slowly picking up the new pile of papers.

"It's okay. I just had to ask," he said, walking towards the door. "We'll leave you to it."

Mick sighed, pleased to be finally left alone again before sticking up a hand as the officers exited his house for the second time.

CHAPTER FOURTEEN

Dan drove towards the outskirts of town before heading for a small, country cottage where his mother lived. All the evidence gained from the library was burning his brain, with some reminding him of his childhood, so needed to see her urgently. He remembered a story his grandfather told him about the murders but thought it was just a tale of some kind, a made-up piece of nonsense to scare him when he was naughty. His grandfather knew how to scare him back then, back when he was seven years old.

His grandfather was around a lot in those days, back in nineteen-ninety-seven. At fifty-eight, he retired from his job with the government. A role he had kept secret all this time. But Dan couldn't stop his mind from drifting back to his childhood to the stories his grandfather told him.

Why did he tell me about the murders in my town? Murders that sound similar to what's happened recently, he thought, turning off down a side road.

He tried concentrating on the journey, but memories of

his grandfather wearing a suit and holding a briefcase now rushed to the front of his mind.

He passed a few cottages, slightly hidden with overgrowing trees; smiling because he knew he was close to his mother's house. He glanced at the snow all around him, fresh and untouched to appear like ice clouds on the ground.

He saw the house, so drove up to park outside, scanning for signs of life inside before slowly exiting the car. He walked up to the door to the sound of it opening; his mother ushering him in to get out of the cold.

"Hi, son, this is a bit late for a visit," *Maureen* said, as Dan moved past her and into the house.

He looked at his watch, noticing it was nearly *11:00 pm.*

"Sorry, Mum...I didn't realise the time," he replied, as she closed the door.

He was ambushed with a hug as he entered the living room; his mother squeezing tight to show how worried she was as the hug went on longer than normal. Dan smiled and sat down before placing the back of his head against the soft backrest of the chair. He closed his eyes to the sound of Maureen leaving the room, only opening them again when she returned with two mugs of hot chocolate. He watched her place them on a small table nearby before quickly wrapping his hands around a mug to feel the heat warm his fingers. Maureen sat opposite, desperately waiting for him to speak, but Dan just remained soaking up the hotness.

"What's wrong?" she asked. "I know there's something wrong, so what is it?..."

Dan took a sip of the drink; his tongue burning as the liquid slipped down his throat. He was thankful for the pain, the distraction needed so he could gather his thoughts before coming back to the here and now.

"...Does it have anything to do with the murdered child?"

"Yes, it does," Dan replied, staring sadly at a wall.

He was shattered emotionally as well as physically and his mother knew it.

"...I don't know if I can solve this case," Dan splurted out, wiping his eyes before sipping his drink again. "I've seen too much in a short space of time and it's torturing me. I'm going to fail. I know it."

"Dan, you can do this...The boy's parents need you to solve it," Maureen softly said, hoping he wasn't about to have a breakdown.

"I know, I know, and I'm trying." Dan felt more old memories creep upon him, kicking him into finding out the truth. "I need to ask you about Granddad's old job."

"Old job?" Maureen replied; feeling lost as to why the concern. "He's had many old jobs."

"The one he did for the government. Before I was born."

"You mean back in the late sixties when he looked stylish in a suit." Maureen sighed as memories of her father sent her on an emotional ride, but nothing came up relating to his job. "He was only there for three years. I was three when he started, so know nothing about it."

"Not even one story about what he did?"

Maureen became on edge, fearing Dan was onto something she had no idea about.

"What's going on? Why the sudden interest in your grandfather's work?"

Dan knew he had to maintain the pressure on her, even though she was turning pale. He felt sad about doing it, but it was something that needed doing.

"Did he mention anything to you about murders in this town? Back in the late forties. When he was around eight."

Dan leaned forward in his seat, sensing his mother knew something. *But how much did she know?*

He watched her shiver like a dead person just woke up to touch her, her hand trembling as it clasped his.

"I didn't want you to worry."

But her words did worry him.

Dan felt angry with himself for not knowing about what his grandfather did, thinking that maybe it could've prevented the recent slayings if he'd known before visiting the library. But had a feeling he was clutching at straws to even get close to finding the killer.

"So, you do know about the horror of seventy-three years ago," he said.

Maureen felt smothered, with no way out. She knew if she kept quiet about it more questions would arrive, but telling Dan would open up some very dark secrets that were meant to be buried forever. Dan waited for her to say something to help him solve the case, but she found it hard to dig into her past.

"...He told me about murders, but I thought he was just trying to scare me."

"Your grandfather wasn't lying to you," Maureen said, rising from her seat to walk towards the window. "He lived on the street when it happened, and saw the medics take the bodies away. It's a childhood memory I wouldn't want to have...He's still having nightmares about it." She looked out into the night sky before adding, "But why do you want to know about his job?"

"Because I think something happened there. Something bad. That's why he left."

"He retired!" Maureen blasted out. "There's nothing more to it." She stared at Dan like he was a puzzle she needed to solve. "What do you know that I don't?"

Dan rose from his seat before flicking up a cushion in anger.

"Retired before he was sixty. Do you honestly believe that?"

Maureen flinched after Dan's words sent her spiralling even deeper into her father's old job. In truth, she always wondered why he retired so early, but he never let slip the actual reason. She sat Dan back down and explained it to him, but her eyes gave out clues that she was keeping something back.

Dan listened to her talk about her father for the next fifteen minutes, but most of the conversation only related to what he was like outside of his job. Then suddenly, the conversation shifted over to her *mother*. She was the one who'd slipped up a few times after feeling emotional. Maureen remembered bits and bobs of information from her about her father's job before she sadly passed away.

She sent Dan back in time to her teenage years. The year *1980* when she was sixteen years old. But, according to her mother, what happened in *1947* was best left forgotten. She'd told Maureen about the nightmares her father was having, the awful night terrors from what he witnessed as a child plus others related to his job. Things he'd seen, stories he'd heard being passed between staff members of awful incidents resulting in deaths, and him screaming *"BUG"* repeatedly whilst asleep.

"Bug?" Dan questioned.

"Yes, bug...But my mother never knew why he was screaming the word."

Dan thought about what Gina told him until his adrenaline exploded again. He needed to know more about the murders, but Maureen stopped the conversation dead by saying there was nothing to add. There were no witnesses, no clues, no motive, and no explanation as to why it happened, but it happened, and it happened in Lemonsville.

"I'm sorry if it's too upsetting for you, but I need to work out why those murders were done in a similar style to what happened to the young boy."

"Maybe you should visit your grandfather?" Maureen said, touching Dan on the shoulder. "He may say more now he's older."

"But I won't be able to see him at this hour."

Maureen smiled. "You're an officer of the law. You can do anything."

"But it's very late," Dan said, smiling back.

"We both know your grandfather will still be awake. He's a right night owl...I'm sure the staff at the nursing home will understand."

"Maybe you're right, but still, it'll be past midnight by the time I get there."

Maureen nudged him. "I'll go with you. You need to do this..."

Dan nodded before relaxing after the tension of keeping everything inside was finally released. He still felt emotional and angry, but, after his mother confirmed most of what he'd read at the library, was happy to keep on digging into the past.

"...Give me five minutes," she said, walking towards a door.

CHAPTER FIFTEEN

Jon and Marek arrived in Lockscroft, hoping to find out more about the attack on the couple. They entered the police station to be stared at by the night shift officers, with some tapping their watches to remind them how late it was, but Jon and Marek just smiled as they reached the information desk.

"Have you come for the file?" the on-duty officer asked, touching it.

"We sure have," Jon replied, reaching out to take it from him.

"You do know I could've emailed it to you."

Jon laughed. "Yep. I know that. But we needed some time away to get our heads around what's been going on."

"Understandable," the officer said, turning away.

Marek watched Jon flip through the pages, noticing his eyes light up before closing the file.

"What's got you all excited?"

"Have a read," Jon replied, passing it over. "Looks like our journey wasn't wasted."

Marek took in everything as he read the contents of the file, blowing out his cheeks after finding out that an unfamiliar numbing drug was used on the victims. He shook his head and smiled, glad to have ignored Dan's order, wanting to find the culprit immediately as he handed the file back to the officer.

"Thanks for this," Jon said, shaking the officer's hand. "He seems like a right piece of work."

"He is," the officer replied. "I'm just annoyed that he's slipped beneath our radar."

"Don't worry, we'll catch him."

Jon walked towards the exit door, waving at the officer as he left. Marek raced to catch him up as he neared the car.

"What do you make of the drug used on the victims?" Marek asked.

"It tells me that it was used to make the attack easier," Jon replied, opening the car door. "That's why an old person got the upper hand so quickly and why no one heard the victims."

"How did he get his hands on a drug unfamiliar in this country?" Marek asked, stiffening after the cold wind crashed into him.

"That's something we need to find out." Jon sat inside the car and took off his gloves. "Let's wait for the lab report to see what happened to the young boy. If there are any un-prescribed drugs in his system then this man could be the person we're looking for."

"But he'll be in his eighties, that's if he's still alive." Marek sighed, now feeling unconvinced as he sat in the passenger seat.

"We need to assume that this man is still out there and still a threat."

"So how do we find out?"

"We head back to base and check the suspect's photo

again." John started up the engine, glad to feel warm air against his skin. "We'll find out who he is once we scan his photo on the database. He's probably had different pseudonyms, that's why he's slipped through our radar. But we'll find him."

CHAPTER SIXTEEN

Nini slowly walked back towards the police station, hoping to rest her aching feet after another traumatic stay inside the house of a recent victim. She had watched the medics bag the body parts but couldn't answer their questions as to how they mysteriously fell from the sky and why the victim was killed.

She turned into another street, adjusting her hat after the sharp wind almost blew it off, sighing after seeing four men walk towards her from the other side of the road, two carrying baseball bats. She glared at them, spotting a silver object glisten as they walked beneath a streetlamp, the man holding it quickly hiding behind the others as she cautiously crossed the road.

"What seems to be the problem here?" she asked, closing in to see the man desperately shove the object inside his coat.

"We're looking for the bastard who's been killing the people of this town!" he shouted.

His name was *Bolton*. An overweight buffoon who loved to be in control.

Nini recognised him from a file she'd read at the station as part of her first day's introduction, so knew what he was capable of. She thought fast to his last arrest, a beating he gave to his wife a year ago; feeling anger towards him because the charges were dropped. She stared him out, waiting for him to look away, but he just winked to cause her blood to boil.

"What bastard? Do you even know who you're looking for?" Nini replied, faking a grin.

Bolton ignored her as he pushed his way to the front of the group, but Nini raced ahead of him to stop him in his tracks.

"...You can't take the law into your own hands, so give me the gun." She stared at his coat, waiting to see if his hands moved towards the weapon. "This will be sorted by the police!" she shouted.

"Don't make me laugh. You, people, can't sort shit!" Bolton pushed her to one side. "It's been all over the news," he said, grunting as he carried on walking.

"Stop right there! We will sort it."

"Too late...We had a meeting and I've been selected to find the fucker before he kills again."

Nini saw the other men follow Bolton like he was the new Messiah, but none were recognised as *Frederick*, a German watchmaker, who wasn't known for being brave, *Solomon*, a nineteen-year-old who felt like a man just by being with the others, and *Jones*, an arrogant man with a scar on his left cheek, walked past her. Nini assumed he was there to bully the other two into helping.

"I will tell you again, and this time you will listen to me!" Nini yelled at the men; her voice becoming hoarse to make them laugh. "You don't even know who is doing this." She ran to the front of the group, facing Bolton before holding out a hand. "Because you are angry, you will probably find the wrong person...Just go home and let the police handle it."

Nini appeared tiny compared to Bolton, but she wouldn't give in. She stared at him even harder, showing persistence, but Jones pushed her hand away before spitting on the ground. Nini turned to him but he ran across the road before she could speak, Bolton closely following to leave her desperately searching for the reason why? She saw someone closing in but they were hidden behind Bolton and Jones' large frames. She knew the person was in trouble.

Clyde was a thirty-something male who was on his way home after checking on his mother for the evening. He'd been worried after hearing the disturbing reports of people being murdered or going missing, so needed to see if she was okay. But he was now facing the angry men.

"Where'd you think you're going?!" Bolton blasted from his mouth before smashing a fist against the side of Clyde's face.

Clyde toppled over in an instant, crashing to the ground to search for two teeth in the snow before staggering back to his feet. He held his mouth to stem the blood flow, but it gushed beneath his fingers as a foot crashed into his stomach to knock him to his knees. He cringed in agony, holding shaking hands out to plead with the men to stop attacking.

Nini nervously ran across the road, screaming at the men as she neared Clyde; her blood boiling again to almost make her cry. But Bolton pulled the gun from the inside pocket of his large winter coat before pointing it at Clyde's head like a paid assassin. He laughed at the sound of Clyde's sobbing, knowing he had him scared.

"You're not going to kill again!" Bolton hollered; his face reddened with rage.

Nini ran in front of him, shivering after staring closely at the gun. "Put that away. He isn't the killer. You know that."

"You don't know who the killer is, so it could be him."

"Look at him," Nini said, pointing at Clyde. "Does he look like a killer?"

She released her gun and aimed it at Bolton, but he didn't flinch. He just laughed at the sight of it.

The other men neared to witness Jones swing a baseball bat at Clyde, but Nini squeezed the trigger to blast him to the ground. He shook for a few seconds, becoming dazed as he got to his knees, his head spinning as he brushed snow from his body. But Nini knew she would need a stronger blast to keep him at bay. She fidgeted with the power whilst observing his next move.

Clyde rose to his feet before slowly making some distance as Frederick and Solomon remained watching. They weren't up for this.

Bolton smiled, happy to see Jones recover quickly, knowing he was just as angry now. They glared at Nini to leave her worried, her hands shaking as thoughts of the gun not recharging in time made her scared.

"We don't want to hurt you, little lady, so just move aside!" Jones shouted.

Nini aimed her gun at him again after seeing it was at full power; watching him back away to let Bolton take over to aim his weapon like he was ready for a duel.

"Is this what you want?" he asked, grinning. "To see what is best. My gun or your weird energy blaster?"

Nini smiled back, knowing if she didn't the men would think she was weak and easy to attack.

"I'm game if you are," she squeaked, not happy to hear her voice change so drastically. "Shall I count down from five?"

Bolton looked at Jones until they both shook their heads.

"Wow! You have some balls on you," Bolton said, almost choking at the sight of Nini. "Or we could just fight? The police are trained to fight, right?"

"We are," Nini replied, feeling on edge.

"Good. Now you can put your gun away."

"Not until you do the same."

"Okay."

Bolton winked at Jones as he dropped his gun in the snow, smirking to see Nini do the same. But she was just playing along. She knew they were up to something, but tackling the men with no weapons seemed her best option right now.

She saw Bolton smile like a sadistic monster, knowing he was doing it to sway her from seeing Jones close in. But she was ready; her breathing controlled as she braced herself for what was to come.

She spun from side to side, clenching fists as both men neared; her seven-stone weight making them laugh as she was easily pushed to the ground. They cracked jokes as she brushed snow from her face, rising to her feet to leave them surprised that she'd come back for more.

"Just give up," Jones said, watching Nini clench her fists again. "We're too strong. We'll crush you."

Nini breathed deeply before grabbing a steel baton from her belt; extending it to its maximum length.

"Back away or I'll use this on you!" she shouted, slamming the baton into the wet ground.

"Ha! Ha! Ha!" Jones laughed.

Bolton did the same, but his laugh faded quickly once Nini cracked the baton against Jones' right kneecap; listening to him squeal like a whimpering child as he fell over to rub his knee and punch the snow.

Bolton snarled and ran at Nini, but she moved swiftly and avoided being hit; kicking snow into his face before swinging her left foot at his head. It connected sharply to knock him backwards, but, after rubbing his skull, he charged again with more intensity, bear-hugging her and lifting her off the ground. He squeezed her lower back, listening to her gasp for air as her bones cracked; the pain almost causing her to collapse as Jones rose again. She saw him close in as fear spread through her body, but Bolton's grip remained tight to stop her from getting away. She wriggled violently to free herself, wincing before slapping hands against the side of his ears; causing him to let go and lose his balance from the uncontrollable ringing now blasting through his eardrums. She saw Jones approach, so turned swiftly before catching him with a superb round-house kick. But it only wobbled him momentarily, as he recovered to throw fists at her in a crazy rage. He came close to connecting but Nini's quickness left him gobsmacked; his energy drained as she ran up his body to crack his jaw with her knee before somersaulting to land back on her feet. Nini's movement was so fast and precise that Jones stood no chance of avoiding it. But he didn't fall. His eyes watered as he swung fists again, but each one hit thin air as Nini bounced from side to side to flick fingers back and forth. She was teasing him now.

Bolton screamed at her as he charged again. But she just stood there like she was giving him a chance to fight back, letting him close in to within a few inches before swiftly moving to one side to see him clumsily crash into Jones. They fell to the ground, exhausted to get up, feeling embarrassed to see Nini smile at them.

Frederick and Solomon just admired her energy, almost clapping after seeing her put on some lipstick.

"A woman needs to look her best when arresting some arseholes," Nini said, laughing.

Clyde bent down to search for his teeth again. He picked them up whilst spitting out blood before producing a goofy smile as Nini handcuffed the two men.

"Are you okay?" she asked him.

"I will survive."

CHAPTER SEVENTEEN

Lemonsville Nursing Home was very quiet when Dan and Maureen entered the main doors. They walked towards reception to see the clock on the wall tick past *12:30 am*. The receptionist nodded as they passed her, happy to see visitors in the early hours.

They entered a private room to find *Eddie Mckay* sitting in a chair, his appearance frail and aged since the last time Dan saw him a few months ago. But Dan didn't want to mention it.

"Have you been eating?" he asked, as Maureen sat nearby.

"Stop fussin'," Eddie replied.

"Come on pops, you know you need to keep your strength up so you can chase all the pretty nurses."

Eddie smiled cheekily as Dan held his hand, but it felt cold to leave him more worried about his grandfather's health. He watched Eddie wearily raise his head, his eyes drained and tired. Maureen noticed; her heart shattered to see her father in such a state. One half of her wanted to stop Dan before he asked any questions but the other knew he needed to get them off his chest.

"Don't you worry," Eddie said. "I can still chase the nurses."

"Dad!" Maureen shrieked. "You do know I'm here, don't you?"

Eddie nodded, pleased that she was. "Yeah. It's good to see you." He stared at her. "But why now? At this time of night?..."

Maureen nervously pointed at Dan, hoping he would start talking about the past. But he was finding it hard to do. Eddie turned to him, sensing something was wrong, the moment sending a shiver down Dan's spine until he released his hand.

"...Is someone going to tell me what's going on?" Eddie asked, feeling the awkwardness in the room.

He coughed and spluttered into his hand to panic Maureen into grabbing a tissue from a nearby table. She handed it to him, becoming close to freaking out. But Eddie stopped.

"Maybe you should do this another time?" she said to Dan.

"Do what?!" Eddie snapped.

"I wasn't talking to you, dad."

Dan looked at the floor, catching his breath before attempting again to say what he wanted to say. He watched Eddie suddenly close his eyes as if he was nodding off, so whistled to grab his attention.

"Pops. I'm here on police business."

"That's so typical of you," Eddie blurted out. "I don't see you in months then you turn up to arrest me."

Dan almost laughed. "Why would I arrest you?"

"Because I did something wrong," Eddie replied, shaking.

A *nurse* walked by, alerting Maureen to bring her into the room. She smiled at Eddie as he babbled on about doing a bad thing, but Maureen felt confused.

"What's he talking about?" she asked.

"He's just having one of his turns again," the nurse said, checking Eddie's pulse. "It's his Alzheimer's. It makes him say strange things. There's nothing to worry about; he's not done anything wrong...Eddie is always good." The nurse looked at him. "Aren't you."

Eddie smiled, allowing his top false teeth to slip. But the nurse just put them back in.

"How long has he been like this?" Maureen asked, lost as to why she didn't know.

"A while now...You may not have noticed because he's usually very good at hiding it, but it's been getting worse the past few days."

"So, I'm wasting my time asking him some questions?" Dan popped up to say. "If he can't remember stuff now."

"Dan!" Maureen shouted. "It's never a waste of time talking to your grandfather."

Dan nodded and held Eddie's hand again.

"Ask him what you want," the nurse said, turning to leave the room. "He may remember something."

Eddie wiped the tissue around his mouth, smiling as Dan sat beside him. But, after the *1947* murders were mentioned, he pretended not to hear. Dan sighed and repeated it, but Eddie wasn't budging and the deafness act remained.

"What's wrong?" Maureen asked, noticing him shrink down in his seat. "Dad, are you okay?..."

Eddie looked scared.

He grabbed Maureen's arm to leave her wanting to cry, his expression the same as it was back when she saw him having nightmares. Everything had calmed down as he got older, with no reports of him having one at the nursing home. But right now he was struggling.

"...What's wrong, dad?" Maureen asked again.

Eddie gripped her arm tighter, wincing as he stared hard.

"I've been having the same dream from that year for the past few days."

"From nineteen-forty-seven? But you were only eight back then," Dan said.

"Eight I may have been, but I'll never forget what happened." Eddie let go of Maureen's arm. "How could anyone forget?"

Dan knew he had hit a nerve after Eddie began to cry, so thought about cancelling the need to dig deeper into his frail mind.

"Pops, don't cry. I'm sorry for mentioning it."

Maureen hugged her father as Dan became lost with what to do next.

"Best if we let him sleep. It's late, son," Maureen said, kissing Eddie on top of his balding head. "We'll come back tomorrow, talk to him then."

"But there is no tomorrow! Tomorrow could bring many more deaths," Dan muttered, wiping a hand across his face. "I seriously can't handle that. Can you?"

He produced a stony stare that rocked his mother, but she stood strong, refusing any more questions aimed at her father. She knew Dan understood, even if it meant him not knowing the truth for a little longer.

"You're right. I can't do this to him," Dan calmly said.

They watched Eddie dry his eyes, but his mind had released the horrid memories that he wished were still buried. He shook from thoughts of what had kept him awake the past few nights, a dream that was turning into something more, a nightmare that nipped at his flesh.

"They won't let me sleep," he softly said.

"Who won't?" Dan replied.

"It's not a who..."

Maureen turned away, holding her mouth to muffle her cries as Dan's heart beat fast.

"Not a who?" he questioned, breathing deeply.

Eddie began to relive his childhood horror, making it clear that he never saw the murders, only the aftermath; the carrying of body parts as the medics took them away. He said the night before was the weirdest night he'd ever witnessed. A strange light appeared in the sky that he'd never seen before or had seen since. It wasn't bright, but it flashed past his bedroom window at a very fast speed, and then it was gone.

"Then what happened?" Dan asked, writing it up in his notepad.

"The sky was back to normal again."

Eddie mentioned he'd told his parents about it, but they just said he'd had a weird dream. The bodies in the street had erased the memory of the light, replacing it with the new, grisly, and sickening one.

Maureen hugged Eddie again, as Dan said, "What did you think the light was?"

"Some kind of plane maybe," Eddie replied.

Dan tried to remember what he'd read at the library, but nothing about a strange sighting or a plane was seen in the files. He knew his grandfather was struggling to talk about the past so thought his mind was muddled up to produce fake news, but Eddie didn't change his story.

"So, did you think there was a plane crash nearby?" Dan asked.

"I did think this for a while," Eddie said, yawning. "But if there was then nothing was found...It made me question myself, so maybe it couldn't have been that?" He stared at Dan. "The light was extremely fast, and I mean lightning quick."

"Meaning?"

"If it did hit the ground then it could have shot hundreds of feet below the surface."

"Whoah! Calm down!" Dan shot back to his feet. "Are you telling me that you think some kind of plane smashed into Lemonsville and no one but you noticed?"

"I don't know. All I know is what I saw." Eddie smiled at Maureen, pleased to be finally letting out the past. "And the next day five people were found dead."

Dan huffed before walking around the room, imagining many scenarios of what may have happened to leave him breathless. It was a lot to take in, especially if it was true.

"But don't you think it's just a strange coincidence?" he asked, returning to face Eddie. "Maybe the flash of light killed them?"

"I seriously don't know, but nothing happened afterwards," Eddie said.

"Nothing happened afterwards, but it's happening *now*."

"What do you mean?" Eddie replied, baffled.

"Have you not seen the news or read today's paper?"

"There's a rule in this place and that's not to let any trauma from outside be talked about...It upsets people, so we don't watch the news or read about it."

Eddie sluggishly tried to exit his chair, but Maureen stopped him.

"Dad, you need to take it easy."

"But I need to know what's been happening?"

Eddie shook, looking more scared than before, as the sadness in Dan's eyes caused him to cry again.

"He doesn't need to hear it now," Maureen said, hugging her father again.

"I do," Eddied softly replied, staring at Dan.

"There's been a bunch of deaths since last night...All

similar to the ones from when you were a child," Dan said, hoping Eddie wouldn't freak out again. "But the only difference is it's gone on longer than one night."

"The murders?"

"Pops, do you honestly want to know more?" Dan questioned.

Eddie nodded.

"...Yes. That, plus people have gone missing without a trace."

Eddie cringed, gulping as he wiped his eyes again; feeling *weak* to remain upright as Maureen sighed.

Dan looked at the clock on the wall to see it was *1:00* am, knowing it was the right time to let Eddie rest. He watched him yawn again and close his eyes, as Maureen tapped his head and smiled.

"Let's leave him to sleep," she softly said, walking towards the door.

CHAPTER EIGHTEEN

Neal and Ben sat in the staffroom, hoping to catch a bit of shut-eye after helping Nini bring the men in responsible for the attack on Clyde. They looked exhausted; their eyelids almost closed, but Nini entered to shake them awake. She was still pumped up after the fight, her hands waving as she explained again the moves she did on the men. But Neal and Ben just kept yawning.

"Hey! Guys! Come on!" she said, watching them lose interest. "You needed to be there. Then you would be as excited as me."

"Yeah, sure. Whatever you say," Neal replied, hoping she was finished now.

Nini huffed as she sat down, but the comfy chair relaxed her to stop talking before she suddenly fell asleep. Ben sighed, almost laughing at how quickly she did it. Her body was now motionless as he wiped his eyes.

"No way," he said. "She stops us from sleeping and now she's out of it." He got up and walked towards the sink, splashing his face with cold water until feeling revitalised, but squinted after staring at something on the notice board.

"What's that?" he said, walking over to it. "It's a photo of old Mick."

Neal blinked as he slowly got up to look at it; scratching his head as Jon entered the room.

"Why's there a picture of old Mick on our wall?" he asked Jon.

"Do you know this man?"

"Hell yeah! I sure do know him. He's the guy we went to see. The man with the newspapers."

Jon smiled, feeling thankful to be one step closer to revealing who the man was.

There's no way he's just an old man with newspapers.

"You two come with me," he said, leaving the room. "Let Nini sleep for a bit. She's had a tough day."

"She's had a tough day!" Ben said, sighing. "Where are we going?"

"To my office," Jon replied, glancing at Nini.

He walked quickly before entering the room to see Neal and Ben awkwardly catch up. But they shied away after spotting a worn-out Marek sitting at the computer.

"What have we done wrong now?" Neal asked.

"Nothing. You've done nothing wrong," Jon said, closing in on Marek. "You've done something right." He ushered them over to the computer to see a hardcore breakdown of Mick's violent past. "Take a good look at the man on the screen...Is this the guy you saw recently?"

"I already said it's him," Neal replied.

"I just needed to be certain."

Everyone stared at Mick's criminal record. It was a list longer than most, with a crime spree stretching back over fifty years. He had been caught many times stealing and had spent a lot of time in prison.

"Wow!" said Marek. "He's a disgrace."

"Are you sure he did all those things?" asked Neal. "I mean, he looks harmless."

"He looks harmless because he's very old!" snapped Jon. "We need to have a word with him."

"A word. A word about what?" Ben said.

"A word about why this town is missing some people."

"You want me to tag along?" Ben asked, curious to know more about what Mick had been up to.

Jon nodded, leaving Neal annoyed to be left out.

"But what about me?"

"It's about time you two had some time apart," Jon said, walking Ben towards the door. "Don't worry though, I'll bring him back."

Neal gulped and sighed after hearing Jon laugh, feeling sad to see Ben disappear.

Jon pointed at Ben's weapon as they approached the reception desk until Ben noticed.

"What?" he asked, feeling spooked as he shrugged.

"Nothing...Just reminding you to keep it charged." Jon rushed towards the main door. "That old man you like so much might try something stupid."

Ben kicked himself for believing Mick's bullshit before scrunching his lips in disgust after realising the old man never did any of the paintings and had probably stolen them. He shook his head to rid the thoughts of Mick being a funny guy, convinced now that he was just another criminal as he followed Jon outside.

CHAPTER NINETEEN

The dark shadow floated up the side of a building until slipping beneath the crack of a window, scurrying inside a house where the owner had recently gone to bed. It split in two, racing along walls like silent slithering snakes until suddenly halting after a floorboard creaked upstairs. The bugs split into smaller groups after the noise intensified; their senses tingling as they hid in the darkness waiting to pounce. They closed in on the stairs after someone coughed, becoming excited from the sound of the steps being trodden on as the person walking down them entered the living room; their bare feet only inches from touching the bugs as a yawn echoed in the air.

But a loud 'whack' on the front door caused the person to jump and stub a toe on the side of a table.

"What the fuck! Who's that knocking on my door?!" Mick shouted.

He reached out to switch on the light, but bugs covered his hand to make him itch, scaring him to the point of freaking out. They bit deep and hard, peeling away the skin before cracking the fingers at the knuckles to leave him in tears. He felt them snap off like Kit-Kat chocolate biscuits before screaming to grab the attention of who was behind the door.

"Hello! Are *you* okay?" Jon shouted.

But the screams intensified to spook him and Ben.

"...Hey! What's going on in there?" he shouted again. "I'll break this door down if you don't reply."

Mick was now smothered with bugs, all biting into him to leave the floor covered in blood. He felt his intestines slip out of his stomach, hearing them flop onto the ground; his hands turning red as he nervously tried pushing other organs back inside before crashing against a wall.

"Hey! Are you okay?" asked Ben, leaning against the door before shrugging at Jon.

He moved out of the way as Jon kicked the door open, but he slipped over as he rushed inside.

Ben caught him up and turned on the light before squirming after spotting Jon's trousers and boots soaked in Mick's life fluid; his face turning green after finding the gruesome remains on the floor.

"Search the room," Jon said, getting back to his feet. "Where's the rest of this person?..."

Ben felt his stomach heave after spotting parts of Mick's intestine hanging off Jon's thigh, but Jon's anger overpowered the need to be sick as he knocked it away.

"...Find me something!" he yelled.

Ben searched the room but stopped swiftly after shockingly seeing something out of this world. He locked onto a dark, ghost-like shadow sneaking away from the lighted area, rubbing his eyes and not believing what he saw as human body parts floated across the floor. But, as he opened his mouth to tell Jon, the body parts vanished. He whimpered as he raced back towards the broken door before quivering to suddenly vomit over Mick's face.

But Jon was struggling to stand upright.

He grabbed the wall to stop from slipping before cringing as Ben puked again; seeing him swallow hard as he wiped his coat sleeve across his mouth.

"...Is this the man in the photo?" Jon asked, wiping blood off his boots. "Is that Mick?"

Ben stared at the body to almost throw up again. "I don't know...Mick never had puke on his face when I last saw him."

"Stop being a dick!" Jon snapped. "Is this him or not?"

"Yeah, I think so. But half of him is missing."

"If this is him then our target for the murders was wrong."

"Too right it was wrong. I've just seen something carry bits of him away!" Ben shouted.

"What do you mean?" Jon became edgy as he reached for his gun. "Is something in the room with us?..."

Ben shook his head before staring at the spot where he saw the shadow; shock still etched on his face as he sat on the sofa. He wanted to speak but no words came out.

Jon watched him closely, waiting to see if he would clown around, but Ben had a look of fear that couldn't be faked.

"...What did you see?" Jon softly asked. "What was carrying bits of him away?"

Ben slowly looked at him, whimpering to shed a tear.

"A dark shadow."

Jon gulped before shaking his head as he glared at the same spot. He said no more about it, just let Ben rest; knowing he was struggling to come to terms with what he'd seen.

"I'm just going to let Dan know," Jon said, reaching for his phone. "But how do I explain it?..."

He heard Dan sleepily answer to remind him of just how tired he was, looking down to sigh at the mess he was in as he tried to explain the last five minutes. But Dan didn't act surprised.

"...How come you're not freaked out?" Jon questioned.

"It's hard to explain, but my grandfather may have seen what happened in nineteen-forty-seven."

"Shit me! No way!"

"I know it sounds unbelievable, but you should've seen him. He looked petrified like he didn't want me to investigate it."

Jon heard Dan stir a drink. "How old is he now? Are you sure he's not losing the plot?"

"Jon, if you'd asked me this before he broke down on me, then I would've agreed. But I know my pops. He wasn't making it up..."

Dan took a sip of coffee as he waited for Jon to reply, but all he heard was Ben in the background saying something about people becoming a nuisance outside before Jon shouted towards him.

"...You guys okay there?!" Dan yelled down the phone.

"Not really," Jon replied, trying to drown out the noise. "Looks like the old man's death has attracted attention. Ben is on it now."

"Get it sorted. I need you both back at the station..."

Dan looked at his mother's frowning face, knowing she was upset because he was stressed. He smiled at her and nodded to show he was calm again.

"...I'm leaving my mother's house soon," he said to Jon. "So meet me at the station."

"Okay, will do."

Jon turned off the phone to hear Ben struggling to keep everyone away from the house, their frantic attempts to enter becoming annoying as he rushed to give Ben a hand. He knew, that if one person got inside to see the blood and the remains of Mick then an avalanche of chaos would start that neither of them could handle.

He stood by the door blocking the dent made by his boot, as Ben told the people to go home before sighing after knowing it could take longer than planned. He cursed under his breath after realising the time, fearing it was too late for the under-staffed medics to bag the body tonight.

He watched the neighbours stare at the blood on him until cringing at the thought of an ambush of questions, but no one spoke as he re-entered the house to drag Mick's corpse into the kitchen. He felt queasy after more organs dropped out of the body before panicking to the sound of Ben scuffling with a man by the door. But it went quiet within seconds to please him as he filled a bucket with water. He placed it down and grabbed a mop as he waited impatiently for Ben to return before tripping over the bucket to splash water over the puke on Mick's face.

He quickly mopped the floor to see the mop steal the blood to turn the water red; glad of the silence outside as Ben returned.

"All sorted?" Jon asked, placing towels over the body.

"For now...But I think they'll be back."

"Let's hope they don't come in here," Jon said, sweating. "I don't think the medics will arrive until the morning."

Ben shrugged.

CHAPTER TWENTY

Dan entered the station to find Chantelle snoozing in the receptionist's chair; his face fuming as he slammed a fist down on the desk to wake her up.

"Are you having fun?" he asked, glaring at her as she returned to an upright position.

She wiped her eyes and smiled at him to see if it softened his glare. But his expression never changed.

"...Where are the others?!" Dan snapped, scanning the area.

"Not sure," Chantelle shyly replied.

"Not sure? Was that because you were asleep?"

Dan slammed a fist down on the desk again before huffing as he headed off to find the others.

He heard snoring coming from the staff room; entering to find Neal and Nini fast asleep, but his face reddened with rage after seeing them so out of it. He bit his lip after finding no sign of Jon or Ben; his anger fading after a reminder of where they were caused him to shiver. He sighed as he watched the sleeping duo before shaking his head after letting them rest;

leaving the room to enter others before finding Marek still glued to his computer.

"...Have you seen them?"

"Seen whom?" Marek replied, sitting back in his chair.

"Jon and Ben...They were meant to meet me here." Dan checked his watch to find it was *1:45 am*. "Where are they?!" he shouted, racing out of the room.

Nini shot up out of her seat before stretching her tired body to see Dan standing in the doorway.

"I think they're still at Mick's house," she said, closing in on him to calm him down. "You know, the guy with the newspapers."

"Yeah, I know. I've already spoken to Jon. I told him to get back here."

"I'm sure they're fine," Nini replied, grabbing Dan's arm.

He tapped her on the hand and smiled, nodding as he reached for his phone. "I'll just give him a call."

Nini watched him closely; feeling he wasn't as calm about Jon not being there as he let on. But at least he wasn't shouting now. She turned to Neal, surprised he was still asleep before throwing a cushion at him to stir him into action as Dan held the phone to his ear.

Neal groaned, stretched, and sauntered out of the room like he was still half asleep before looking lazily at two figures closing in.

"There you are!" he shouted.

Dan heard other voices nearby as the phone went to voicemail. He followed Neal to see him wave his hands in the air like a lovesick puppy before spotting Jon and Ben close in.

"I was just about to call you."

"Yeah, sorry about that, chief" Jon replied, leaving a trail of bloody prints on the floor. "We got caught up with the neighbours...They saw us trying to leave."

"And the *body*?" Dan nervously asked.

Neal froze as sadness erupted inside of him, feeling the urge to faint after a reminder of Mick making him laugh entered his mind. He looked at the blood still attached to Jon's clothing, breathing deeply before gathering himself to see Nini arrive. She hugged him, feeling his pain.

"I had to leave the corpse in the kitchen. Couldn't wait any longer for the medics...I have no idea if they turned up," Jon said, shaking his head.

"Do we have to feed the fat fucks in the cells?" Ben said, changing the subject to confuse Dan.

"We have people in the cells?"

"Yeah, chief. Nini got caught up in a scuffle in the street and arrested two men."

Dan looked at her as excitement overtook her again, her body glowing from the adrenaline rushing back to bring a broad smile to her lips.

"What happened?" he asked.

"They were out witch-hunting," she replied, flashing her hands in front of the others to show some of the moves she did on the men. "They picked on a defenceless victim, claiming he was behind the murders, so I had to intervene."

"Intervene?!" Marek said, laughing. "You fuckin' kicked the shit out of 'em."

Dan didn't want to laugh, but he couldn't help it. "You beat up two men?"

"Not beat up exactly...I only tapped them."

Marek almost wet himself from laughing so loud as Nini told Dan about the vigilante-style group. She explained she was worried that more groups would follow, especially now the first attempt failed. Dan agreed. He knew if things got out of hand then the town could be overrun, meaning he would have to call in backup. But right now he prayed it was a one-off. He could see that his officers were whacked and needed to rest, knowing they would struggle to contain another bunch of wannabe heroes tonight.

"Listen up...It's coming up to two in the morning, so I want you all to go home and get some sleep." Dan saw the baffled look on their faces but had a feeling deep inside they agreed. "I know we've had a crazy couple of nights, but we're useless to the people if we don't sleep." He closed his eyes for a few seconds as flashbacks from the past two days made him *cringe*. "I just pray that no more deaths happen tonight...We have a better chance of cracking this case once we're fully recharged."

"But what about the clowns in the cells?" Nini asked.

"Fuck them! A good night in the cells is the least of their worries," Dan replied.

CHAPTER TWENTY-ONE

U p by the park, near where old Mick lived, stood a group containing four men. Solomon and Frederick were back with more worried family members, but none were vigilante material like Jones and Bolton. They were just out because they wanted to help keep everyone safe. They didn't believe that the police were sorting things out so needed to stand up and protect their families.

The residents from their street were on edge and didn't understand why Bolton and Jones had been arrested, so, the men were chosen to find answers. But the two newcomers seemed more excited to be out.

Enrique, a twenty-five-year-old man of Spanish origin stood next to *Bob*, a West Indian man in his mid-forties. He was chubby and slow but preferred to be out in the cold than indoors with his nagging wife.

"I think it'll snow again soon," Solomon said.

"How do you know?" Enrique replied.

"Because I do."

"Okay. If you say so."

The men split up, leaving Bob to walk down a back street

leading to the side of Mick's house. He stared at the sky as he neared, thinking Solomon could be right about the snow as he shone a torch at the ground; feeling shocked after noticing red spots in the slushy ice. He knelt to inspect it, touching the sticky liquid to feel sick, as the bugs swooped with the silence and speed of an assassin to slit his throat. He desperately gripped the stinging wound as blood gushed out to paint a picture in the snow; his energy fading quickly to collapse in a heap as the bugs pounced on his back to burrow into his skin.

He reeled around in pain, desperately searching for someone nearby. But there was no sign as a faint groan escaped his mouth. He cringed, gurgling blood; his hands letting go of his throat to produce a silent scream as his spine snapped.

Then the bugs ripped his legs clean off.

Frederick closed in, shining his torch to follow the same path. But chattering noises forced him to beam light up the side of a building. He shook his head after seeing nothing, thinking the dark was playing tricks on him.

"Can you see him?!" shouted Solomon.

Frederick stared at the building until the chattering faded, shrugging his shoulders before walking up the same back street to stand where Bob was last seen. He turned to see Solomon wave before turning back to suddenly disappear.

"Did you see that?!" Enrique shouted, breathing heavily as he raced over to Solomon.

"See what?"

Enrique, still panting, pointed towards the back street, but Solomon was lost as to why he was upset and breathing like someone who'd just completed a workout.

"...See what?" he asked again.

"He disappeared. He just vanished!" Enrique hollered.

"I know he did. He's gone round the back of the houses..."

But Solomon's sentence was cut short after Enrique began to cry.

"...What's wrong?"

"He never got that far because he vanished into thin air."

"What are you talking about?" Solomon asked, shivering more than usual.

He shone a light at the same area before darting his eyes from left to right, now fearing something he had no idea about.

Enrique was petrified; his courage low as he slowly walked towards the same spot.

"...Be careful," Solomon said, watching him closely.

Enrique turned to him, nodding; his knees trembling more and more after each step until the darkness swallowed him up.

Solomon smiled as Enrique's torch lit up the side of a building, the sight giving him the strength to follow before screams blasted through him, causing him to panic and lose control. He stared into the distance, seeing Enrique sob beneath his fingers before catching him up to find Frederick's arms on the ground.

"...What is...happening?" Solomon mumbled after noticing blood spatters trail off in the snow. "But I saw him walk up here."

"He never got far." Enrique thought only of his family after staring nervously at the arms. "Something from the sky took him. I saw it."

"Saw what exactly?" Solomon became more scared and close to retreating.

"I'm not sure now. Some kind of black cloud," Enrique spilt out, almost crying again. "It covered his body and then he vanished."

"It's dark out tonight, darker than most nights, so how do you know for sure?"

"It doesn't matter if you believe me. All that matters is what's in front of us." Enrique glanced upwards as the chattering sounds whizzed past his ears. "This is bad. Something happened to him. I can't stay here."

Solomon also didn't want to stay, but somehow wasn't turning to head home. He pointed ahead, pleading with Enrique to keep on searching, cautiously walking off in the hope that the other man would man up and follow. He did, but they stopped quickly after approaching a large puddle of blood.

"This is fucked up!" shouted Solomon. "Looks like a fuckin' red pond."

He was close to giving up and hiding, but the chattering increased to cause him to jump. He shone a light towards the beam coming from Enrique's torch to see nothing as the bugs trapped him inside a circle of evil to leave him defenceless. He attempted to run away, but they smothered him, injecting his calves with the paralyzing liquid to make him sway on the spot.

Enrique watched on with tears in his eyes, but his legs stiffened before giving way, leaving him dropping to sit on the ground, as the hairs on the back of his neck stood up. He saw more bugs cover Solomon before choking and closing his eyes; too scared to attempt an escape.

Solomon fell into the thick blood to feel the warmness wash over him, but, as he tried to pull himself out, the bugs entered his mouth to sting his tongue, gums and lips.

Enrique opened his eyes as a cold sweat raced over him before shivering to see Solomon hold his face to whimper beneath his fingers. He watched Solomon struggle to get to his feet; his hands lowering to reveal a hideously swollen mouth that scared Enrique into almost screaming.

He cringed after hearing Solomon's muffled moans before seeing his face shake violently as a bug bit its way out of the swollen mouth. It crawled across his nose as others followed, splitting his face wide open to release blood spatters onto the ground.

Enrique felt faint as he slowly got up, but the bugs chattered, forming into a shadow again to surround him before he could retreat. He lashed out with his feet, kicking up snow to cover them, but they smothered his left boot, leaving him in tears. He agonisingly shook his foot to get them off until frantically kicking at thin air, seeing they were gone to feel glad they'd left him alone. But his adrenaline faded to leave just screams of agony.

He stared at his leg as a fountain of blood gushed out; his heart pounding as he reached for his trouser belt. But, as he searched for the bugs, saw his boot fall from the sky to bounce off his head. He fumbled to remove the belt as blood streamed down his face; his complexion paler as he collapsed back to the ground. He sat up, wincing from the pain, feeling sleepy as he reached down to tie the belt around his leg; sweating rapidly at not knowing where the bugs were. But a sharpness shot through the back of his head until his eyes fell from their sockets. The bugs fed on his face as he toppled over.

Solomon slid along the ground to try and escape as his teeth protruded where his cheeks had been; his face a mess of red as he focused on the houses nearby to gain someone's attention. But he was lifted into the air to float like a magic carpet.

He saw people inside houses, so hoped someone saw him before spitting out blood in an attempt to speak as the bugs lifted him higher to edge closer to a bedroom window. He flapped his arms to gain a woman's attention as a sharp pain flashed across his stomach, leaving the contents dropping rapidly to the ground.

Then, the men vanished in a flash like they hadn't been there at all.

CHAPTER TWENTY-TWO

Bolton and Jones shivered inside the prison cell, annoyed at only getting one blanket to keep warm. They lay on their beds as the temperature dropped even more; the blankets pulled up to their chins as they nursed their bruises. But they acted more like innocent victims than trouble-making thugs.

"What time is it?" Jones asked.

Bolton flicked the light on his watch to reveal it was *4:00 am*. "Too fuckin' early. What time do those morons get back?"

"Soon, I hope. This is torture."

Bolton touched his nose, feeling the bone crack to make him cringe. "I think that bitch bust it!" he raged.

Jones sat up to see him touch his nose again as the light on his watch slowly faded.

"My jaw feels like it's crushed," Jones said, rubbing his chin.

"It's not crushed, you dick!" Bolton snapped. "If it was you wouldn't be able to talk properly."

Jones sighed. "But it still hurts."

"Don't mention this to anyone," Bolton said, feeling

embarrassed. "I don't want my family finding out that a skinny pig fucked us over."

Jones tried to smile, but it stung his face. "I'm not stupid. I feel as humiliated about this as you do."

"I'm going to sue her arse. This is police brutality. She can't get away with it."

"You did attack that bloke, so she'll use it against you."

"Oh fuck!" Bolton had forgotten about that. "But there's four of us and only one of her. We'll stick to the story that the guy attacked me first."

Jones agreed.

He lay down again to pull the blanket over his head, closing his eyes to think nice thoughts in an attempt to get some sleep.

Bolton tried to do the same but a chattering sound grabbed his attention.

He grunted as he stared at the wall behind Jones, squinting upon failing to see the shadow, as the noise became irritating to make him more restless.

Jones shook from beneath the blanket as his legs itched; his feet now ticklish to leave him kicking out.

"What the fuck is that noise?!" he hurried from his mouth, as the chattering increased. "It's truly pissin' me off."

Bolton placed a pillow over his head to drown it out, but Jones' fidgeting annoyed him to the point of screaming.

"Just go to sleep!" he hollered. "Ignore it..."

But Jones huffed.

He pulled the blanket off his head before leaning over to scratch his legs but was close to touching the bugs as they slid off him. He smiled, feeling pleased that the itching had stopped before lying back down.

The bugs split into two groups as the men lay quiet, with one sliding off the bed to nestle on the floor as the other stayed put. But Jones became restless again as his legs itched once more. He quickly sat up to be pounced on by the bugs as Bolton rose to say, "And anyway..." Not noticing anything coming from Jones' bed. "When we get out of here, I'm gonna pay a visit to fuckin' Frederick and that pipsqueak of a kid, Solomon. They did fuck all to help us; the fuckin' cowards..."

He waited for a reply but Jones was silent.

The bugs covered his face to suffocate him, leaving Bolton staring hard into the darkness; his eyes straining to find no clue as to what was going on.

"...Sorry, mate, I'll let you sleep..."

He rolled onto his side but heard Jones' bed shake violently; the legs bouncing off the floor to freak him out.

"...Fuckin' hell, Jones!," he hollered, sitting upright again. "This isn't the time to be tossin' off. You're a sick man."

He saw the outline of Jones crash to the floor as the bugs below bit into him. The sight sent shudders down Bolton's spine as he leapt back against a wall.

He saw Jones get up and run around the cell, not speaking to scare him.

"Stop messing about and get back to bed. This isn't funny."

But, as he stared, Jones suddenly stopped in the middle of the cell.

What's he up to?

Bolton clicked his watch light on again to expose Jones' figure, but, as he slowly turned to face Bolton, bugs raced over his face to make his head swell.

Bolton feared for his life after hearing something thud to the floor. He knew he should leave off the light and just crawl into a ball and hide, but needed to see what had made the sound. He shone the light at the floor until spotting Jones' arm, almost vomiting as he raced to the other side of the bed to suddenly feel blood on his lips. He choked and shone the light again, shaking to see Jones' throat was slit.

"AAAAARGGGHHH!" he shouted. "What are you doing?..."

He wiped the blood away but was too frightened to run for the cell door; becoming a blubbering mess as Jones crashed to the floor to be torn apart.

"...Let me out of here, please! I need help in here!" Bolton belted from his mouth as the shadow hovered over his bed. "What the fuck are you?!"

———

Inside the spaceship appeared a more powerful-looking queen, as two extra mouths snapped from within her body. She was pure muscle, her legs like swords, sharp and dangerous. She was alert, not sluggish anymore, flapping her wings with freedom, ready for the outside.

She watched the bugs move away from the recent food they'd brought back before skewering the human meat with three of her legs; dropping a torso, arm and head into the mouths to be crunched with razor-sharp teeth. She shrieked loudly after swallowing pieces belonging to the men from the cells; the noise alerting the bugs to say she was back in control.

CHAPTER TWENTY-THREE

Dan was woken by shouts coming from outside his house; his name was mentioned alerting him to check the time. He sighed, slowly rising to see his bedside clock turn *7:00 am*, as a pebble hit his window to force him to rush with anger to put on his trousers. He reached for a shirt and placed it on before racing towards the pane, hearing another pebble strike as he drew back the curtains to see *four* frightened women, all crying into each other's shoulders. They looked up at him with sad eyes, confusing him with their body language; his head nodding to signal that he was on his way down.

He left the bedroom, kicking himself for leaving the station unattended before walking down the stairs to open the door. But the women barged their way in to almost knock him over. They rushed their words, speaking loudly upon talking over the top of each other as Dan found his bearings to shut the door.

"Okay. Just calm down," he said, hoping they would stop. "Will one of you please tell me what's going on?"

He saw three of the women hush as they awkwardly

stared at the fourth, Frederick's wife, before nodding to get her talking again.

"My husband's missing," she whispered, clearing her throat before repeating it.

"Missing?" Dan asked, feeling unsure.

He waited for a reply but the other women butted in with their own stories of how their family members hadn't arrived home since last night. Dan knew this was going to be another tough day even before arriving at work.

He listened to them spill out what their men had been up to, shaking his head at how stupidly brave the people of this town were, as hopes of Bolton and Jones' fiasco being a one-off crushed him.

"Were they also out looking for trouble?" he asked.

"No!" Frederick's wife shouted, tearing up again. "They were just trying to help...My husband told me about the copper who arrested Bolton and Jones...He was disappointed in their behaviour...He was just out to try and help you."

Dan felt a lump in his throat, knowing he was partly to blame for the men going missing.

"But why did he go back out after the arrest?"

"Because I told him to," Frederick's wife replied, crying again after feeling guilty.

The other women consoled her as Dan tried working out who exactly was out the night before. He wanted to ask but the moment became too sad for him, his heart in pieces as he waited for someone to speak.

"My son, Gilder's husband, and Sophie's son were also out," Solomon's mother said whilst pointing at the women in turn.

Gilder was Bob's wife and Sophie was Enrique's mother.

Dan huffed as he broke down the hours from when he left the station to the present time, but his head and body still ached from tiredness as he slowly entered the living room to find his shoes. He placed them on to hear the women talk amongst themselves, knowing he may not find an answer as to where their loved ones could be.

Surely they weren't snatched like the missing girls.

He breathed in deeply to more cries coming from the women. He shook his head as he grabbed his work jacket from a hook in the hallway, placing it on and wrapping a scarf around his neck before reaching for a hat as he neared the door.

"When was the last time any of you spoke to them?"

"Around two this morning," Gilder answered. "That's when Bob phoned to say it was cold out."

The others nodded in agreement.

"I too had a call around that time," Solomon's mother said.

Dan grabbed his car keys and sighed, knowing it was close to the time he shut down the station.

He opened the door to lead the women back out, smiling weakly as he followed to shut it.

"I want you all to go home...I'll find out what's going on."

He watched them slowly leave before feeling their eyes bore into his back as he locked the door.

———

Jon slowly stirred in his bed, reaching for the alarm clock to see it was *7:20 am*. He was drained of energy so wasn't looking pleased to see what the day had in store for him. He checked his phone messages to listen to a recent one from Dan, his voice raspy as he mentioned more missing people. Jon knew it was his cue to quickly get back to work.

He yawned as he sat on the edge of the bed before

LEE ANDREW TAYLOR

reaching down to pick up his work clothes from last night, sighing because he never had time to iron anymore. He got dressed quickly and grabbed his boots, seeing blood on one to remind him of last night's horror show before rushing into the bathroom to switch on the light. He walked towards the sink and turned on a tap, but, as he flipped the boot over to wash away the red sticky fluid, saw tiny insects stuck within the deep grips of the sole. He squirmed as they struggled to get free before lowering a finger to prod one. But they burst into flames to spook him.

———

Marek popped a headache tablet into his mouth before drinking an energy drink to his alarm going off at *7:30 am*. He smiled, feeling pumped up to face the day, laughing because he was awake thirty minutes before the alarm. He finished off the drink, puffed out his cheeks and left his house.

———

Nini seemed bright-eyed as usual; the trouble from last night not affecting her as she prayed in silence. She gathered her thoughts to think only of positive news before wrapping up to face another freezing day; bracing herself to find the killer as she left her house.

———

Neal and Ben woke up in synchronised timing to the sound of their alarms, both appearing as clueless as usual upon rushing to get dressed.

"Still can't believe he's gone," Ben said, leaving his bedroom to see Neal coming out of the bathroom.

"I can't either," Neal replied, standing by his bedroom door. "I'm not looking forward to today. Something bad is going to happen."

"Neal, something bad has already happened. Just don't do a Nini on me and go all premonition minded..."

Neal sighed as he re-entered his room, leaving Ben worried that he wasn't going to cope.

"...It'll be okay!" Ben shouted. "I'll look after you."

He entered the bathroom to the sound of a phone ringing momentarily, the sound of Neal's voice talking to someone leaving him intrigued. He heard Mick's name being mentioned so left the room, hearing Neal say – 'will do' – before putting down the phone.

"Who was that?"

"Dan wants us to go back to Mick's house, and check to see if the body was taken by the medics."

"He could've just phoned the hospital for that."

"I know, but he's worried that nosey neighbours may try to get inside the house. He needs us there to keep guard until forensics arrive."

Ben huffed as he stormed back to his room. "He just wants us out of the way!"

————

Dan parked his car outside the station before rushing to open the door; whiffing a strange smell that caused him to choke. He assumed it had something to do with the bins, with the blame for the stink being aimed at Ben or Neal, but, as he walked closer to the cells, the smell intensified.

"I bet you two want to go home about now!" he shouted,

holding his nose as he closed in. He waited for a sarcastic reply but scratched his head after receiving none. "I said, I bet you would like to go home about now."

But the silence caused him to panic.

He thought the prisoners somehow escaped, so moved swiftly, reaching the cell. But retched after seeing a bloodstained skeleton lying on a bed. He slowly looked away before retching again to almost crash against a wall, as the sound of officers closing in grabbed his attention. He moved away to wipe his mouth as the urge to be sick was still felt before heading back to the front of the station to see Nini and Marek talking to Marion.

"Hey, chief," Marek said, as Dan ignored him. "Chief!"

Dan stared at him, feeling emotionally pained as words floated towards him again. He was lost with what to say and Nini noticed.

"Dan," she said. "You okay?"

He slowly looked at her, squinting his eyes. "How many men did you say were arrested last night?"

"Two!" Nini replied. "Why?"

Dan glanced towards the cells; his heart racing. "Because there's only one there now..."

Marek attempted to run past him but was stopped in his tracks.

"...Prepare yourself. It's not a pretty sight," Dan whispered.

He moved Nini and Marek away from the prying eyes of Marion, knowing she was looking for more gossip to spread, as Marek became worried that the killer may still be inside the building. Dan knew what he was thinking as he'd already thought the same, but he was convinced they'd gone.

"...It's empty down there," he said, walking them into the staff room. "There was no sign of forced entry."

"It doesn't make sense," Marek replied. "The killer couldn't have got in here, not with our security."

"Not only got in but got in and out without opening the cell door." Dan stared towards the cells again. "And took one of the men whilst leaving the other just a pile of bones."

"Just bones?!" Nini said, quivering from the thought. "How can this be?"

Marek interrupted her. "How can a boy be ripped to pieces? And also the old man?"

Dan listened to them, feeling their concern; his mind going over recent events until convincing himself that the killer couldn't be human. He reminded them about the strange sighting at the top of the stairs inside the house of the headless man, just before the head bounced down next to him. He was convinced that a shadowy figure pushed it. But, it wasn't until after seeing his grandfather and listening to him talk about the light that he truly believed in what he'd seen.

"Come to think of it, I had a creepy experience when I bagged those dead ants at the store," Marek said.

"What do you mean?" Dan asked.

"I swear I saw a shadowy figure lurking in the corner, but it vanished rather quickly."

"What happened with your grandfather to make you so jumpy today?" Nini asked, wanting to find answers before losing her mind.

"Let's just say, that whatever he said, it seems to be more linked to what's going on than anything we've been able to come up with..."

But the sound of a frustrated Jon entering the station stopped Dan from talking about his grandfather.

"...What's up with you this morning?" Dan asked, leaving the staffroom to see him talking to himself.

Jon seemed fidgety.

He wiped a hand down his clothing like he was getting rid of something that wasn't there.

"Not much, apart from an unusual encounter with a few weird bugs."

Dan almost laughed but knew Jon seemed spooked by what he'd seen.

"Bugs! What kind of bugs?"

"I don't know what kind." Jon stopped wiping his hand. "But they freaked me out. They were stuck to the bottom of my boot."

"Did you bring them in?"

"I would've done if they hadn't set on fire."

Dan stared at him, waiting for a smile, but Jon remained stern.

"What was it you said to me before? Something about what Ben saw at the old man's house...A weird shape carrying parts of his body."

Jon was still in two minds about that. "You know what he's like, chief. He's always had an overactive imagination."

Nini and Marek closed in to find Dan lost in thought, as news about the skeleton in the cell was pushed aside by the story of a shadowy figure that took parts of Mick away.

"I've seen something weird, Marek's seen something as well, and you've heard a story from Ben that sounds similar to what we thought we saw." Dan looked over at Marion before adding, "Also, Gina claims to have seen bugs escape her husband's mouth."

"It can't be coincidental," Nini said.

"No, it can't. There's a link between the sightings and what my grandfather told me...So, we need to work fast to find out exactly what happened back in nineteen-forty-seven."

"So, what do we do about the body in the cell?" Marek asked, knowing he was probably going to be the one who moved it.

Jon just sighed as Dan smiled at Nini before hinting for her to take Marion away from the station. He knew the less she knew about what went down in the cell, the easier it would be for everyone.

Nini walked back to the reception desk to find Marion checking emails.

"Looks like I'm taking you for breakfast," Nini said. "You need a good feed today because it will be another busy one."

"Really? But I've already had breakfast," Marion replied, waiting for the punchline.

"Trust me, you will need another."

Nini stuck a thumb up behind her back to let Dan know the plan was working whilst Marion placed on her coat, as the others watched them leave before racing off towards where the stench was still strong.

"Have you checked the CCTV?" Jon cried out; feeling queasy after seeing the remains of Bolton.

"Not yet," Dan replied. "First we need to sort this mess out."

He watched Jon and Marek enter the cell to cover the blanket over the bones, seeing them carry it towards the back door before puffing out his cheeks as he walked towards the staff room. He filled a bucket with water and bleach, grabbing a scrubbing brush before racing back to the cell to scrub away the dried blood off the floor, walls and cell door. But Marek interrupted him.

"Where shall we put them?"

"Just keep them away from Marion." Dan shrugged, wishing he had a better answer. But he knew there was no right answer to give.

Jon closed in as Dan sprayed the cell with air freshener, but the situation made his blood boil.

"Fuck this! ...Let's just throw the bones in the skip outside..."

But Dan looked at him oddly. He knew it was wrong to do, but he was running out of time. He knew if news got out that another body was found, or worse, a bag of bones, then it would be too traumatic for the townsfolk to take, meaning a pandemonium outbreak could happen and more people would likely die. Dan didn't need that right now. He couldn't handle it.

Jon watched him walk around the cell like he was thinking of doing something that was way out of his comfort zone.

"...Yes?!" Jon snapped.

"Okay. Just do it," Dan said, surprising Jon. "But neither of you says anything to Marion."

"My lips are sealed," Marek replied smiling.

He aimed for the back exit, dragging the blanket out of the door, as Dan and Jon slowly walked back to the staff room.

"Do you think you'll be able to recognize the bugs you saw?"

"Maybe," Jon replied.

"Maybe is better than a no...So go online and locate them."

Jon nodded as he turned to leave the room, but Marek entered to smile like a naughty child.

"Where did you put the bones?"

"In the place you suggested."

"I hope you kept them inside the blanket," Dan butted in. "I don't want someone's dog finding em'."

"They won't."

"Good." Dan closed in on Marek, placing an arm around

him. "I want you to keep our two clowns company. Make sure they aren't up to mischief at the old guy's place."

"And you? What are you doing?" Marek asked.

"I'm off to check out the CCTV. I just hope no one turned it off last night." Dan grimaced from the thought after thinking back to a few times when someone did.

He sat in his office, turning on his computer before clicking on the CCTV file; rewinding it to the early hours of the morning. He saw the two men talking, not noticing anything out of the ordinary, but something covered the lens. He scratched his head upon rewinding and playing again before slowing it down to pause on a shadow smothering the camera. He gulped, kicking his desk as he raced from the room.

CHAPTER TWENTY-FOUR

D an drove through the town, still feeling queasy as he pulled up outside the library; his head spinning from too many agonising thoughts as he exited the car. He reached the main door before sighing to find it was still closed; about to walk away until spotting a figure moving around inside.

He banged on the door and waited for it to be opened; jumping back and feeling nervous as Sabrina appeared.

"Good morning," he said, smiling.

Sabrina smiled back before inviting him inside, shutting the door to walk him past where she was recently standing.

"...Am I keeping you from your job?" Dan asked, noticing a pile of books not placed on the shelves.

Sabrina looked at them and waved a hand. "It's okay. I can finish that when you leave."

She stared into Dan's eyes to feel the warmth from them. She knew he was back for a reason.

"Sorry for doing this to you, but I need your help again."

Sabrina scrunched her lips. "What do you need today?"

"More help with the archives of this town," Dan replied,

as they neared the 'Staff Only' room again. "I need to know if a plane crashed in this area in nineteen-forty-seven...I've read newspaper reports but saw nothing to confirm it."

"You're still talking about nineteen-forty-seven?..."

Sabrina seemed excited.

She hated the mornings at work, sorting through the returned books and tidying up from the day before. It was boring. But this was like an adventure.

"...A plane crash?" she questioned, opening the door to lead Dan to the computers.

She watched him aim for the same filing cabinet like he was now a pro with how the library worked; smiling again as he booted up the computer before silently leaving him alone. But a few minutes later she was back with a cup of coffee.

"Thanks," Dan said, scrolling through the file.

This time his concentration didn't fade as the drink was placed next to him.

Sabrina watched him write notes on his pad, pleased to see him committed before tapping him on the shoulder and leaving him alone.

————

Dan stared at his watch as the time reached *10:00 am.*

He listened to the faint sound of people inside the building, so knew Sabrina had opened up; smiling like a schoolboy with a huge crush upon staring at more newspaper archives and reports. He read the witness statements from the various stories' dated back to the needed year but saw nothing about a plane or any other flying machine crashing in town. But still, he needed to, wanted to believe his grandfather's story.

But how when there's no evidence to support it?

He switched files, opening up some from later years until spotting an article about a housing development happening in the year of his birth; in the vicinity of where Eddie said the light from the sky came down. He didn't want to think the worst, that something was underneath Cassidy Street, but that street was smack bang in the centre of all the recent murders and was the starting point of the investigation.

Is something buried under that house?

He questioned himself for minutes over it before deciding that nothing could have survived for that long underground, human or otherwise. He printed off the information about the houses, even though he wasn't convinced it had any connection to the deaths before shutting down the computer and keeping hold of the stick.

He saw a dozen people browsing books as he walked past, feeling miffed as to why? when the town was battling to find a killer until it dawned on him that maybe reading was their way of escaping the trauma.

He closed in on Sabrina, still feeling nervous as he waited for her to finish with a customer.

"You are done now?" she asked; turning to him after the customer walked away.

"Oh yeah," Dan replied, showing her the stick. "But I need to borrow this for a while."

"You found any clues on it?"

"Maybe. But I need my team to take a look."

CHAPTER TWENTY-FIVE

Marek walked around Mick's living room, checking out the paintings before switching his attention between Neal, Ben and Cliff, who were still gathering evidence after the man's body was taken away. Marek watched him sigh deeply as he handed Rob some tubes, so figured he was stressing over something.

"Any clues?" he asked, hoping for some positive news.

Cliff sighed again and shook his head. "Nothing! It doesn't make any sense."

"You're telling me." Marek gulped after a flashback hit him. "I still haven't recovered from the night of the boy's murder."

"None of us has, mate...Rob and I spent a good few hours in that house after you left. It was scary witnessing how gruesome the scene was."

"And it's not stopped," Rob interrupted. "It's carrying on right on our doorsteps."

Marek sensed Rob was on the verge of losing it, but in truth, so were three of the five men in that room.

He looked over at the dumb and dumber officers before

grimacing as they posed in front of the paintings, taking selfies like social media freaks to drive him nuts. He knew they were bored but they needed to snap out of it.

"Guys! It wasn't so long ago that you admired the old man, but now, before his body is even cold, you are back to acting like utter twats..."

Neal stopped what he was doing after realising Marek was right, but Ben had to take one more selfie before putting his phone away.

"...Have you finished?!" Marek snapped at him.

"Yeah," Ben replied, showing Neal the recent photo. "What do you want us to do now?"

"Not much left you can do apart from speak to the residents; see if anyone saw something suspicious before you arrived with Jon last night."

Ben nodded, feeling alert again as he left the house with Neal. But Marek waited until hearing them knock on the neighbour's doors before swearing under his breath.

He shook his head and bit his lip. "I needed to get those clowns out of the way before telling you this," he said to Cliff. "It's even happened at the station, inside the cells."

"Was someone in the cells?" Cliff replied.

Marek gulped hard. "Yeah. Two people were arrested last night. But only one was there this morning."

"A witness?"

"No, Cliff, he was just bones. A skeleton."

Rob dropped an ornament after the words made him feel woozy.

"This can't be right. People in cells have been killed. Cells, where no one but you guys has a key to...This is fucked up."

"How'd you think this could've happened?" Cliff interrupted.

But Marek couldn't answer him.

It wasn't a case of wouldn't. He actually couldn't give him an answer.

"All I know is, if this case isn't solved soon then one of us could be next."

Marek's words left an eerie feeling floating around the room until scaring the men to quickly look around them. They feared he was right and that anything was possible right now.

"Did you know that the boy was eaten from the inside?" Cliff said, surprising Marek. "After being paralysed by an unknown liquid."

Marek did know but needed to hear it again. "Did you find out more about the liquid?"

Cliff explained that it was unrecognisable and something not discovered in this country. But it had all the attributes of an anaesthetic.

"So, the boy felt no pain?" Marek asked, watching Cliff cringe.

"I want to believe he didn't, really I do, but we'll never know for sure."

Marek froze as his mind started racing. "Hold on a minute! Are you saying that some maniac brought the drug in from overseas?"

Cliff shrugged his shoulders as the moment became too much. And Rob noticed.

"We don't think it's been invented yet...Well, not that kind of drug," Rob said, closing up his briefcase. "The chemicals used couldn't be traced to any other country either, so it's a mystery how it was found inside the boy."

"What do you mean, not invented yet?" Marek became nervous. "You found it. It had to be invented."

"We couldn't find anything on it. Meaning it's probably not of this world."

Marek waited for Rob to smile but he just took his briefcase to the door.

"Aliens? You think aliens have landed in this town?"

"Okay, Marek, listen closely. We tested the sample on a lab rat, and within seconds it was paralyzed. It could see us because we saw its eyes follow our movements, but not one muscle moved," Cliff said, closing his case. "What if the boy did the same thing?"

"Are you saying he may have felt something when being butchered to death?"

Marek was close to falling apart, as the more Cliff spoke, the more memories of seeing the boy's body tortured him.

"I don't know, but if the rat was still able to move its eyes then it may have been able to feel pain. Same as the boy."

Marek choked loudly as the sound echoed into the hallway to alert Neal and Ben.

"So, the parents didn't do this to him?" he said as the oddball officers returned.

"The murders are still happening, so there's your answer," Rob replied.

Marek cursed again, feeling embarrassed for accusing Tommy Senior of murder.

———

Jon looked at the bottom right corner of his computer screen to see it had just gone *10:30 am*. He wasn't a huge fan of computers, but kept at it, clicking on photos of small bug-like insects as they appeared to wince at how hideous most of them looked.

But the phone rang to spook him.

It was Marion, letting him know that someone from the hospital was on the line. He thanked her and took the call.

"Hello," he said, feeling curious.

"Is that you Dan?"

"No, it's Jon. Who's this?"

"Sorry. It's Charles West. I'm phoning because the boy's parents have snapped out of their trance."

Jon became alert, happy with the news. "Do you think they're ready to talk?"

"Talk, my friend. They haven't talked in a while, so I think they're more than ready."

"Good. I'm on my way."

Jon replaced the phone to stare at a photo on the screen before writing a note and grabbing his weapon as he left the room.

———

He arrived at the hospital, waving at Charles as he exited his car before rushing over to follow him through the sliding door entrance.

"Have they said anything?" he asked, catching Charles up.

"They're talking, but it doesn't make any sense," Charles replied, appearing haggard as his eyes strained to focus.

"What do you mean?"

"You'll have to see for yourself..."

Jon suddenly felt butterflies as they reached the room, becoming excited as Charles slowly opened the door. He knew there was a better chance of catching the killer once he spoke to the couple, but the closer he got to them, the more nervous he became.

"...Are you ready?"

"Ready," Jon replied, walking into the room.

He almost broke down after seeing the couple cry before breathing deeply to nod as Charles watched on. But Jon felt shy to speak after the couple's tears left him fumbling to almost fall into a seat opposite. He waited until the sobbing faded before attempting to question them, but Wendy nervously gripped his hand.

"What happened to my son?" she asked, sniffing and wiping her eyes.

"That's why I'm here," Jon said, feeling confused. "I need to know what you saw?"

"I was asleep….downstairs." Wendy cried again. "So never saw anything."

"But did you hear something?"

Wendy shook her head. "No. I heard nothing."

"I came home from work to find him in his bed," Tommy senior interrupted, hugging Wendy tight.

"And he was already dead?" Jon asked, wishing he hadn't.

Tommy Senior rubbed his puffy eyes and nodded before saying, "Whoever did this didn't come through the front door."

Jon already knew that but didn't want to say it because he needed them to keep talking. He listened, hoping for news that insects had been seen, but nothing on who or what could've done it arrived.

He wrote notes on his pad as he kept up with both parents talking at the same time, but nothing concrete was being said. He watched them closely upon checking for a sign of weakness, but their version of events remained strong, with neither flinching as they spoke.

Tommy became more agitated, as his words increased in volume and speed. But Charles placed a hand on his shoulder until he calmed down.

Jon smiled and closed his pad.

He knew the statements given were all he was going to

get, but, as he attempted to read back what he wrote, the couple hugged each other again.

Jon nodded, knowing they never touched their son before exiting his seat to usher Charles to stand beside him.

"I'm off back to base to type this up." Jon shook Charles' hand. "I'll make sure their son's death is solved."

CHAPTER TWENTY-SIX

The abandoned railway carriage that Nini nearly checked out was being visited by a creature, not of this world. The queen moved around it, spiking two cats with her legs, as the loud screeching after eating them rattled the inside of the carriage. She spread her wings as the freedom of movement made her feel more alive before ripping into other carcasses with each mouth; screeching again as her wings flapped.

———

Ben, Neal, and Marek walked nearby after leaving old Mick's house, checking over the old ground to find recent clues. But neither seemed happy to be outside again.

Marek looked at the other men, wishing now for some foolishness to arrive to take his mind off how cold he was feeling. But neither Ben nor Neal was up for it.

Ben swiftly turned around, feeling alert and frightened like the music in a horror movie had just scared him, his eyes wide as he stared into the distance.

"What's up with you?" Marek asked.

"Did you hear that?" Ben replied, shaking.

Marek looked at Neal, seeing if he would giggle to prove that Ben was messing around. But Neal looked on confused as he rubbed his hands to keep warm.

"Hey! I hope this isn't a prank," Marek said, staring in the direction of where Ben was looking. "I can't hear anything."

Ben placed up a hand. "Shush. Wait."

But the others laughed at him and carried on walking.

"Hear what?" Neal asked. "I can't hear anything."

"I'm not surprised with those furry pink earmuffs on," Ben replied, catching him up.

Neal laughed again.

He was used to everyone mocking him for wearing them, but he didn't care. All that mattered to him was keeping his ears warm.

Marek listened out for the noise, but the late morning wind penetrated his eardrums, almost freezing them.

"What did it sound like?" he asked, pulling down his hat to cover his ears. "Maybe you heard the wind blow a road sign or something."

Ben almost agreed with him, but another loud shriek whistled past to leave them nervous and close to retreating. Marek pointed to his left, picking up courage before racing off towards the noise, leaving the others to stare in the direction of the old railway track.

"Fuck that!" Neal shouted, not feeling as enthusiastic. "If he wants to act like some Superhero then fine, but I'm too cold to move."

Ben agreed, but, after Marek glared at him, he sighed and moved forward.

"Come on you two!" Marek shouted, charging up his gun. "It could be the killer…"

He set it on stun, smiling as the others closed in. But another shriek brought Neal and Ben to their knees.

"...Get up!" Marek yelled. "And charge your guns."

"Is it a bird?" Neal asked, rising.

"The only bird big enough to make that noise is the one from Sesame Street," Ben replied.

Marek shook his head and steered to his right before lowering his weapon in frustration at the silence. He frowned as Neal and Ben drifted closer to the carriage, but the echoing shrieks were back to leave him pumped up again. He raced off to the other side, leaving the others twitching their ears in the hope he was going to speak; their guns raised as they nervously gawped at a sliding door. But Marek said nothing as Neal's sweaty hand closed in to touch the handle. He felt excited now, eager to know what was inside the carriage, but Ben was still shaking.

"Come on, Ben," Neal whispered, nodding as he gripped the handle tightly. "All we need to do is to arrest who's behind this door and we can put our feet up."

Ben gulped, nodding back as Marek shouted, "Ready!"

Neal slid the door open at speed but a choking stench wafted out to make his eyes water, as Ben manned up to cover his mouth before climbing inside the creepy dark carriage.

He lowered his gun and held out a hand upon waiting for Neal to grip it, but something shuffling through the blackness at the far corner of the carriage scared Neal to retreat.

Ben panicked, sweating profusely to feel a vibration race up his legs, as the shuffling closed in to leave him fumbling to raise his gun.

"What is that?" he whispered, slowly shining his torch.

But he almost wet himself after seeing a pile of animal remains, put there by the bugs for when the queen arrived.

He hovered the light over cats, birds, rodents and dogs

until his stomach heaved; shaking from the thought of seeing something alive. He gulped, looking at Neal, but he was too statue-like to help as the shuffling continued.

Ben heard a slapping sound like something was eating, his heart racing after seeing the queen's leg spike through a dog before dropping it into a mouth.

He froze, as Neal snapped out of his trance to light up the queen, but the mouths snapped at him in annoyance for being seen.

But he kept the beam on her, hoping it would prevent her from eyeing up Ben.

It worked, as the mouths just snapped at thin air; not attempting to attack as she sniffed and flapped her wings.

But that changed when Marek closed in.

The queen shrieked at him before using a wing to flip animal carcasses in his direction; leaving him ducking for cover to avoid being struck. He was still high on adrenaline as he dived across the ground, but a flying dog suddenly knocked him on his arse, leaving him wincing for breath.

"Get that...door...closed!" he yelled.

But Neal and Ben were too frightened to do it.

Marek fired his gun at the queen, but she didn't flinch as the energy blast bounced off her. She became more ferocious upon shrieking louder to scare Ben into pulling Neal onto the carriage; both shivering as they turned off their torches to huddle in a corner. But seconds later they tripped over the carcasses and fell onto the pile.

"...Just shoot it!" Marek shouted, turning up the power on his gun. "And stop messin' around."

"I'm on it!" Ben said, rising from the pile to aim his weapon. But he was now unsure of where the queen was.

He waited for Neal to respond, thinking he would back him up, but, as he fired his gun, a blast hit Neal in the back as he stupidly charged the queen. He was thrown across the carriage with force to land unconscious on the cold and mouldy floor.

Marek yelled at the creature until she turned to face him before shining a light to witness all her tongues slap at thin air; her grotesque form causing him to cringe.

"Is it re-charged?" he nervously asked Ben, watching him fumble with his gun.

But Ben sighed.

He shook his head upon urging the power light to come on, raising his gun in the hope it would recharge quicker as his mind spun at a thousand miles an hour with sad thoughts about Neal.

"...Hey! Over here! Whatever you are!" Marek screamed, watching the queen closely in case she went for Neal. "What the fuck are you?" he said, now trembling in his boots.

He kept eye contact as he cautiously climbed onto the carriage before waving his torch from side to side to confuse the queen into retreating, her heavy steps sounding like thunder as she moved. But the sight of Neal excited the mouths to open and close.

She moved towards him before raising a leg to aim at his head; panicking Marek and Ben into desperately punching extra energy into their weapons until firing a double blast that knocked her backwards. But she shrieked and flapped her wings before charging Ben, wrapping a tongue around his leg like a coiling snake to pull him onto his back. Her tongue retreated towards the mouths to leave Marek awkwardly watching on, his hands shaking to almost drop his gun as Ben screamed in agony.

His leg tightened to the point of snapping as he was dragged along the carriage floor; his tears flowing as he struggled to loosen the grip. But the sound of the queen's teeth grinding alerted Marek to attempt a rescue.

He sweated fast as the tongue lifted Ben off the ground to pull him closer to the mouths; his heart racing to see Ben in agony upon diving towards Neal's gun. He tapped in his code and smiled as it unlocked before firing quickly at the tongue to split it in two; happy to see Ben drop to the ground to untangle it. But it slithered along the floor before climbing up the queen to reattach itself.

Ben choked, feeling terrified as the queen smashed a wing against the side of the carriage, his leg sore as he aimed his gun to fire again. But a swarm of deadly bugs jumped on him, biting him until he screamed again.

Marek eyeballed the queen but panicked to the point of jumping off the carriage as she closed in. He waited for her to attack, but she didn't. She just ran for the exit door, spreading her wings to take flight once reaching the outside.

Ben screamed again after feeling teeth saw through his bones. He sweated fast as the agony shook him before firing an energy blast into himself; crying when flames appeared on his clothing before fainting as the bugs ignited to disappear like a magic trick.

Marek rushed to Ben's rescue, taking off his jacket to smother the flames before hearing Neal wake up.

"Oh, my God!" Neal cried out, shaking his head after seeing the coat over Ben. "He's dead. Oh my God. It was my stupid fault."

"No, mate. He's not dead. He's just knocked out," Marek sadly replied, as Neal wept like it was Ben's funeral.

"What happened?"

But Marek didn't explain. He was too concerned about where the queen was.

"At least we know what the weapons can do when not on

stun mode," he said, sighing as he moved towards the entrance.

"Shit, Marek, what mode was Ben's gun on?" Neal asked, staggering over to pick it up. "He had it on halfway."

"Wow! If that's what happens when only on halfway mode then just imagine if it was on full?" Marek stared at the sky and rubbed his chin. "I think we need maximum power to stop that thing."

Neal sat next to Ben and held his hand, glad to see he was breathing as the smoke escaped beneath Marek's jacket. He sighed, knowing Ben was extremely lucky.

He lifted the jacket and gave it a good shake, making sure no flames appeared before tossing it over to Marek. He had a feeling Marek would need it again soon, fearing he was planning to look for the creature.

Marek nodded as he caught it but was soon sighing after spotting holes all over it.

"Dan will kill me for ruining it," he said, placing it on to curse himself after mentioning the K-word. He then smiled at Ben. "How is he?"

"You saved him. Dan will understand," Neal replied.

Marek climbed down off the carriage and reached for his phone, waiting for Dan to answer his call.

"Chief, there's been a sighting of something creepy at the old railway," he spluttered, not sure of how to explain it.

But what he saw was real and that's what mattered.

————

Dan looked over at Nini sitting opposite him in his office, but his expression changed swiftly to worry her. She listened in on the conversation, watching him nodding and shaking his head before suddenly slamming a fist onto the desk.

"...We saw this large thing. Well, a sort of large bug," Marek told him.

Dan put the phone on speaker.

"Did you say a large bug?"

"Yes!" Marek snapped, panicking. "It's escaped and is in flight somewhere over town." He looked over at the injured man again, annoyed with himself for not keeping him safe. "Ben's hurt...We need an ambulance pronto...I'm going to look for the thing."

Dan and Nini gulped as the line went dead.

"Call him back!" Dan shouted, rubbing his eyes.

Nini nodded before grabbing the phone to reach out to Marek. But he didn't answer. She tried again to feel Dan's eyes on her; shaking to see him put on his weapons belt.

"...If he's being serious then that thing may be the killer."

"But we would've seen it by now," Nini replied, unconvinced.

Dan yelled into his hand, knowing she was right.

———

Neal moved away from Ben to pick up his gun before showing Marek respect for his bravery; knowing he wouldn't have been able to do the same.

"Thank the lord you remembered your password," he said, attempting a smile. "Be careful."

Marek turned to walk away, puffing out his cheeks. "Just make sure you keep your gun fully charged...Find me once the medics get here."

"Are you sure you don't want to wait for backup?"

"No time...You saw that thing. It needs to be found and stopped."

Neal wasn't going to argue over it. Not now, not when

Marek was angry. He had a feeling that Marek's extra surge of determination was down to what happened to Ben, knowing he felt guilty. Now he needed to save everyone from the flying monster.

Neal watched him race off, gaining distance quickly in his quest to fight a one-man war.

———

Dan rushed into Jon's office to find it empty, but a note stuck to the computer screen grabbed his attention. He pulled it off, clicking the keyboard to light it up, surprised to see an image of the common household bedbug.

A bedbug is our killer?

He saw Nini close in, appearing eager and ready to help Marek; her eyes focused to leave Dan feeling proud of her courage. He smiled at her, about to speak, but Jon rushed into the room to spook him.

"Is that what you saw?" Dan asked, pointing at the screen.

"Yeah, that's roughly similar to the ones on my boot," Jon replied breathing heavily.

"But they're just bedbugs."

"I know, but it's what I saw. Or something close to it."

Nini shook her head, feeling confused that a bedbug could be involved in the murders, but Jon wasn't taking back what he said.

"This is all too crazy!" Dan yelled, rubbing his face hard. "Do we need to look for tiny bugs now?"

"I think the word bug has come up more than enough over the past day or two, so yes, they have to be involved in some way," Jon replied.

"I've just had Marek on the phone. He said something that confused me."

"What was it?" Jon asked, feeling nervous.

"He said he saw a large bug at the old railway line."

Jon gulped. "Then what are we waiting for?"

———

Marek stared all around him, feeling tense as he waited for a sign of the creature. He walked slowly so as not to miss anything, sighing at the silence before speeding up to move towards the centre of town as a *shrill* was heard. He almost dropped his gun after it happened again before rotating to see no one around; shivering from the sound of his phone ringing as his legs buckled beneath him.

"Fuck!" he yelled, regretting it instantly after fearing the creature could strike.

He stared at the sky before answering the call.

"Yep."

"Where are you?" Nini asked.

"Heading into town," Marek replied sternly, attempting not to worry her. "The route from the old railway tracks. Why?"

"We're nearby. Will be with you soon."

Marek nervously smiled as he looked ahead. "Did you hear that scream?"

"What scream?"

An incoming alert beeped on Marek's phone to send his mind crazy. It was a call he couldn't refuse.

"Nini, hold on a sec. Neal's trying to get through."

Marek switched calls, listening to Neal scream out words of no meaning; his voice choking from fear.

"It's taken Ben!" he rushed out. "It's fuckin' taken him."

"Taken him where?" Marek asked, listening to Neal cry. "I'm on my way."

He switched back to Nini to fill her in on what Neal just said, as the voice of Dan shouting:- "Tell him we're heading for the railway," brought a little comfort his way. He didn't want to see that thing again by himself.

He ran again, but the road became icier to slow him down. He cursed as he swiftly shone his torch, hoping to see the person who screamed, until it dawned on him that it must've been Ben. So, dug his boots into the ice and picked up speed, keeping his balance as he closed in on the carriage. But all he saw was Neal kicking it in rage.

"What happened?" Marek asked, gulping.

"That thing was walking along the roof, so I got up to investigate."

"Then what?"

"It tricked me...Got me outta' the way." Neal wiped his eyes. "Then it came inside and dragged Ben out."

"So he could be nearby?"

"No!" Neal bellowed. "Because it disappeared, taking him."

Marek was left stunned.

"What's happened here?!" Dan shouted, closing in with Jon and Nini to see Neal in pieces.

Marek shook his head before explaining where Ben was, or where he could be, but Dan found his words hard to believe. He looked at Neal again until it sunk in that Marek wasn't making it up, but still, the thought of Ben being scooped up and flown away into the night unnoticed was creeping him out.

"Right. We need to split up," Dan said, comforting Neal. "We'll head for Cassidy Street...That's where it all began, so I'm hoping that's where it'll end."

"And us?" Jon questioned.

"You head south. Marek and Nini will head north."

Dan watched everyone gather their thoughts as the moment got to them, pleased to see neither refusing the order.

CHAPTER TWENTY-SEVEN

Marek parked up on the outskirts of town, still feeling angry and motivated as he stared at the beam blasting from the car's headlights.

He turned to Nini, watching her quiver like she was having another flashback of the horror from her country before gently touching her until she calmed down; nodding and smiling as he exited the vehicle. But he squirmed after the derelict housing estate he now looked at brought back memories from his past.

"Are you okay now?" he asked, hoping she was so he could fire up his gun and shoot something. "We need to do this."

Nini nodded as she braced herself to step out of the car.

She fiddled with her Cossack hat, feeling pleased with it as it became like a new best friend, but Marek sighed because he'd left his hat at the carriage.

"Didn't you live around here once?" Nini asked, watching him stare into the distance.

"Yeah, but we had to get out due to mould. The whole estate was crawling with it and it was making people sick."

Nini walked ahead, stepping over snow-covered rubble. "Do you think the thing you saw could be here?"

"Maybe. It's a good place to hide. But I can't hear anything...The creature makes a loud sound, so, if it is here then it's suddenly learnt not to."

Nini cautiously pulled out her gun, setting it to full power before slowly nearing the first house.

"This creature you saw."

"What of it?" Marek replied.

"Does it look like you explained?"

"Why would I make it up?!" Marek snapped at her.

Nini backed off, feeling he was just as scared as she was about seeing it.

"It sounds pretty scary," she said, switching on her torch to light up the house.

"It is." Marek caught her up, smiling nervously. "I nearly shit my pants when its large tongue coiled around Ben's leg."

Nini gulped after imagining being in the carriage with them, becoming teary-eyed for a few seconds before entering the house. She was about to speak, but Marek raced past her like he was back at the police academy doing a physical exam; taking control of his mission to pass. So, she left him to it.

Nini breathed in deeply before spitting out the mouldy fumes floating in the air. She saw Marek kick out at everything in his path, seeing his emotions change rapidly as he fought with the rage eating at his insides. She knew he was on the verge of a breakdown.

She caught him up as he smashed his way into the living room, finding him glaring at spray-painted gang symbols and used hypodermic needles before flinching at how many were laid out on the floor.

"Watch your step," Marek said, pointing at them.

Nini shook her head. "Do you think people still live here?"

"Nah...It's too cold," was all Marek said as he disappeared into another room.

Nini heard his boots smack loudly against rotting steps so knew he was heading up the stairs, but, as she closed in, she quivered when they shook beneath Marek's weight. But he didn't care. All he cared about was finding Ben.

"You okay up there?!" Nini shouted.

She headed for the kitchen to the sound of the stairs creaking loudly, hearing them suddenly collapse to leave her worried. But, as she turned around, saw Marek sweating at the bottom to brush dust away. He was lucky not to have been injured. He puffed out his cheeks as the adrenaline circled inside him before catching her up to give her a cheeky wink.

"...You could've been killed."

"Nah. Don't worry about me. I'm fine...It's the stupid stairs that aren't." Marek stared at the damage. He shuddered after realising Nini was right, as thoughts of being like a cat with nine lives made him chuckle. "Let's keep moving."

Nini agreed, happy that his arrogance and confidence were back as he walked into the kitchen.

They left the house to enter the next one as Marek raced off again. But this time he was yelping within seconds to leave Nini more nervous. She gripped her gun and shone her torch, feeling on edge to find him hopping; his boot leaking blood as tears filled his eyes.

"What's happened now?"

"I fuckin' stood on a nail!" Marek shouted, raising his boot to pull the nail out. "The damn thing went right through."

"You had me scared..."

Nini punched him in the arm before helping him to a dusty chair, sitting him down to watch him take off his boot like it was a booby trap that could go off at any time. He dropped it to feel the blood seep through his sock; his face squirming in pain as he took it off before holding up the nail like he'd won it in a competition.

"...Are you okay to walk?"

"I'm fine!" Marek snapped back, throwing the nail across the room. "I just need to tie something around the wound."

He winced as he stood up again, but the sound of glass breaking in the next room almost caused him to topple over. He saw Nini shudder before raising her gun to fire at anything coming towards her; her sight firmly focused on what was ahead.

"Nini," Marek whispered. "I need to stop the bleeding."

"There's no time for that. Just man up, put your boot back on and help me find out who broke the glass."

Marek bit his lip and shook his head.

He soaked up the pain before wrapping the bloodied sock around the wound, quickly replacing his boot to leave a nasty sting shooting up his body as he gripped his gun and hobbled towards the noise. Nini slowly followed, feeling cautious as they

entered the room.

They stood back-to-back to perform a move they'd rehearsed many times, walking sideways like a crab as Nini aimed her gun whilst Marek shone a light. But nothing was seen moving around.

Marek grumbled to himself after spotting a broken bottle on the ground.

"That didn't fall by itself. Something's in here with us," Nini said, swinging her gun nervously from side to side.

She feared a sighting of the dreaded bugs that everyone else had seen before scratching herself after a thought of what they looked like crossed her mind. She stayed focused as Marek broke away to walk over to the other side of the room.

"...You see anything?" she asked, pointing her gun at his torchlight.

She was about to speak again when something brushed past her foot, causing her to shriek.

"What?" Marek said; his patience wearing thin.

"Sorry," Nini replied, turning to run away. "I need to get out of here."

Something brushed past her foot again making her feet stamp like they were doing a crazy dance; her face pale as Marek's torchlight covered her. He knew something had scared her.

He saw her stumble like she'd been tripped as the light caught sight of a rat on the floor trying to nibble at her boots. But, as he reached out a hand to grab her, he was nervously ignored.

"Have you got this?!" he shouted, keeping the light on the rat. "I would kick it away but I might fall over."

Nini glared at the rodent.

She cringed after listening to it squeak before stepping back to fire off an energy blast; almost puking to see its body explode.

"Now let's get out of here before more arrive!" she shouted.

CHAPTER TWENTY-EIGHT

Dan and Neal rushed to the house of the Tanker family to find the police security tape still in position on the doors and windows. Dan smiled, thankful that no one had penetrated it to get in, but his smile faded quickly after the creature Neal saw vanishing into the sky crept into his mind. He pulled down the tape from the front door and opened it, slowly peering inside to find nothing but quiet.

"Anything here!" Neal shouted as Dan pushed him.

"for God's sake, why are you making a noise?" Dan asked, clearly frustrated.

Neal shied away, knowing he was being a complete idiot again. He was nervous, Dan knew that. But still, he had to think before speaking.

Dan aimed for the stairs with his weapon ready to leave Neal looking on. He was worried he would make too much noise if he moved again.

"...Search down here," Dan said, approaching the first step. "And be careful."

Neal nodded as he pushed the front door shut, but the

sound of it clanging annoyed Dan even more as he reached step five. He sneered at Neal to see him cowardly walking towards the kitchen before shaking his head as he neared the top of the stairs; feeling his heart pumping fast against his chest to mess with his breathing. But he stopped, caught his breath and slowly moved along the landing before getting angrier after imagining what the creature looked like.

Neal entered the room to find a police issue boot on the floor, the sight bringing with it worry as he scoured the area. He shook as he picked it up, seeing the initials *B.D.* on the inside of the tongue, but was left confused as to whom it belonged to. He saw the other boot a few yards further with the same initials.

B.D.? Boris Decker? Bradley Dalton? Who? he thought, feeling frustrated.

But then suddenly he shrieked, becoming white as he raced around the kitchen.

"Ben! Ben! Where are you?"

He dropped the boot and aimed his gun, but cringed after his hand became cold; feeling like the blood had drained from it. He shook it to warm it up, staring at the boots again upon trying to make sense of it; the moment too unreal to grasp. He breathed deeply, almost fainting as he bounced off a kitchen cupboard before rubbing his face to walk back into the hallway.

"Chief!" he yelled. "I've found Ben's boots."

Dan raced along the landing, feeling baffled as the words sunk in; storming down the stairs to say, "And Ben? Is he okay?"

Neal gulped. "No sighting of him."

Dan slammed a fist against a wall before heading back upstairs, shouting under his breath as Neal nervously followed. But he kept looking behind as he reached the top until nearing Dan as he entered one of the bedrooms. They moved at speed, searching for a sign that Ben had been there, but were left disappointed to find nothing.

"We keep looking," Dan said, hugging Neal. "We will find him."

They exited the room to stare at the tape covering Tommy Junior's bedroom door, as a moment of pure sadness washed over them to make them quiver before Dan anxiously tore it away. But Neal's stomach turned over from the sickening thought of what happened inside.

"How can Ben's boots be here but not him?" Dan asked as he struggled to enter the room.

"No idea." Neal shrugged, puffing out his cheeks. "He has to be somewhere."

But the faint sound of someone trying to speak downstairs spooked them, becoming more noticeable within seconds. They raced back down to find Ben pulling himself along the hallway floor, his body battered, burned and bruised as he tried speaking again.

"Hey, mate," Neal whispered, lifting him off the ground.

He gulped hard after seeing how serious the burns were, the clothing around Ben's chest now entwined with his skin to leave a cloth tattoo. But there were no injuries made by the flying beast.

"What happened?" Dan asked, unsure if Ben would answer.

He helped Neal carry Ben to a chair inside the living room before rushing off to fetch some water, handing a glass to Neal to watch him bring it closer to Ben's blistered mouth. He tried sipping the water, but his throat hurt to leave him spitting it out.

"I don't...know," he croaked. "I was with...Neal...but I ended up in this room." Ben's eyes flickered rapidly as the stinging pain left him choking. "It was dark...very dark, like nothing I'd witnessed...before."

"Do you want to take a break?" Dan asked, knowing Ben was weak.

"No!" Ben coughed; his eyes filling with fluid. "I need to... tell you."

Neal comforted him to see tears suddenly fall, as Dan turned away for a second to compose himself before waiting for the injured man to continue.

Ben took another sip of water, allowing it to sting his throat before adding, "...I felt its...wing on me and smelled its breath."

"And?" Dan asked; eager to know more but sad that Ben was hurting every time he spoke.

"I couldn't see it anymore...It had me then it dropped me off here." Ben shivered, coughing up water. "Was it keeping me here...until it was hungry again?"

"This house could be its lair," Dan quickly said, hoping he was wrong.

Neal gulped, sweating after fearing the creature could be nearby; feeling suffocated from the tension in the air to want to escape. But he couldn't leave Ben.

"...There's something about this house," Dan said, standing by the door.

"What do you mean?" Neal asked.

"As far as we know this is where the first murder took place." Dan stared into the hallway, listening out for the slightest of sounds. "There has to be a reason as to why that thing brought Ben here."

Neal checked Ben's pulse, but a faint beat left him worried. He shook his head towards Dan before slowly seeing Ben's eyes close. He felt scared he wouldn't live.

CHAPTER TWENTY-NINE

News spread as quickly as a forest fire that all residents should remain indoors until further notice, but in one house, a house a few streets away from Cassidy Street, the news had no effect. A young boy of around ten years old stood in his back garden, playing in the snow. He looked over at his house, knowing his parents were watching TV; imagining his father brushing the news off and laughing because he thought it was a hoax.

The boy's name was *Angus.*

He had moved here with his parents from Scotland in search of a better tomorrow. The promise of jobs was the main reason why they sold up and invested in property in Lemonsville, but that promise was a lie because jobs were just as hard to find here. Factories were mostly shut down as a recession gripped the nation, so Angus' father was out of work.

A better future for what?- Had been the most asked question, *Connor,* his father had mentioned to his wife, *Jackie,* ever since they moved here.

Depression had kicked in for him, leaving him another victim to drink and drugs. Now, most of the household appliances were gone, sold off to pay for his habit. But Jackie stayed by him. She believed a change would come and he would get better, but that was over a year ago. Angus was left with just a reminder of a time when he had a games console, computer, and many friends. Now he was just a quiet boy who moved around the house unnoticed by his spaced-out father and sad mother.

At the top of the garden stood the guest house. Well, according to Connor it was. But it was just a wooden shed that Angus sometimes slept in during the summer when visiting family members arrived. He was happy to sleep there. It was his peaceful place. He had pimped it out with posters and drawings, even painted the inside himself. He stared at it as he watched the snow sparkle from the early afternoon sun, pleased to feel no wind.

He gathered some snow off the grass and crunched it into a ball, throwing it at the shed to nervously jump after a thunderous crash echoed from the inside; forcing the snow on top to plummet to the ground. But Angus shook his head, not feeling scared as he threw another snowball; laughing when the crashing sound happened again.

"Todd is that you in there?..."

He looked back at the house, curious to see if his parents were watching; kicking snow in the air after seeing no one there before turning to the shed again to feel slightly annoyed that the boy from next door wasn't showing himself.

"...Todd!" he shouted. "I know it's you. You can't prank me today..."

He closed in, throwing more snowballs, but the noise had stopped.

"...You can come out now, Todd. I know it's you in there..."

Angus stepped closer and closer, feeling partly excited and partly nervous; shouting Todd's name again before shivering from the silence. He reached for more snow but the shed door swung open to leave him falling into the pile that had fallen off the roof. He felt scared after hearing something sniff. He slowly searched for what was making the sound to see nothing as he returned to his feet; glaring at the shed and wiping the snow off his body to find the door still open.

"...Todd!" he shouted again, closing to almost cry after seeing some of his posters torn.

He felt something *eerie* creep upon him to make the hairs on his arms stand up before slowly turning around to be hit hard in the face by a wing; smashing against the inside of the shed to lie dazed as his nose bled heavily.

"...Please, don't hurt me. I'm a good boy," he said, rubbing the back of his head.

He whimpered loudly as the queen hovered outside; mouths snapping together in excitement as she closed in to wrap a tongue around his neck; pulling him towards her as the door slammed shut.

His mother appeared at the top of the garden wrapped in a thick coat, shaking her head after spotting footprints in the snow leading to the shed. She sighed, feeling guilty that her son preferred to hang out inside it than be in the house.

"Angus!" she shouted. "Get inside. I've made some food..."

The queen twitched her head upon stabbing a leg into Angus' chest; tearing it open to pluck out his heart before eating it as his mother called out again.

Jackie cursed under her breath, annoyed that he wasn't answering; staring at the shed in disgust as thoughts of it being too much of a hassle to check on him crossed her mind.

She looked at the sky, not wanting to be outside as she lost her patience.

"...He's in trouble when he gets back here," she mumbled, turning to go back inside.

CHAPTER THIRTY

J on put his phone away after a lengthy conversation with Nini; smiling after hearing about her brush with the mighty rat. It was just what he needed, something to take his mind off the traumatic day.

He walked to the end of a road, stopping at every lamppost to search the area; not happy that no clues were found. He grabbed his phone again, holding it to his ear to the sound of Dan's voice, but a moment of sadness took over after finding out Ben was injured.

"How is he?"

"Not good. He's off to the hospital," Dan said, waving the medics on. "I'm still trying to make sense of it all."

"I bet you are." Jon turned the corner to see the local junior school, the thought of what happened to Ben burning him up as he neared it. "I'll keep you updated."

"Sure thing," Dan replied.

Jon put his phone away again as he reached the school entrance, confused to find the padlock on the gate unlocked. He held his gun ready in case someone ran at him, feeling nervous for not having any backup as he entered the school grounds.

The lock should be on when the school is closed, he thought, reaching the main doors to see no one around.

He stared through one of the windows, spotting movement, not sure if it was someone or something as it swiftly left a room.

"Fuck me! What's in there?" he said, shuffling over to the next classroom to see a shadow fade out of sight.

He was scared and close to backing away, but his courage kept him moving as he turned up the power on his gun. He reached the main door again, taking a deep breath before gripping the handle; shoving it open to sneak inside as a guilty feeling washed over him. He knew he should be calling it in but felt there was no time. He needed to stop the creature now.

He calmed down as he walked along a hallway, glancing inside every room he passed with his trigger finger ready to fire; reaching a corner to see a sign that read – Go right for the main office – so aimed left to check out more classrooms.

But he became indecisive as panic crept in.

He stopped to listen closely to the silence; his heart pounding as he neared the first room to look inside as a faint sound sent his ears twitching. He knew it was coming from nearby, so bent down to crawl below the window before nervously sweating as he reached the next one. He listened out again, unable to hear the sound, feeling annoyed as he slid along to another room. But a door closed to confuse him.

No monster is going to open and close a door.

He heard footsteps closing in, so gritted his teeth and waited; his heart beating faster as he tackled the school caretaker.

"Get off me!" he cried out as Jon rose to his feet.

"Why are you here when the school is closed?" Jon angrily asked, watching the man get back up.

"I'm fixing a leak in one of the classrooms," he said, feeling shaken up.

"Oh! Sorry for jumping on you," Jon embarrassingly said. "But why have you got a leak?"

"No idea...I heard a strange noise coming from here when I was sitting in my house over the road, so came to check it out."

"You're brave," Jon replied. "Especially with what's been happenin' recently."

The caretaker sighed, knowing Jon was right. "Yeah, I know, but I didn't think anything bad was going to happen, seeing as the school was close by."

"Just get the leak fixed quickly and get home." Jon stared down the corridor. "How bad was the damage?"

"It's bad...I heard a loud crash when I arrived here like something heavy had just smashed into the school."

"And what was it?" Jon asked.

"I didn't find out...When I got to the room, all I saw was a hole in the ceiling with a broken pipe gushing water all over the floor."

"Show me."

The caretaker walked Jon back into the room he'd just left before opening another door, stepping into a puddle of water as they entered the room.

"I got the water turned off," the caretaker said, pointing to the ceiling.

Jon saw the pipe hanging down, feeling stunned by the damage as he noticed an area on the floor not soaked in water; just small puddles leading to another door.

"Did you do this?" he asked, hoping for a yes.

"Nah! I never went over there," the caretaker said, shrugging his shoulders as he packed up his tools.

Jon followed the puddles before opening the door with caution; aiming his gun as he moved into a hallway. But the puddles stopped after another few feet.

"What the fuck!"

The caretaker heard Jon talking to himself, so smiled after more swear words came from him. But, as he carried his toolbox towards the door, was hit with an intense pain stinging his cheek. He froze, feeling blood leak down his face; scared to move after seeing it splash into the water on the floor. He touched the wound to see his hand covered in blood, his mouth quivering as he tried to call out for help. But he staggered as the side of his face peeled away. He was close to fainting as the pain ripped through him before sweat seeped into the wound to make it sting even more as he slowly looked at the ceiling. His eyes filled with tears after seeing the queen hang above him, his colour swiftly changing after spotting a wing dripping blood. He tried to run but the wing penetrated his right eye to pluck it from its socket; the juice painting his face as he screamed in agony.

Jon raced into the room to see the queen eat the eye, leaving his confidence gone as she shrieked. He saw the caretaker walk in a daze, holding a hand over his face in an attempt to quench the avalanche of blood gushing out. But he became weak; falling to choke on the blood stuck in his throat.

The queen dropped from the ceiling, landing next to him to snap mouths; clamping down to tear him to pieces as Jon was almost sick. He watched her swallow the man's legs upon fearing a meltdown closing in; shaking as he fired to see the blast rip away ceiling tiles.

But the queen shrieked again to force him to back away.

He cringed as she chewed on the caretaker's head before rattling his gun in the hope of a recharge; turning to run to slam the door shut as he escaped the room.

He heard the creature as he raced down the hallway, feeling his heart beating too fast to leave him breathing heavily as he searched for somewhere safe to hide. He never looked back to see where it was but felt it was near as he closed in on the main doors; shaking like a leaf to see the queen appear in front of him to smash her wings against the walls. Jon gulped after seeing bricks and plaster smash to the floor, leaving his stomach aching as he tried to catch his breath. He felt sweat drip from his hand, leaving him fumbling with his gun as the recharge light came on. But the queen scraped a wing across a radiator to bring a sharp pain to his head before he could fire again. He squirmed as his teeth shuddered before biting his lip to make it bleed, the sight of the queen terrifying him to drop his gun.

He watched her closely as he bent down to pick it up, thinking only of his life ending as she charged. But she stopped after his phone began to ring; the tone confusing her to allow him time to retrieve his weapon.

Jon scrunched his face after seeing her head follow the sound; the mouths snapping at thin air until shrieking again. He knew she was getting angry.

He fired his gun quickly at her before spreading his arms over his head, ready to give in to his death as she charged. But she vanished before reaching him.

He *shook* as he slowly reached for his phone.

"Hello," he whispered, sweating nervously.

"Are you okay?" Nini asked.

"I am now."

"I'm on my way to you."

Jon sat on the floor, close to crying.

CHAPTER THIRTY-ONE

The time had reached *1:15 pm* when Jon checked his watch. He was drained, nervous, and too scared to leave the school. He breathed in deeply to the sound of people closing in on the main doors, wiping his eyes as he rose off the floor to see Nini and Marek enter.

"Am I glad to see you two," he said, as they reached him.

"What happened?" Marek asked, knowing Jon had witnessed more than he'd let on whilst talking to Nini on the phone.

"That thing you saw savagely tore the school caretaker apart." Jon almost crumbled back to the floor after the sight of what was left of the man entered his mind. "I just stood there and watched."

Nini hugged him, knowing he needed it. "Do you know where it went?"

Jon kept the hug tight. Marek watched him, pleased to see him still in one piece.

"Did it vanish?" he asked, seeing Jon nod. "Fuck! How can we find something that keeps disappearing?"

Jon let go of Nini.

He composed himself to look back at where the caretaker was killed; gripping his gun like he was afraid to let it go again.

"I think I would've been next if my phone hadn't rung."

"What do you mean?" Marek asked.

"It was about to attack, but my phone went off to spook it."

"So you saw the creature up close?"

"Yes, Marek, it was right in front of me. But it vanished before attacking."

His words baffled the others, but he wasn't prepared to explain it again. He needed to find the creature and fast.

———

Dan's phone rang from inside his pocket; the sound causing him to jump as he stared at Neal. He reached for it, hoping for positive news, glad it was Jon calling.

"You got anything?"

Neal listened in, tensing every time Dan opened his mouth. The words - "That's all we need," was enough for him to know this wasn't over.

Dan walked around the room, nodding and shaking his head to confuse Neal, his posture alert after finding out where the creature had recently been.

"How's Ben doing?" Jon sadly asked.

"Not heard from the hospital yet."

"It was a stroke of luck that you found him there."

"Yeah, it was..."

Dan shuddered after a loud THUD shook the wall, causing him to swiftly look at Neal to see if he was behind it. But he wasn't. Dan gulped, scratching his head as the banging continued.

"...I think next door is doing some house renovations," he said to Jon.

"What do you mean?"

"Just heard loud banging. Almost brought the wall down."

"I heard it from here..."

Jon slowed down to almost stop after making some distance from the school, allowing Marek and Nini to walk away as he spoke to Dan again.

"...Do you know who lives there?"

"Can't say that I do, but if they keep up the racket then I'll soon will." Dan heard Jon nervously chuckle. "Hey, just a thought. If that thing flew here without being seen then it could've killed the boy."

"Yeah, but we've heard it. It's fuckin' loud. The Tankers would've heard it also."

"Good point," Dan replied, rubbing his chin. "What about the insects?"

"Vanishing you mean?"

"Yeah! What if they can do it too?..."

Dan watched Neal move towards the wall to place an ear against it, but he cringed after hearing a strange vibration. He turned to Dan, confusing him to leave him worried.

"...Sorry, Jon, I need to go," Dan said, walking towards Neal. "Just keep me updated."

He put his phone away to see Neal touch the wall, noticing his hand bounce off.

"What's wrong?"

"Check this out. It's shaking."

"It's the people next door. I think they're working on the house."

"Do you honestly think someone will be doing house renovations with a creature lurking about?"

Dan was impressed, and it wasn't because Neal used a big word like renovations. What he said made sense.

Dan also touched the wall to feel the vibration crash against his palm, stunning him as he tried to work out what it was. He placed an ear against it, hoping to tell if it was some type of drill. But the THUD sounded again to frighten him. He retreated as pictures plummeted off the wall and cracks appeared, but his courage came back to motivate him into action. He raced to the front door feeling frustrated from nervous anger, gripping his weapon to the sound of Neal closing in before cautiously stepping outside to stare at the other house. He puffed out his cheeks and nodded before slowly sneaking up to a window. But the curtains were drawn.

"I can't see what's in there," he whispered.

"So, what's the plan?" Neal asked.

Dan aimed for the front door to see dried-in bloodstains on the doorstep before angrily turning to push Neal.

"You did the house-to-house, so why didn't you report this?" he asked, feeling disgusted.

"I didn't think it was important at the time," Neal said, bowing his head to listen to more angry words.

"Not important?"

Dan stared at him, close to yelling before calming down to see blood-soaked scratch marks engraved into the door.

"Stay alert. Someone's pet was killed here..."

But Neal stood open-mouthed like the word '*pet*' had freaked him out.

"...What?" Dan asked, confused.

"That giant freak was eating dead animals back at the old railway."

"Then it may have come here," Dan said, hearing the

thudding noise vibrate through the door. "Hey! Is anyone in there? Let me in!" he yelled, banging on it.

He nervously lifted the letterbox to peer inside the house, but a torn to pieces body freaked him out as he held up a hand to gain Neal's attention. He saw the queen scuttle down the stairs, leaving his eyes wide from shock; her many tongues curling around the body to drag it scaring him into letting go of the flap.

"It's inside, isn't it," Neal said.

Dan nodded, coughing up spit as he reached for his phone.

———

Jon pointed down the street as his phone went off again before watching Nini and Marek shuffle off as he took the call.

"What's up? You sound out of breath," he said to Dan.

"Just get everyone down to Cassidy Street fast. The beast is next door to the boy's house."

Jon was about to reply but the phone went dead.

———

Dan and Neal stared at the door, cringing at the sound of the queen snapping through bone. Dan wasn't stupid, he knew he needed help before entering the house, but felt tempted to lift the letterbox again. He moved closer, but Neal shook his head and grabbed his arm.

"Don't! You may spook it."

Dan felt nervous as Neal pulled his hand away.

"Is it still there?!" Marek shouted, hobbling towards them.

"Where's the car?" Dan asked, spotting Marek's weird walk.

"Down the street. I didn't want that thing to hear us arrive."

"Cool, but why are you walking funny?"

"I stood on a nail. But don't worry, I've cleaned and dressed it. I'll be fine."

Dan frowned upon hearing Jon and Nini arrive before slowly smiling at his four able officers. He was glad they were with him, knowing now there was a chance they could pin down the creature before it attacked someone else.

"We need to be quick," he said, pointing to where he wanted the others to go. "Marek, take Nini and go round the back."

But more crunching sounds stopped them from moving.

"Is it behind the door?" Nini nervously asked.

Dan nodded, knowing she was freaking out.

"If it's too much for you just say?"

Nini stared at the door, imagining what the creature looked like as fear spread through her. But Marek wouldn't let her quit.

"Hey, you've got this," he said, grabbing hold of her to snap her into action. "We need to do this for Ben."

Nini sighed and checked her gun, smiling at Dan as she followed Marek to the other side of the house, as Jon approached the letterbox. But he shuddered after remembering the feel of the creature's breath on him back at the school.

"Be careful," Dan said, hoping the creature didn't hear Jon nervously grip the flap. "Just don't scare it off."

Jon almost laughed as he lifted it.

He bent down to peek inside as Dan and Neal watched on.

"Are you sure it was there?" he asked, rising again.

"Yeah!" Dan replied, shocked by his words. "You heard the crunching sound. It was definitely in there. I saw it." He was close to collapsing as he moved Jon out of the way. "Fuck! Fuck! Fuck! Even the corpse has gone."

He saw Nini enter from the kitchen so closed the flap to be let inside. But his face dropped after spotting Marek eating a slice of pizza, grinning as he took another bite.

"What the fuck you got?!" Dan shouted, losing his cool.

"I was starving, so took this from the kitchen," Marek replied. "But it's a bit stale."

Nini gave him a filthy look. "You make me sick...That's probably full of bacteria."

"But it still tastes like pepperoni."

Dan slapped the pizza out of his hand. "Have you finished behaving like a prick?" he said, fuming. "You do know why we're here, don't you?"

Marek stood to attention, feeling Nini's glare. "Yeah, sorry, chief. I wasn't thinking."

"We could all end up dead because you weren't thinking..."

Dan stared at the floor to see bloodstains lead up the stairs, his ears twitching, waiting for another sound as Jon and Neal entered the house.

"...We can't let it escape this time," Dan said, as the front door was closed.

But Jon looked towards the kitchen, eager to enter after seeing Marek pick up the pizza.

"Any left?" he asked.

"No more pizza talk," Dan said, clicking his fingers. "We have a creature to kill...."

A loud CRASH from upstairs forced the ceiling to crack as everyone stared at a light shade swinging; the moment bringing them to their knees in fear of the ceiling caving in.

They rose again to check their guns, gulping at the sight of the stairs before looking up at the top to the sound of something thrashing about as Dan stood on the first step. But his courage faded after hearing it creak.

"...It's time, so get ready," Dan said, moving forward. "We take it down with everything we have..."

The queen shrieked to scare them even more, but they remained firm, aiming their guns as they followed Dan as he reached halfway. He turned to see Nini shivering behind him; her nerves freaking everyone out as he told her to breathe.

"...We will get through this," Dan softly said, wincing from the sweat leaking through his uniform. "Just remember to not cross beams...I don't want it bouncing back to hit you."

Nini smiled but flinched when Marek touched her shoulder; wanting to quit after feeling her heart race. She thought about being last in the line, knowing how easy it was for her to slip away whilst the others fought with the creature. But, after seeing Neal and Jon close in behind Marek, knew she had to brave it out.

She saw Dan reach the top to hold a finger against his mouth, pointing down the landing to where the noise was coming from as she cautiously climbed the rest of the stairs. But Jon stopped after a strange whiff caused him to choke.

"What the fuck! You filthy little shit," he whispered to Marek whilst wafting a hand across his face.

"Sorry...This is what happens when I mix pain meds with pizza. It goes right through me," Marek replied, sniggering.

Dan glared at them as they caught him up, close to losing his focus as he pointed again.

"It's in the end room," he said, slowly nearing it.

He reached the door to hear the creature eat before looking through the gap to see more bones snap; his stomach churning as the queen perched on a bed to savagely rip at the remainder of Cain's corpse. But it glared at the door to scare him into retreating.

He raised his gun to mime – 'It's inside' – before the others followed suit. But the queen stopped glaring to carry on eating.

Dan breathed deeply as he raised a hand before clenching a fist to drop it swiftly. He charged the door to fire at the queen but she sensed the attack before it happened, avoiding everyone's blasts to bounce from wall to wall to leave them close to crumbling as a wing clipped Neal to fling him across the room.

"...We need to put it down!" Dan shouted, avoiding the wing to see Neal roll back onto his knees.

"How can we when it's dodged everything we've fired at it," Marek replied, nervously backing off.

The queen slapped tongues at them as her mouths groaned, the sight of flesh still embedded in her teeth causing everyone's knees to shake as they huddled in a corner to see her piercingly glaring at Nini. She sensed Nini's fear as she watched her tremble to the floor, nervously rolling under the bed whilst the others sadly watched on; neither moving until their guns recharged.

But a leg flipped the bed to send it hurling into Marek, knocking him against a wall as Nini curled up in a ball. She was close to crying after seeing the mattress filled with body organs drop on top of him, whimpering as she waited for him to move. But he wasn't.

Dan shouted at the queen, but she ignored him to focus back on Nini. She groaned as she closed in, panicking Dan into throwing a cup resting on a chest of drawers.

"Nini, you okay?" he asked, eyeballing the queen as the cup hit her on the head.

Nini moved, close to getting up, but the queen shrieked at

her before stabbing a leg into a floorboard. Nini winced as another leg crashed down to miss her by inches before crying to confuse the queen; kicking out to snap the leg to see green liquid cover the floor. The queen shrieked again as more legs aimed for Nini, but all of them narrowly missed.

"...You need to get up!" Dan yelled as the queen attempted to strike again. "And do it now!"

He saw Nini shudder, too frightened to move; knowing she would die if a leg pierced her. So, he dived on the queen's back. But he was thrown from side to side like a rodeo bull until spiralling through the air to crash into Neal, as Jon pulled Marek off the floor.

"Are you fit to continue?" Jon asked him, glad to see he was okay.

"Let me at the creep," Marek said, shaking himself before reaching for his gun.

But the queen glared at him to stall his attack.

Dan and Neal appeared slightly dazed as they slowly rose off the floor; happy to see Nini stand next to them to scrub mascara off her face as the queen's glare stayed strong. Nini thanked Dan for his outburst, knowing his words were the motivation behind why she was still alive before composing herself to lift her gun; pointing it at the queen with anger in her eyes upon waiting for his order to fire it. But Dan wasn't saying anything. He was lost with what to do after seeing the queen's mouths snap together like shredding machines.

"Hey!" Jon screamed, stepping in to grab the queen's attention before she ripped into Marek. "I've got something for you."

He removed his phone, pressing keys as the others strangely looked on.

"This isn't the time to phone a friend," Dan said, shrugging as Nini's phone went off.

The queen backed away after the music floated around her. She sniffed the air as she did at the school in an attempt to pinpoint where it was coming from, as Jon closed his eyes to think back to a drunken night out when he last sang. It was a time he swore he would never attempt again. But, as he opened his eyes, began to sing along to the ringtone, urging the others to do the same after sensing the queen become more confused.

Dan sighed, hoping it was a joke, but Jon's terrible attempt at singing wasn't coming to an end. So Dan gulped and joined in. Neal and Marek followed to make the song sound worse, but it worked as the queen lost her bearings to walk into a wall. She snapped out her tongues upon shrieking with less ferocity as she whipped her head from side to side; the terrible din sending her in a spin until her muscles tensed, ready to attack again.

That was until Nini sang in an angelic voice.

It hypnotised the queen to rock her back and forth as the others stood surprised; their eyes opening wide as Nini grew in confidence to sing louder.

Jon smiled, glad to be able to stop as his weapon beeped to show it was recharged. He fired at the queen to send her crashing against a wall as more blasts smashed into her. Marek grinned to see her quiver as his shot ripped into her stomach whilst Neal spat as his energy blast kept her at bay. He saw Dan fire at her face to send pleading yelps through the air; the mouths shuddering to leave teeth falling to the floor as Nini kept up with the pace of her ringtone. But it stopped swiftly after Jon's phone died.

Nini saw the queen slowly recover, forcing her to tremble again. But this time she didn't cower, she just blasted the creature until its wings began to smoke, watching it crumble to the floor before shutting its eyes.

"It better be dead," Marek angrily said.

"Why don't you touch it and check?" Jon replied.

"Fuck that!"

They watched the queen closely to see if there was a flicker of movement, everyone still on edge in case she woke up. But she wasn't moving as Dan kicked her.

"It's over," he said, feeling exhausted as he walked towards the door.

CHAPTER THIRTY-TWO

Neal was close to falling apart as he collapsed into a chair inside a hospital ward, pleased to see Ben stir in his bed.

"Where am I?" Ben asked, cringing from the pain.

"Hospital," Neal replied, glancing up at a clock on the wall to see it was now *2:30 pm*. "You need to rest."

"What happened?"

Neal could see that Ben was still very weak because his eyes were constantly closing, so wasn't sure if telling him would be heard.

"I shot you," he whispered, wiping a tear from his eye before touching Ben's hand.

He waited for a reply, but Ben's silence worried him to slowly exit the chair. He walked away, gaining some distance but smiled after hearing Ben move.

"Where are you going?" Ben said, coughing.

"Outside to let Dan know you're awake."

Neal smiled again after Ben closed his eyes, but his heart was in pieces as he backtracked out of the ward to follow the exit sign pointing to reception. He moved quickly as he fought his emotions to reach the outside before shaking as he grabbed his phone.

"Where are you?" he blurted out as Dan picked up.

"Back at the station," Dan said, hearing Neal struggle to get the words out. "How is he?"

"He's stable." Neal gulped. "I'll stay with him for a while if that's okay?"

Dan needed Neal by his side but knew he would only get half of him if he forced him back now.

"Make sure he's fine then report in," he said, hoping Neal didn't fall apart.

"Will do." Neal sat on a snow-drenched bench. "Are you sure that thing is dead?"

"It was dead when we left, so it's dead now...Stop worrying and get back to Ben."

Dan stopped the call and left his office to find Marion playing mother to the tired-out officers crashed out inside the staff room. She was still trying to make sense of it all.

"Thanks," Dan softly said, tapping her on the shoulder. "But we need to carry on."

"You need to rest." Marion stared at the others, feeling lost as to why they couldn't take more time out. "Look at them. They can't carry on today."

Dan sighed.

He felt tempted to tell her everything but knew he would be a hypocrite if he did after warning the others not to. So just smiled and hugged her.

"I know you're worried and you want to help, but being here right now is what I need from you," he said, letting go to watch her leave the room.

Jon tiredly rose from his seat, yawning to stretch before grabbing a coffee.

"Will I get time to drink it?" he said, staring at the coffee like it was the best drink ever.

"I know you want to rest your aching bones, but the truth is you can't. Not now anyway," Dan replied, frowning as he closed in.

"Will this ever end?" Nini asked.

"Yes, when those bugs are found." Dan picked up a notepad and pen from a bookcase and sat next to her.

He began to write, intriguing everyone to pay attention; their eyes glued to the pad as he concentrated. He never spoke or looked at them, just wrote until finished before putting the pad on a nearby coffee table.

"...I've written down all the sightings of the bugs. Well, the ones I know of," Dan said, as everyone stared at the list. "If anyone can think of another place where they were seen then add it."

"You've got the sighting at Lovells' shop, at Mick's house, and the one I told you about with my boot," Jon said, scratching his head to think of another. "But nothing from the boy's house or from next door where that thing was."

"Nothing yet, but we all know there's a connection there. We just need to investigate more."

Marek grabbed the pad as the others watched him closely. "I'm adding the sighting from the stockroom," he said, writing it on the list. "It fuckin' creeped me out."

"But you weren't sure you said," Nini interrupted.

"Not sure can still be added," Dan replied. "What Marek thought he saw is close enough."

Marek smirked at Nini, knowing she couldn't contribute because she hadn't seen any of the insects. She shrugged her shoulders and ignored him to see Jon write on the pad.

"I'm adding the sighting in the street when I was with you," he said, pointing at Dan.

"You mean when we entered the house of the dead dog?" Jon nodded.

"Then I'll add the creepy sighting at the top of the stairs." Dan reached out to take the pad. "I swear a black shadow pushed that head down the steps."

He wrote it down before adding the deaths of the men inside the cells, knowing everyone would agree that the bugs had something to do with it.

"This doesn't make any sense," Marek said, staring at the pad again. "We know they may be able to disappear, but how can they carry people?"

"You know Ben saw them do it, so why bring it up?" Jon asked.

"Because you said the ones on your boot were very tiny."

"And? ...We don't even know what they are, so how can we know what they can or can't pick up?" Jon sighed, feeling angry that the bugs were still out there. "Maybe they're stronger than we think?"

Dan soaked up the conversation before standing back to listen to the other's recollections. He was glad to see them find their fighting spirit again.

"Right, I'm off to speak to my grandfather. See if I can get more information on what happened all those years ago."

"Would you like some company?" Nini asked.

"That would be great."

"But what shall we do?" Marek asked.

"Get rid of that beast," Dan replied. "I don't know how but we can't have people snooping inside that house." He looked over at Jon. "Go with him, please, then stop off at the hospital to see Ben. He's woken up."

"Will do," Jon said.

"What about the bugs?!" Marek cried out, as Dan and Nini were about to leave.

"Keep it down. Do you want Marion to find out?"

Marek placed a hand over his mouth to see Nini shake her head at him again.

"Soz, chief," he said from beneath his fingers.

"Just grab the keys for the police van, drive over to the house, cover the creature the best you can and get it out of there." Dan shuddered, feeling queasy about what the creature nearly achieved. "Get help if you need to. I'm just glad I'm not touching it."

"Me neither," replied Nini.

"But where do we take it?" Marek asked, feeling the pressure of the job.

Talk to the medics, and see if the hospital can store it in their large freezer until we know what to do with it...It's not like they don't know what's been going on."

"Do we tell them what it is?" Marek asked.

"You won't need to tell them. They'll see it for themselves." Dan walked away but stopped to say, "Once the large creature is in storage the bugs hopefully will be easier to find."

Jon and Marek sighed as Dan and Nini moved out of sight, but their tiredness and aching bones crept back to almost make them want to sit down again.

CHAPTER THIRTY-THREE

Dan parked his car outside the nursing home, pleased to find that none of the trauma he'd recently encountered had been seen there. He watched as workers escorted the elderly around the grounds, all wrapped up to get some fresh air before chuckling nervously to surprise Nini.

"What's so funny?" she asked, zipping up her coat.

"Nothing...Just something my pops said when I was last here."

"Don't keep me in suspense. What did he say?"

Dan told her about the rules of the nursing home, and that no outside news was to be mentioned especially bad news. But he frowned, gulping after remembering he'd spilt the beans to his grandfather about what was happening in Lemonsville.

"Damn. I hope he hasn't told everyone what I said."

Nini opened the door, smacking her hands together to keep warm. "Look at the place. It's quiet. He hasn't said anything."

"I agree. He's probably been sleeping since I left and hasn't woken up yet."

Nini shrugged and exited the car.

She waited for Dan to slowly follow, knowing his mind was somewhere else as they walked towards the entrance; seeing him nod at the person in reception before making his way down a corridor. He knew where his grandfather would be if he was awake.

He led Nini to a lounge room, seeing her smile at the elderly people watching a movie on TV before searching for his grandfather; finding him at the back of the room nestled snug in a chair.

"Hey, pops, how are you doing today?" Dan said, lifting a blanket to Eddie's chest. "You look tired. Have you been sleeping okay?"

Eddie smiled as he stared widely, but his appearance seemed weaker than last night.

"My memory must be rubbish today," he said, staring at Nini. "I can't remember who you are."

Dan almost laughed. "You don't know her, pops. She's new to the force."

Eddie held Nini's hand to receive a warm smile as Dan pulled up a chair. But the sound of it scraping across the wooden floor annoyed the residents.

"Hoy!" Eddie shouted, scowling at them. "Watch your movie...My grandson is the law. He will arrest you all."

"Okay, pops," Dan interrupted, holding up a hand towards the residents as he sat. "You need to calm down."

"I don't even know who they are." Eddie grinned and coughed into his hand before returning to look at Nini.

"How are you?" she asked.

"Now that's sweet," Eddie said, glancing at Dan. "A stranger asks if I'm okay but not my grandson..."

Nini looked awkwardly towards Dan as he shook his head, but relaxed after Eddie laughed.

"I'm bored," he said, coughing again. "There's nothing to do here."

"You're eighty-one, pops," Dan interrupted. "There's not much you can do."

Eddie trembled as his eyes filled with fluid; the sadness pouncing on Dan to leave him turning his head so as not to show his vulnerability. He couldn't let Eddie see he was feeling his pain.

Nini felt sweat leak from Eddie's hand to make the hairs on her arm stand up before gasping to see him suddenly crumble, bringing pain to her heart as he wept.

"I can do anything, I can," Eddie spluttered, letting go of her to clamp a hand onto Dan. "You just need to get me out of here."

He tried lifting out of the chair but struggled to make him angry before coughing again to send his breathing out of rhythm. It scared Dan.

"Right, I'm getting a nurse," he said, gripping Eddie's arm. "You're not well."

But Eddie shook his head and squeezed Dan hard.

"Don't," he whispered. "I'm fine."

"Come on pops," Dan said. "You don't have to prove anything to me. I know you're not well."

Eddie tried to ignore him as he attempted to leave his seat again, but he squirmed in pain when his elbows wouldn't lock.

"Help me get out of here," he pleaded, as sweat burst from his face. "They're coming for me?"

"Who is?" Dan asked, fearing Eddie was in trouble. "The nurses?"

"I tried telling you before but you wouldn't listen. It's not a who. It's them."

"Come on pops, you're worrying me now," Dan said, as a memory flashed in front of him of their recent chat. "Are you talking about the strange plane?"

"It wasn't a plane," Eddie said, releasing more tears as he held a hand over his mouth. "I know what it was. I've seen something like it..."

His words gripped Dan and Nini.

"...When I worked for the government."

Dan didn't know whether to ask about it or steer the conversation onto something less traumatic but knew there was a chance his grandfather could open up about his time when he wore a suit if he kept pushing.

"I thought the government job was private, so why do you want to talk about it now?"

"Because I did something wrong." Eddie glared at him like he was about to explode.

Dan thought he was confused again as he was last night and hadn't done anything wrong, but his mind swiftly changed when Eddie mentioned *bugs*.

"I should've reported them. I should've told someone before it was too late...I knew this day would come."

Eddie shook even more after feeling imaginary insects crawl over him, the sweat soaking through him to leave Nini sad and confused.

"Tell me what you remember," Dan softly said, not wanting to put pressure on in case Eddie retreated into his shell.

He told Nini to write it down, even if what Eddie said sounded farfetched. He knew anything was possible right now.

He held Eddie's hand and waited, feeling a vein vibrate

against his skin upon fearing something bad being said, whilst Nini stood nervous with a notepad and pen in her hands.

Eddie went back to the year *1969* when he worked in an underground facility. It was his first week there so had no clearance to enter the **TOP SECRET** room. But he was foolish and nosey back then so found a way inside.

"And did you find anything?" Dan asked, intrigued.

"Yes."

Eddie went on to say that men with jumpsuits and masks occupied the room. And they all had a specific job. Some were checking machines, others were writing notes, whilst others were staring at a large, glass window.

"And were you caught?"

"No," Eddie replied, holding back more tears. "I hid so they couldn't see me."

"So what was on the other side of the window?"

"A large tarpaulin. I couldn't see what was behind it."

"So that's the end of that story then."

Eddie shook his head to leave Dan surprised. "There's more."

He went on to say that he snuck inside another room, nearing the tarpaulin to see what was hidden; almost freaking out after witnessing a type of plane he'd never seen before.

"And it wasn't used by the military?"

"Nope...I would've recognised it if it was...It was a UFO?"

"How do you know for sure?"

Eddie *gulped*. "Because I saw a dark shadow come out of it to rip apart the men inside the room."

Nini dropped the notepad to cause Dan to shiver, as his head spun from thoughts of the shadow being behind the gruesome deaths back in *1947*. But Eddie put him straight by saying it couldn't have been that as the shadow hadn't surfaced before then. He said he was very lucky that it didn't attack him, and to this day still wasn't sure why? But he felt a connection to the UFO after that.

"What happened to the shadow?"

"It was frozen."

"So the bugs inside it could still be alive today? ...It could be them that's doing this now."

"The UFO we had was found in the same year as those awful murders, but what was inside it wasn't the killer."

"Meaning?"

"There had to be more than one."

Dan shuddered from the thought of there being more alien landings back then, as the words – 'Just how many?' – smashed against his brain.

"Where was the spaceship found?"

"North. Somewhere in Scotland, I think." Eddie coughed again. "The UFO took twenty-two years to breach. None of our tools got close to opening it. But when it finally did, it was like everyone's worse nightmare."

Dan glanced at Nini to see her turn over a page, pleased to see her concentration intact as she kept on writing. He knew she could so easily laugh it off and do some doodles instead but she was keen and excited to know more.

Dan sighed, feeling anger towards the people responsible for keeping the secret. Not his grandfather, but the people higher up. He knew their secret could end up destroying all of mankind, especially if more of those things came out of hiding.

"Just one more thing I need to mention," Dan awkwardly said. "Did you see a flying creature?"

"I never stuck around to find out. The sirens went off so I ran."

Dan nodded, knowing anyone would've done the same.

"That's why you left. You never retired, you quit."

"What would you have done?!" Eddie barked, feeling stressed again. "I couldn't tell anyone about it. It's been haunting me for over fifty years."

Nini hugged him, knowing he needed it as Dan glanced at the notes.

"Pops, do you think the shadow from nineteen-forty-seven is back?"

"Yes. I do. But why come out of hiding after seventy-three years?"

Dan shrugged, knowing he would have to find out soon.

He just hoped that now Eddie had released the demons from his past he could sleep properly again.

CHAPTER THIRTY-FOUR

Marek drove a large police van towards the house. He was alone; a choice he'd made just before leaving the station. He wanted to act cool to show Jon he was capable of handling the creature without him watching his every move. He said he would arrange for other officers to help once he'd secured the area, so Jon accepted before heading towards the hospital. But the real reason behind Marek's decision to go solo was that he feared hospitals, and had done since childhood. He'd seen too many family members die in them, but couldn't mention it to Jon.

He pulled up outside the house to a sudden increase in nerves, staring at the bedroom window as he turned off the engine. He looked around to see the street bare of people but knew some could be hiding in the shadows as he exited the car; slowly walking to the house to take deep breaths as he touched the door.

———

Jon entered the hospital at speed, moving through the corridors until reaching the ward Ben was on. He saw Neal still sitting next to him, his face plastered with sadness, so knew all wasn't good.

"Hey...Just checking on the patient," Jon said, closing in to sit in a chair. "How long's he been out of it?"

"He's in and out of consciousness, but at least he's alive."

"Thank God."

Jon yawned, almost nodding off within seconds of taking a rest. But he jolted upright, stretched and shook his head; exiting the seat to walk towards the exit.

"You fancy a coffee?"

Neal nodded, thankful he was there.

————

Marek psyched himself up to enter the house; opening the front door to feel a coldness in the air before quivering after realising he'd made a huge mistake by going alone. He shut the door and looked at the stairs, cautiously closing in to hear nothing as he stood on the first one. But his heart thudded against his chest. He was close to turning around to wait for backup, but, after climbing a few more steps, felt okay to continue. He was scared and excited to see the fallen creature, knowing he was part of the reason behind its demise. But he stalled as he reached the bedroom door before turning white as he gripped the handle; breathing deeply as he opened it to almost collapse after finding the creature was gone.

Where is it?

He reached for his phone, sweating upon smelling burned flesh, becoming cowardly after feeling breath against his neck before crouching in pain from something sharp penetrating his back. He collapsed to the floor, dropping the phone to touch the wound, feeling blood on his hand as his legs stiffened. He was petrified, fearing for his life.

He twisted his head from side to side, desperately trying to catch a glimpse of what attacked him, but nothing was seen as blood seeped out of the wound to form a puddle on the floor.

He pressed down on the injury and winced as he crawled towards his phone, twitching his nose as the burned flesh smell returned before looking up to see the queen in front of him, her missing teeth now replaced and her skin blistered.

Marek's heart sunk as the queen pierced a leg into his thigh, his screams echoing around the room as she licked the red juice off before stabbing him in the thigh again.

"I saw you...die," Marek weakly said, cringing in agony. "We killed you."

He winced as the queen thrust a leg into his stomach before coughing up fluid as tongues licked his body.

Marek was defenceless.

He reached for his phone again but the pain increased to slow him down, his screams becoming deafening after feeling his bones break through his skin. His eyes became drenched with tears after the queen slapped a tongue around his neck; his face bulging, turning blue as it tightened. He struggled to breathe as he was lifted into the air to spin around like he was on a fairground ride before his hands slapped at thin air as he was thrown violently against a wall.

He lay still on the ground, hoping it would put the creature off to leave him alone. But the blood loss left him feeling faint. He knew he was doomed.

The queen flapped her wings and shrieked as Marek's phone rang, but her frantic movement allowed him time to desperately attempt to stem the blood from escaping. He watched her move around the room, so waited to gain some distance before shuffling towards the phone to leave bloody handprints on the floor. He waited for the queen to attack, hoping it was a quick death, but she was still fascinated by the ringtone to allow him time to answer. His mouth quivered as he heard Dan on the other end, but a wing swiped the phone from his grasp before he could speak. He could still hear Dan's voice as the phone landed on the floor before tears fell, the mouths gripping his body and face.

"Marek! Marek! What's going on? Where are you?!" Dan shouted as the queen tore Marek apart. "Stop messing about!..."

The queen carried on eating as Dan shouted, "If you keep this up I'll be taking your badge. I'm being serious. Marek! Marek!"

She moved closer to sniff the phone, shrieking before crushing it with a leg.

CHAPTER THIRTY-FIVE

an bowed his head as he parked outside the house, as the thought of Marek messing about faded to leave him sad. He charged his gun and glared at the front door as Nini sat next to him, almost in tears as she did the same.

They got out fast, leaving the doors open to rush towards the house, sensing a creepiness hovering over them as they reached it.

"Don't open it!" Dan shouted, gripping Nini's arm. "We don't know what's inside."

"But we can't leave him in there," she replied, worried. "Do the others know?"

"Jon does. He's on his way."

"We don't have time to wait for him. We need to get in there now," Nini replied, taking charge after Dan almost broke down on the doorstep. "Chief! Snap out of it..."

Dan shook his head to release the tension building up inside before smiling at Nini as he pushed open the door. He entered with caution, checking the hallway for signs that Marek had been there as Nini stepped into the house. But a ghostly shiver raced through her, leaving her crying as she stared at the stairs.

"...He's dead."

"Don't say that. Marek's a fighter. He'll be fine."

"He's not!" Nini snapped back.

They turned to the sound of people piling out onto the street, all feeling confident after spotting the police car. But Dan grimaced as he shut the door. He had no idea what to tell them so hoped they would return home, but, as he walked towards the stairs, voices were heard closing in on the door.

"What's going on?!" a man cried out, whilst a woman shouted, "Is this town in trouble?!"

Dan looked over at Nini but the people shuffling behind the door annoyed him to glare at it. They started banging on it, wanting to be let inside, arguing amongst themselves to leave him close to opening it. But the letterbox flap lifted to stop him.

"Why is there blood out here?!" a woman yelled, rapping it.

Nini raced towards the door, hushing the woman to back away, but her attempt failed as more people slammed fists against it.

"Don't tell me to be quiet. I have a right to know what's going on..."

Nini saw the woman's eyes eagerly stare at Dan, her anger increasing after he ignored her to walk the stairs.

"...Hoy! Don't ignore me. Tell me what's going on?!" she screamed, kicking the base of the door.

Nini gulped after remembering the awkward moment with the arrested men, hoping the neighbours didn't break in to force her to fight them off.

She followed Dan up the stairs to leave the irate woman still kicking before catching him up as he reached the bedroom door. But she flinched when he opened it, shuddering from the fear of the beast attacking again.

"Where is it?" Dan whispered.

Nini choked before saying, "And where is Marek?..."

She picked up the pieces of Marek's phone to feel the dried blood, as her head spun from seeing no sign of him.

"...We blasted that thing with all we had. It shouldn't have survived."

"But it did," Dan replied, shocked to see no more blood inside the room.

He watched Nini tremble as she tried putting the phone back together, holding the battery like it was a bomb ready to go off before throwing it against a wall. She was close to screaming but stopped after seeing something glisten from beneath the mattress; bending to pick it up to see it was Marek's police badge before becoming queasy after feeling his soul in the room.

"He died here," she said, placing the badge inside a plastic bag. "Why was he so stupid to come here alone?"

Dan wanted to reply, wanted to make sure she was okay, but the shouts coming from the unsettled bystanders ripped through him, causing him to lose his temper. Nini noticed he was on the verge of racing back down the stairs so hugged him tightly, hoping the distraction would drown out the swearing now being aimed at him. But Dan flipped, kicking the wall before leaving the room in a hurry. Nini raced after him to more insults coming from the people behind the door, fearing Dan could lash out at any time.

"Go home!" he shouted. "There's nothing to see here."

Nini rushed past him, closing in on the door, as Dan's phone began to ring.

"What's going on?" the woman said, trying to listen in as Dan answered the call.

"He's told you to go home. Now go...You're not safe outside," Nini ranted, hoping her strict approach would work.

She smiled after the woman shut the letterbox, breathing easier at the sound of people moving away from the door. She wanted to tell Dan but he had gone into the kitchen, as the faint words of, "Yes, I'm Daniel Boone," convinced her it wasn't someone from the police station on the phone.

She entered the room to find him standing against a table, looking ashen as he listened to the caller; his heart beating fast as the words, "Your grandfather passed away," sent a cold shiver down his spine.

"But I was with him not long ago," Dan said, frowning.

"I know you were," the reply came. "But he passed away during his afternoon nap...He died peacefully..."

Dan found it hard to take, the fact that his grandfather suddenly died peacefully after knowing he was upset, but he stayed quiet and listened.

"...I found something odd in his bedside drawer."

"What was that?" Dan asked.

"He had drawings."

"Drawings? You think my grandfather's drawings were odd?"

"Yes...He had drawn disturbing images of bugs attacking people, plus a flying ship of some kind with a larger bug inside."

"Really?" Dan asked, curious.

"Do you know why?"

Dan never answered the question but he knew.

"I'll come over now to look at them."

Nini saw him tremble after the reality of the call hit before seeing him replace the phone to hold a hand up to his mouth.

"Is everything okay?" she asked, knowing it wasn't.

"No, not really." Dan paused and rubbed his eyes. "My grandfather's just died."

"Oh, my God. I'm so sorry."

Dan sighed as a tear dropped, but the irritating woman slammed on the front door again yelling for an answer.

Dan glared beyond Nini before racing to the door, pulling it open to see the woman embarrassingly almost tumble inside the house as he stormed towards his car.

CHAPTER THIRTY-SIX

Nini raced inside the hospital as the clock above the reception desk ticked to *4:15 pm*. She was annoyed at being left on her own to talk to the neighbours back at the house but understood why Dan did it upon holding back tears as she closed in on the ward. She assumed he would be visiting Ben after leaving the nursing home, but had a feeling the awful news about his grandfather and the disappearance of Marek had crushed his spirit. She had tried to call him several times, but every call went straight to voicemail.

She felt soreness around the eyes as an image of Marek walked towards her, but the closer the person got, the more it wasn't him. She stared at the person as they walked past, hoping it was a sign that Marek was okay, that the creature had left him unharmed as it did with Ben, but that hope faded by the time she reached the ward. She gulped upon glancing at Jon, leaving him worried as he attempted to comfort her. But she brushed him off and backed away.

"Why weren't you with him?!" she snapped.

Jon tried to hug her again but she swiped at his hands.

"Marek wanted to go alone," he said, regretting what he did. "You know what he's like."

"You saw that monster," Nini interrupted. "And you still let him go alone. It's unforgivable..."

Neal grabbed hold of her, pulling her close, letting her *sob* into his chest as Jon sadly watched on. He tried apologising but Nini was too upset to listen; her eyes drained as she looked over at Ben.

"...Where's Dan?" she asked, calming down to wait for an answer.

"He's not here," Neal replied. "What happened to him?"

"He just flipped out and rushed off." Nini collapsed into a seat and held Ben's hand. "His grandfather passed away recently."

Ben stirred in his bed, waking up to groan after having a bad dream.

"You okay buddy?" Neal asked, closing in to comfort him.

But Ben writhed, slapping at his chest. "Get off! Get them off me!" he screamed.

"It's okay," Nini softly said. "You're safe now."

"You need to get them off me," Ben said, slapping at his chest again. "They're on me...Please get them off."

"There's nothing there," Neal said, touching Ben's chest. "See? If those critters were on you then they would be on me too."

Ben opened his eyes wider to see Neal's hand move around his body, as confusion etched across his face. He was lost as to why no one else could see what he was seeing.

He quickly sat up, trembling as he ripped at his hair, screaming louder than before to worry the others into finding some help.

"Those bugs are on me! Get them off!"

A *nurse* appeared, moving closer to check on Ben; calming him down before ushering the others to back away.

"It's time to let him rest," she said, staring at the bedside monitor. "Haven't you got somewhere else you need to be?"

Her words left the others feeling ashamed for not doing their job.

They backed off, knowing it was time to go, but Nini felt pain shoot across her head as she glanced at Ben.

"Did the bugs attack you in the carriage?" she asked.

"He's probably still in shock," Neal said, shrugging towards Jon. "It was a large bug he saw, not those small ones." He walked back to the bed feeling more confused. "Tell them, Ben, it was just the large one."

Ben reached out and gripped his arm. "I saw them on me," he whispered, staring deeply into his eyes.

Neal sighed.

He turned to see the nurse holding a stethoscope tight to her chest like it was some kind of a religious cross before seeing her check Ben's heartbeat.

"And?" he asked, feeling strained. "Is it bad?"

"No," the nurse replied. "His heartbeat has slowed again... I'll take care of him now."

Neal saw Ben's eyes flutter to almost make him cry, as Jon pulled him away from the bed.

"It's time to go," he calmly said before flicking his head at Nini. "We need to finish this."

He nodded to the nurse before sadly smiling at Ben as he walked the others out of the ward. But a flashback of the bugs on his boot began a whirlwind of random theories that stuck with him until they reached the outside.

"Don't get your hopes up but I may have found a way to

destroy those freaks," he said, looking around to see if anyone was listening. "Ben seems adamant that they were on him back at the carriage."

"But I didn't see them." Neal seemed sure that it was just the large creature but doubt crept in once Jon shook his head. "So why didn't I see them?"

"I don't know, but what if Ben only fired his gun into himself to get rid of those things?"

"Go on," Nini said, hoping Jon had a point. "What are you getting at."

"His gun evaporated them, burned them off, just like the ones that caught fire on my boot."

"But you didn't shoot them, so how did they?" Nini asked, thinking back to what Jon told everyone. "The light maybe?... You said you turned your bathroom light on."

"But how can a light bulb kill them?" Neal jumped in, feeling even more confused.

Nini shrugged her shoulders. "I don't know, but a light bulb acts like fire. It's bright and hot, so could be a clue?"

"Daylight!" Jon yelled, surprising everyone. "Why have all the attacks happened at night? It's because those little fuckers hate daylight."

"What?" Nini questioned. "But Gina's husband was murdered in the daytime. It doesn't make any sense."

"But was it light where he was?" Neal asked, worried that his question would be overlooked. "Daylight outside doesn't always mean it's light inside..."

Nini and Jon stared at him like he'd just answered the million-dollar question; their faces glowing in agreement with what he'd said.

"...It was dark inside the carriage when Ben was attacked so maybe the stockroom was also dark?"

"Neal, you could be onto a winner," Jon said, aiming for the car park. "The bulb inside the stockroom needed changing. It was very dull. Only lit up part of the room."

He sighed as he reached his car but felt happy with the theory of how to destroy the bugs.

CHAPTER THIRTY-SEVEN

The queen lashed out her many tongues as she moved towards two figures inside the UFO; both hanging upside down encased in a cocoon-like web. She sniffed them, shrieking with delight, acting as a protector as she lay between them, the bugs crawling over her to settle on her back as she watched the cocoons slightly move. She then snapped all mouths and shut her eyes.

———

Dan had sat inside his car outside the nursing home for a while as painful memories of his last visit to see his grandfather stalled him from entering. He thought of him suffering torturous dreams recently, dreams that he'd kept a secret, but hoped that the pictures he drew would help work out why?

Fresh snowflakes landed on the windscreen to grab Dan's attention, helping him to fight the sad emotions. But he shuddered after seeing the darkness creep upon him. He feared another night of terror as he listened to his bones creak, frowning at his stubbornness for keeping it within his district for so long. He had faith in his officers, but that faith had left one injured and another missing, presumed dead, so it was time to give in and find some backup.

He stared at the nursing home entrance as a sudden dose of panic smashed into him, feeling sad from the thought of knowing the truth about his grandfather's death before reaching for his phone to make a call. He spoke to someone for a few minutes upon thinking back to Cassidy Street before sending out an order for extra officers to go to the house. He put the phone away to open the car door, feeling his heart wrench as he sucked in the cold before exiting and walking towards the nursing home.

———

Jon, Neal, and Nini arrived at the Tanker house to find it swamped with *workmen*; shocked to see so many not scared by the recent events. They watched some take tools from a large van to carry inside the house whilst others brought furniture outside.

"What's going on?" Jon asked, closing in to see snow cling to a sofa. "Did Dan call this in?"

"Yeah, bud," a mid-twenties man with a safety helmet on replied. "He wants the house gutted. Floorboards and everything."

Nini and Neal sighed over whether to warn the worker of what happened there, but he acted like he already knew.

"Hey! The pay for this gig was too good to turn down, no matter what you guys saw," he said, grinning as he grabbed more tools from the van.

Jon entered the house to a loud noise coming from the living room, closing in to find a workman sawing through a floorboard. He cringed as the sound made his teeth hurt before raising a hand over his face to stop the dust from entering his eyes.

"Hey!" he hollered. "Put the guard down to stop the dust from blinding someone."

He saw the *foreman* point towards the electric saw until the workman turned it off.

"What's up boss?" he said, unsure of why he had to stop.

"How many times have I told you to keep the guard down when usin' that thing?!" the foreman cried out. "It's not a fuckin' toy..."

The workman gulped as Jon neared.

"...I see you know your tools," the foreman said, approaching him. "We could do with a hand."

"Nice try," Jon replied, turning to leave the room. "But you're right. I do know my tools."

He entered the hallway to see *three* officers inside the kitchen, nodding towards them to notice their lack of confidence as Neal and Nini entered the house.

———

Dan slowly neared the reception desk to feel everyone's eyes on him, so dropped his head to avoid their stares. He knew they felt sad for him, but the more they looked, the more guilty he became. He was close to crying after realising he had visited his grandfather more times in the past day or so than in the past few months, gulping upon reaching the desk to see elderly people smile at him. They bowed their heads, holding hands to perform a silent prayer as he sadly smiled.

"I was told to come down," he said to the receptionist, trying hard not to crumble after making eye contact. "My grandfather had drawn some strange pictures that I need to look at..."

The receptionist nodded before pointing towards a nearby nurse; seeing Dan turn to see her close in like she'd been waiting for him to arrive. But she didn't speak. She just smiled and walked down a corridor.

"...Did you see Eddie much?" Dan asked, catching her up in the hope of getting a reaction. But she remained firm, not saying a word.

He followed her down more corridors until stopping outside a room with the name 'Eddie Mckay' written on the door before watching her take a key from her uniform pocket and opening it to allow him inside. But it took him a few seconds to enter. He examined the room, noticing it was very tidy, now not sure if his grandfather did what he did.

"...So, did you see my grandfather much?" Dan asked again.

"Yeah. He was a pleasant man. Always laughing and joking with us."

The nurse stalled upon staring at the bed, her eyes welling up to spook Dan.

"Are you okay?" he asked, touching her shoulder as she trembled by the door.

She snapped away from staring and wiped her face. "Yeah. I'm fine. But something changed within your grandfather in the past few days."

"What do you mean?"

"He couldn't sleep. He seemed anxious all the time. And he appeared terrified of something."

Dan knew there was a link between the bugs his grandfather saw and the recent nightmares he was having, but he didn't want to let the nurse know. He didn't need her freaking out, so just smiled as she pointed to a chest of drawers.

"The pictures are in the top one," she said, recoiling as she stared at the bed again. "I'll leave you to it."

Dan breathed deeply as she walked away before anxiously staring at the drawer. He hoped it was just fake news. But, as he nervously pulled it open, saw a folder. He grabbed it and placed it on the bed, staring at it like he wanted it to open itself, but the sound of people walking past the room snapped him out of it.

He shook as he slowly flipped it open to reveal a bizarre, eerie picture. It wasn't expected, especially coming from his grandfather, but somehow he had drawn it from his mind. Dan took it out and placed it on the bed but felt sick after seeing the next one, choking to catch his breath as he lay it next to the first. He did the same with the rest, knowing each one told a story about what had gone on recently in town; pointing at them in turn to scowl at how gruesome they were.

But in what order are they meant to be?

He stared hard at the drawings, moving one with a boy in a bed being attacked by small insects next to a young man being pulled from a swing by the same things; shaking his head and close to tears after seeing a picture resembling a storeroom. It was mostly blacked out, but a figure was lying on the floor with insects coming out of the person's mouth.

He rubbed his chin as he placed the pictures in some kind of order, hoping to work out the timeframe from when each incident took place. But his mouth became dry the more he studied them.

He must've been having nightmares before the first murder. But how did he know? Could he see what they were doing?

Dan reached for his phone and dialled Nini, taking a deep breath as she answered.

"Hey, what's happening?" he said, hearing loud banging crashing through his phone. He tried listening to Nini's reply but the noise made his ears burn. "Go outside. It's too loud."

He waited for the sound to fade before Nini said, "Sorry, chief. I was inside the boy's house...There are loads of workmen here smashing up the floorboards and the noise is attracting attention. But don't worry, the situation's in hand."

"That's great news...Has Jon spoken to them yet, told them what the dangers are?"

Nini looked back at the house, watching the workmen whistle like it was just another day. "He did, but they don't seem to care...Too macho."

She heard Dan breathe heavily like he was lifting something before the words: "Holy shit! There's more," entered her ears.

"Chief! Chief! You okay?"

"Yeah, yeah, I'm fine," Dan replied, placing more pictures on the bed. "Everything's just a little too weird right now. I've just found more drawings under the mattress."

"What did he draw?" Nini asked, showing concern after a bad feeling washed over her. "It's bad, isn't it."

"Yes, it is," Dan said, feeling more queasy after the last drawing landed on the bed. "He's drawn every death that we know of."

"Is there any that we don't?"

Dan stared at a drawing. "Yes, but don't freak out."

"I've done my freaking out. Just tell me."

"It's a drawing of that large creature."

"And?" Nini questioned, not understanding why Dan would mention it when she already knew it existed.

"There's a man in a police uniform below it, and he looks dead."

"It's just a drawing, Dan. Marek could still be alive."

"Nini, my grandfather has drawn every death we have witnessed recently, including the ones from the cells, so why would he add one of Marek if he was still alive?"

Nini froze as she watched the backup police keep the growing crowd back, her head aching upon knowing what Dan said was true. She heard him apologise for freaking her out as her legs came close to crumbling. But, after seeing the residents stare at her, regained her focus to leave them confused.

"Do you know why he was able to do this?" she asked, sniffing.

"I have my theory," Dan replied. "He mentioned something about having a connection with the UFO he saw all those years ago, so I'm guessing it happened again with the bugs."

"Like some form of telepathy, you mean?"

"Yeah, something like that."

"So why didn't he draw pictures before now?" Nini asked.

"Maybe he was? Or maybe there was no reason to until now?" Dan placed the pictures inside the folder before adding, "The light he saw as a child may have hypnotised him, allowing the bugs access to connect with him now...It's the only explanation I have..."

Dan felt a cold wind suddenly race around his feet until another drawing was seen blowing out from under the bed; attaching itself to his thigh.

"...Hold on, Nini," he said, pulling it away. "I've found another one."

Nini waited anxiously for Dan to describe it but all she heard was him choking on his hand.

"Dan! Dan!"

"I'm here," he slowly said, as a tear fell onto the drawing.

"It's a picture of an old man lying in bed, staring up at a lightbulb."

"Your grandfather?"

"Yep...I think he drew his death just before he died. It wasn't a peaceful death. The fuckin' creatures did it."

He ended the call before Nini could reply. He placed the drawing inside the folder with the others, scratching his head as he walked towards the door, but something burned inside his mind to slow him down. He felt guilty again for not listening to Eddie, knowing he should have paid more attention when being told about the recent nightmares upon closing his eyes to be hit by a train of horrid thoughts linked to Eddie's death. He shuddered, close to punching something; feeling his adrenaline explode to revenge his grandfather's death.

CHAPTER THIRTY-EIGHT

Jon watched the foreman give out orders as the living room was dismantled; listening to his deep voice echo around the room to keep everyone on their toes. He closed in on him before staring into a hole; his heart beating fast as more of the floor was taken away. He waited for someone to ask questions about why they were digging below the house, but no one was. He was pleased to not have to deal with any more stress as he made himself useful, but the sound of workers laughing with each other like they were bonding down a pub, with each seemingly taking it in their stride, became annoying.

Jon pointed at a piece of floorboard as Nini and Neal closed in. He grabbed one end as Neal grabbed the other before they carried it out of the room.

"Take it outside," Jon said, putting his end down in the hallway. "Best to keep busy until Dan gets here."

"And when will that be?" Neal frustratingly asked. "That large beast could be anywhere."

"I know you want to find it, and so do I. But, if Dan's right about something being buried below the house then we need to get to it...If we destroy it then we destroy that thing."

"But what if he's wrong?" Neal asked, angrily dragging the floorboard towards the front door. "I don't want to end up like Marek."

Nini and Jon sighed as Neal took the wood outside; fearing he was close to losing it as he threw it down on the grass. They saw him grunt before talking to himself as the wind blew against his clothing, knowing he was lost without Ben.

"He doesn't look good," Nini said, moving towards the door as Neal spoke to one of the workers. "We need to keep an eye on him."

"I know...I just hope he keeps busy," Jon replied.

The neighbours edged closer to the house, feeling more confident to surround Neal as he tried to back away. But he became flustered as they bombarded him with questions. He couldn't breathe as the words – 'What happened to poor Tommy?' – 'What the fuck was that thing inside the house?' – and – 'Are we safe?' - blasted into him.

Jon and Nini raced outside after seeing Neal try to keep the residents back, pushing their way through the crowd to pull him away as the workmen nearby became spooked.

"What are they saying?" one asked, whilst another shouted, "I thought it was just a hoax! Did someone truly die here?"

They dropped tools once it sunk in that the reason why they were being paid so much was because of how dangerous the job was before coming close to running away as more shouts aimed at the truth hit them.

"Can everyone stop screaming at each other," Jon said, moving towards them. "I thought you guys knew what went on here?"

"So did we," one of them replied, staring at the house. "But no one told us about a creature being inside there."

"But you all came here with an attitude like nothing scared you. Don't tell me you're scared now."

"Of course we're scared. That thing may still be in there."

Neal broke away from Nini to prod the worker in the chest before yelling, "The house is fuckin' empty!..."

The worker backed off, becoming more worried, but Neal wouldn't calm down.

"...You wouldn't be alive if that thing was still there." He quivered as he looked at the house before shedding tears after seeing a flashback of Ben being found there. "You all need to know."

But Nini stepped in to hold him tight, shaking her head towards Jon as other workers left the house. She knew the plan would fall apart if they all became too frightened to carry on, so was glad to see him step up.

"Okay, guys, gather round," Jon nervously said, watching the workers wait for someone to make the first move. "We need you." He pointed at the house, slapping his chest upon feeling emotional. "Do you honestly think we'd be here if something bad was going to happen?"

He smiled as they closed in, staying relaxed to produce the right words to keep them focused. But someone screaming – 'HELP' - from down the street caused him to shudder.

He swiftly turned to see the crowd split open like the Dead Sea to reveal a woman wearing a heavy coat over a bathrobe running towards him in her slippers. He sighed as she neared, seeing her almost topple over as she tried catching her breath.

"My boy's not come home!" she shouted. "He's not come home."

Angus' mother was frantic as she stumbled into Jon, pushing him before crumbling to the ground. She lay in the snow to shed more tears, rubbing a hand over her face to smudge her eyeliner as Nini helped her up.

"Come home from where?" she asked.

"From where he was last," Jackie said, knocking snow off her body. "He never came in from the garden. He's gone missing."

Nini listened to her story about how she called Angus in to make it sound like she was worried. But, after hearing that it took another five hours to check on him, Nini almost lashed out.

"You've only just told us after five hours?!" she yelled at Jackie. "He's your son. Your son."

Jackie's face exploded into redness to make her appear more like a clown; the moment grabbing hold of her, reminding her of how neglectful she was to her boy.

"I was busy," she softly said, placing hands over her face so as not to see everyone glare at her.

She could feel their stares of hate towards her as her mind crumbled from the guilt of not knowing where Angus was. She cried again but received no words of comfort as her tears seeped beneath her fingers to leave her feeling alone.

Jon gulped. He knew it was his duty to take her statement, even though he wished he didn't.

He reached out to hold her hand upon forcing back the hatred he now felt towards her, wanting to get her away from the others before someone did more than glare at her.

"I'll take you to the station so we can have a more formal chat," he said, wincing after seeing Neal and Nini's heads drop. "It's better this way."

He switched off from listening to the crowd echo out

more shouts before rushing Jackie towards his car as the officers kept the peace.

Nini watched them. She shook her head as Jon opened the passenger side door, feeling lost as to why he was leaving when he was needed at the house.

CHAPTER THIRTY-NINE

Dan slowly parked outside his mother's house again to find her waiting on the doorstep; her eyes stinging from too much crying.

He nervously waved at her as he exited the car, but the strength in his legs faded to send him crumbling against a wall. Maureen teared up again to leave him close to doing the same, as he regained his balance to walk towards the house.

"Hi," he said, hugging her. "We need to talk."

Maureen wrapped her arms around him, shaking as she held him tight, but the moment lasted longer than expected. Dan let it happen, realising she needed to do it. She let go and kissed him on the cheek before walking back inside the house, letting him follow until stopping by the living room door.

"How are you feeling, son?" she said, entering the room. "I still think someone's going to tell us it's a mistake, that he's still alive."

Dan sat in an armchair, fidgeting like he needed to say something but was finding it hard to do. He smiled, but Maureen knew he was struggling.

"But it's not a mistake," he spat out. "I've just come from the nursing home..."

Maureen bowed her head, muttering to herself like she was fighting with the truth. She knew Dan had been there but didn't want to believe it. She noticed a folder in his hand, waiting for him to mention it. But he didn't. He just placed it down on the coffee table.

"...Did you know what Pops was doing before he died?"

"What do you mean?" Maureen asked, sitting down swiftly like the words had just blown her over. "What was he doing?"

Dan didn't want to re-open the floodgate of tears that she had already shed but needed to tell her. He stared at the floor to make her anxious, her vision flicking from the folder to him until he cracked.

"You need to look at the drawings," Dan said, pointing at the folder. "But prepare yourself. It's upsetting to imagine what was going through Pop's mind just before he died."

Maureen grabbed the folder. She opened it quickly to be faced with the creepy and disturbing pictures before jumping back in her seat to let go as the drawings fell onto the table. She stared at the one with the old man in bed, feeling confused by what it meant as she slowly became hypnotised by the lightbulb in the drawing.

"He drew all those?!" she shouted. "Eddie couldn't draw. Are you sure it was him?"

"Yes, it was him who drew them," Dan softly said, rushing the pictures back inside the folder.

He watched Maureen sink into her seat upon feeling lost to fight back with words; her head in a daze to see her father draw himself.

"But why?" she asked, becoming emotional again. "Why draw himself lying in bed looking peaceful?"

"He wasn't peaceful. I think he was forced to draw it so it looked that way."

"Dan, you're scaring me now. Forced by whom?"

"By the aliens..."

Maureen burst into tears as Dan tried to explain what Eddie had gone through during the past few days, but it wasn't making any sense to her.

"...He must have either drawn them in his sleep or felt every death as he drew them...I think Pops had a connection with the aliens," Dan said, reaching out to grip her hand.

But Maureen shot up out of her seat, crying so loud that it freaked him out. "Stop! I don't want to hear anymore."

Dan saw her shiver to make him feel guilty for having to leave. But he needed her to stay safe.

"Please go into the cellar and stay there," he said, wiping tears from her face. "Promise me you won't leave until you hear from me?"

"Okay."

CHAPTER FORTY

Dan checked the clock on his dashboard to see it was after *7:00 pm* as he turned his car into Cassidy Street. He cursed from fearing another attack from the creature before cursing again after spotting the street full of people. He honked the car horn at them to let him pass, but most were transfixed on the house so never noticed him until his car almost hit them.

He stared ahead to see a commotion unfold between the officers and the workmen, knowing now that the truth was probably out about what happened inside. He honked again to get their attention before parking next to household furniture, but his car was swamped by people, leaving him struggling to open the door.

"Hey, shift!" he shouted, annoyed at a workman leaning against it. "There's no time to argue amongst yourselves."

The workman huffed before moving to allow Dan to open the door, but he was blasted with questions before his feet touched the ground.

"Can you tell us what's going on?" a man from the crowd nervously asked.

Dan turned to see him holding a child wrapped in a blanket; her eyes wide in an attempt to stay awake. She smiled, leaving Dan close to breaking down, as thoughts of her father keeping her safe entered his mind.

"You need to go home," he said, pushing his way past the workmen. "And do it now."

The father wanted to say more but Dan's tone worried him, so, he gripped his daughter tight and walked away; hearing Dan speak to the workmen as he carried her back home.

Dan shouted at the bystanders again, but his words didn't affect them. They seemed more stubborn, and tenser upon knowing what was going on before feeling courageous to gather closer to the house. But the other officers stopped them as Dan reached Nini and Neal.

"I see you got the workers to carry on," he said, entering the house to show his appreciation after seeing a few workers carry more flooring outside.

"It was touch and go," Nini replied, moving out of the way to let the workers pass. "Jon gave them one of his speeches."

"I bet he bored them into coming back," Dan said, close to laughing. "His speeches have a habit of doing that...Isn't that right, Neal?"

Neal nodded before the sound of a drill spooked him, as Dan entered the living room to see a worker dig out concrete. But he coughed from the dust floating nearby before raising a hand and returning to the hallway.

"Is Jon not here?!" he shouted at Nini. "Thought he would be back from the station by now!"

Nini cringed as the drill crashed into more concrete before letting the words nestle inside her brain. She smiled at Dan as the drilling stopped to be replaced by the sound of spades gathering up concrete, as Dan repeated what he'd said.

"No, chief." Nini shrugged her shoulders.

Dan sighed as he looked back inside the room. He saw the foreman checking the hole, so closed in to pay attention.

"So, how far you got to go?" he asked, watching a worker dig out more concrete.

"Not far now," the foreman replied. "We just need to make sure we don't break any pipes."

"Good." Dan smiled before glancing over at Nini. "I need this day to end."

He stared inside the hole; his heart beating fast after visions of more of those creatures being below the house sent him on edge. It was a reminder to stay alert.

The foreman suddenly huffed as he grabbed some tools to leave Dan lost, but, after he did it again, Dan became angry.

"What?!" he snapped. "If you've got something on your mind you'd better spill."

The foreman cringed, feeling unsure if he should say anything. But, after seeing the sad look on Nini's face he crumbled.

"What's happenin' with the missing girls?"

Dan choked into his hand, turning pale to almost vomit upon hating himself for forgetting about them.

"We're still working on that," Neal said, butting in before nodding towards Dan to give him time to compose himself. "Shouldn't you be doing what you're getting paid for?"

The foreman glared at Neal, but the worker inside the hole screamed to scare him. He moved back, close to hiding behind Dan as the worker was thrown from side to side, his face a quivering mess to leave everyone confused.

Dan aimed his gun whilst the worker continued to bounce around inside the hole, his screaming causing everyone to panic. But he suddenly stopped before flopping against the side, moaning in pain to spit out blood to send the foreman into a guilty meltdown. He cautiously moved away from Dan to reach inside the hole, grabbing onto the worker's hand to see his eyes glaze over.

"Is he dead?" Neal asked; fearing he was.

The foreman sweated nervously as he pulled on the hand, but its limpness spooked him even more. He struggled to extract the worker from the hole so Dan leaned over to help, but the man's stomach tore open to release his entrails, leaving some workers dropping tools to race to the window to climb out as others ran out the door. But Dan froze after seeing the entrails disappear. He held his breath as he struggled to escape the room, but Nini pushed him away from the hole.

"Get the foreman out of here," he whispered. "They're back."

But light bulbs exploded to send the room into blackness.

Dan pushed whoever he could reach to get them to move, but they were slow to react. He heard more bulbs smash from inside other rooms, followed by the sound of workers being set upon, as their screams sent him diving to the floor. He grabbed Nini, pulling her down next to him as Neal did the same with the foreman; each now crawling on their hands and knees to follow Dan towards the door. But he shivered as another worker fell next to him. He held his mouth and retreated but stumbled into the others, as the worker choked out his last breath.

Nini clasped her ears to drown out the sickening noise of the worker being ripped apart, fearing she was going to die upon submitting to the enemy. But the foreman broke rank, rising to race out of the room until being covered by the bugs. They attacked his face as he tried to fight them off before falling like a cut-down tree, but the sound of his eyeballs popping made the others squirm.

Dan huddled Nini as the room became silent before grabbing his torch from his belt to shine a light; aiming it at the foreman to witness the man's eye sockets glow after the bugs inside them ignited.

Jon was right, they do burn.

He moved the torchlight swiftly over the man's body, setting more bugs on fire before they could pounce.

"Get everyone out of the house!" he shouted, lifting off the floor to race from the room.

Nini and Neal gripped their torches and followed, eliminating bugs with the light before they got close. They searched the downstairs rooms, stepping over mangled bodies to find no survivors; choking from the sight as their torches kept the insects at bay.

Dan moved past them as he raced outside to shout at the bystanders still watching on, but some were more curious than fearful. They hovered around to get a glimpse inside the house upon setting their phones to record what was going on, but the queen swooped, shrieking like she knew her babies had been harmed. She stabbed a leg into an escaping man, lifting him into the sky before Dan could react; his hand shaking as he reached for his weapon to find her gone.

The bystanders panicked to leave the extra officers struggling to cope, with most running into each other after staring hard at the sky.

"...Get back inside your homes. NOW!" Dan shouted, aiming his gun upwards. "Unless you want that thing to get you."

He watched them flee the scene, screaming as they raced back to their homes before the sound of a gun firing grabbed his attention. He turned to see Neal pointing at the sky as other officers fired at the queen, but their energy blasts missed her by inches. She swooped again, shrieking louder;

aiming towards a scared teenager running towards the front garden of his house.

He reached his door to fumble with the key after hearing wings flap close by; his knees trembling as he kicked the door before wetting himself after dropping the keys on the ground. He cried and pleaded for someone to let him in before banging on the door like a deranged lunatic; hearing the queen behind him as he felt a tongue on his shoulder. He could smell her toxic breath. He almost fainted after listening to the mouths snap, but his body was now drenched in sweat and piss as he banged on the door again. He felt slime drip off the queen's tongue as it moved towards his neck before suddenly the door opened to leave him falling inside the house. He kicked the door shut and sat on the floor, crying into his knees as his mother watched on.

She heard scratching coming from outside as more shrieks frightened her to stagger back towards the stairs; her heart in pieces to see her son sway. But she couldn't move to help him.

"What's out there?" she nervously asked.

"Don't go outside!" her son yelled, jumping from fear after the door was slammed into.

It tore from its hinges to fall on top of him, leaving him squealing out for help as his mother ran up the stairs. But the queen stood on the door to crush his body before he had time to escape. The mother sobbed as the queen snapped off her son's hand; swallowing it and smashing up the hallway with her wings, but shouts coming from the onrushing officers stopped her from attacking. She glared at them, snapping her teeth before swiftly flying off again.

The mother appeared at the bottom of the stairs, trembling to see Nini and Neal lift the door off her son; her mouth quivering to find he was dead as Nini closed in to comfort her. But Dan's shouts were heard nearby as the woman collapsed onto a step. Nini felt emotional after seeing the woman staring at her son as Neal gripped her arm to whisper, "We need to go. Dan needs us."

They ran outside to see him give out orders to the new officers before hearing him mention putting on the night vision goggles, so released theirs and caught him up. But the sound of a vehicle braking over the road caught their eye. It was Gordon and Terry. They raced from an ambulance looking confused and lost as to what was going on before spotting the boy's mother covered in blood on the doorstep.

"Grab the first-aid kit," Terry said, prodding Gordon to stay focused. "That woman needs attention."

"There's no need," Neal softly replied. "She's fine. It's her son who isn't." He stared at the woman before adding, "He's dead."

"What happened?" Gordon asked, putting the kit back. "We got a call on the radio telling us to get here fast."

"Yeah, probably Marion. She tried calling me earlier," Dan said, feeling the hairs on his arms stand up after a reminder of the foreman's death washed over him. He gripped his gun tight and looked up at the sky. "She must've been worried."

"Are you okay, chief?" Nini asked. "We can't have you falling apart."

"Don't worry. I won't fall apart until this is over," he replied, feeling grateful...

Gordon looked at the sky like he was following something move across it, his actions causing the officers to flinch as they aimed their guns upward. Dan shuddered as his trigger finger came close to firing, but he couldn't see what Gordon was seeing. He began to sweat, fearing the creature was about to strike again.

But from where?

"...You've seen it, haven't you," he said, grabbing Gordon's attention.

"Seen what?" Gordon became tense after seeing the guns aimed in the air; his heart thumping to see everyone freak out. "I'm just admiring the stars. They're bright tonight."

Dan glared at him to make him feel small. "You're admiring the stars when a killer beast is flying around?"

Gordon froze, not expecting to hear what he heard.

He backed away to leave Terry gulping after recent news returned to the front of his mind.

"We were told that something crashed into an empty building opposite the hospital," he said, as Dan turned to him. "No one was sure what it was but it came from the sky."

"It had to be the creature." Dan stared at the Tanker house, cringing at the thought of any bugs still alive. "Do you know if it's still there?"

"Not sure. We were on our way here when we got the news."

"It has to be. It won't go too far from that house," Dan said pointing. "Not when its lair is below it."

He walked back towards the house to feel the screams of the recent fallen with each step he made; holding his head upon trying to stop them from entering his mind. Nini and Neal followed to watch him like they were expecting him to lose it, becoming worried after seeing him spin around like he was fighting an imaginary enemy. They knew he was close to collapsing.

"Chief. Do you need to take a break?" Neal asked as Dan reached the door.

But he just stared inside the house, not noticing Neal standing next to him.

Everyone jumped after screams coming from the recently

killed teenager's house shook them before the mother ran over the road to shout, "Help! It's inside. Please help!"

Terry and Gordon froze after seeing the queen hover over the boy's body, shrieking before stabbing a leg into his torso to lift him towards her many mouths. She tore into him and shrieked again before racing outside to flap her wings; connecting to slice the mother's head clean off as she carried what was left of her son into the air.

She disappeared as the officers fired into the darkness.

Terry and Gordon moved again as the tragedy sunk in, both shaking as they attempted to remove the mother's body. But they were hit by falling organs, leaving them close to crying.

"Right, you two," Dan said, hoping they hadn't surrendered to the nightmare. "I need you to return to the hospital. Warn everyone. Tell them to keep quiet and hide."

They looked at him stunned before wiping themselves down as they returned to the ambulance.

CHAPTER FORTY-ONE

J on turned his car into the street, screeching it to a halt to see everyone staring upward. He opened the door and raced towards the house but Dan was on the doorstep glaring at him.

"What was I meant to do?" he asked, knowing Dan was upset. "She was causing an uproar...Anything could've happened if she'd kept shouting at us."

"Anything did happen!" Dan snapped. "The fuckin' creature came back." He glanced at his watch to see it had turned *8:00 pm*. "This will not go into another day. It'll end tonight."

"What's the plan?" Jon asked, relaxing slightly now Dan had his mind back on the job. "Find that freak and put it down again?"

"First we eliminate the small bugs." Dan tapped him on the shoulder, smiling as he said, "You were right about them burning when exposed to light. I've seen it happen, but I'm not sure if we killed them all..."

Jon smiled back, now pleased he wasn't imagining it. He

watched Dan wave his hands around like he was conducting an orchestra until they stopped to aim at the house.

"...We need to go back inside. That's where they were seen last."

"And then what?" Jon asked. "We shine torches on em'?"

"We may not need the torches if we can get the main lights back on." Dan sucked his bottom lip before adding, "Or we find other sources of light."

"Won't it take a while to fix them? All the bulbs blew," Nini said, feeling worried in case the plan failed.

"Hey, if we can't replace them then we find something that will, like candles."

"Just turn the microwave on," Neal pointed out. "And leave the door open."

"Have you seen a microwave work with the door open?..."

Neal just shrugged at Dan.

"...I can see you're trying," Dan said, smiling as he poked Neal on the arm. "We will end this."

Everyone entered the house to turn on torches, stepping over corpses as they reached the living room. But Jon frowned after shining light over the carnage. He knew he was lucky not to have been there.

Dan smiled at Nini to make her feel uncomfortable. She looked away, fearing he would ask her to do another babysitting job on the dead, but felt confused after knowing that no one was leaving the house.

"Nini," Dan said softly, turning her around to get her attention.

"Come on, chief, I know that look," she replied, backing away. "Please don't say that you want to use me as bait?"

"Wow! You're good."

"I've only been here a short time but I already know how your mind thinks. That look gave it away."

Dan sighed as he reached out to hold her arms. "I promise you'll be fine. There'll be no more of my officers dying tonight..."

His words hit everyone hard, leaving them lowering their heads, as the disappearance of Marek brought more hatred towards the creatures of the night.

"...Are you sure you're okay with this?" Dan asked, feeling Nini tense up. "I can't think of any other way if the power doesn't come back on."

"Yes, chief, I'll be fine," Nini replied, smiling nervously. "Just kill them all."

"Why don't we wait until it gets light outside?" Neal questioned, feeling chuffed with his suggestion.

But Dan glared at him.

"Don't be a complete moron...It'll take hours before daylight...Do you think the bugs will stay away for that long?..."

Neal now felt stupid for mentioning it.

Dan stood by the hole as his body became shrouded in the torchlight, his appearance like someone on a stage as he looked inside it.

"...Okay, Nini, I want you to stand inside here. We'll watch you at all times."

She flinched, feeling queasy for having to stand where the worker was torn apart, wondering where his body had gone upon closing in to see blood spatters nearby.

"Please don't let them get me," she whimpered.

Dan hugged her tight, knowing how scared she was.

"Trust me. They won't get you..."

He let go and patted her on the arm.

"...Check the power circuit," he cried out to Jon and Neal. "If you can fix it then find more bulbs...I want to see this place lit up like a Christmas tree when those critters arrive again."

CHAPTER FORTY-TWO

Vera stood at her window, trying to catch a glimpse of the officers outside the house; waiting for a noise to penetrate through her wall. But it had gone silent, spooking her even more than the frightening screams coming from the victims. She turned up the volume on her hearing aids in case she missed someone talking next door, but there was still nothing. She sighed as she leaned closer to the glass, smothering it with her breath whilst wishing she wasn't so stubborn to move. She knew her glasses were somewhere nearby but she would rather follow the blurred images of the officers than risk missing out on something by looking for them.

She kept off the light so as not to be spotted, fearing that whatever was attacking did so because the people were seen. But her mind produced eerie thoughts to leave her frightened of her own shadow. She wiped the window to notice most of the street in darkness before backing away after a strange chattering sound caused her to check her hearing aids.

"Stupid things!" she cried out, tapping them to see if the noise would stop.

But it didn't. It just got louder and louder to make her shiver.

She took them out, slamming them down on the window sill, angry because her head was pounding from the noise before squinting after seeing a blurred shadow glide along the carpet.

It confused her as she reached for her glasses.

She put them on as her legs began to itch, feeling something crawl up to her knees to annoy her to scratch them. But she never looked down.

She scratched again before walking back to the window, staring out into the street to see the officers more clearly. But the bugs were still unnoticed as they crawled up her body.

She laughed, becoming ticklish upon swiping a hand across her thigh, but a sharp sting caused her to yelp, making her feel agitated to rush her breathing. She staggered after bringing her hand up to her face, freaking out to see it covered with bugs. Some leapt off to cling to her lenses, scaring her to want to escape, but more stings brought tears to her eyes as one side of her body became numb. She toppled over, crashing her face against the floor as she desperately tried to move and scream, but neither was achieved as the bugs tore at her face to leave half of it gone.

———

Clyde sat nervously on his bed, trying his best to ignore what was happening in the Tanker house across the street. He listened to music through a pair of headphones whilst reading a novel about a town being attacked by zombies, the front cover showing 'Clifton Falls' as the title. He was still in pain, his bruises a reminder of how lucky he was that the attack on him wasn't worse.

He turned over a page, keeping his concentration as the bugs appeared in a darkened corner of the room, staying unnoticed as they avoided the light beaming from the bedside lamp. But it smashed seconds later, showering glass over Clyde to make him jump. He shook as he removed the headphones, staring into the darkness to listen out for movement. But all he heard was the faint sound of the tune coming through them.

"Hello," he said, feeling more nervous by the second. "Is anyone in here?..."

He dropped the novel onto the bed before placing his feet on the floor but cringed after standing on something wet.

"...This isn't funny. I'm not in the mood for jokes..."

He bent down to touch the item, feeling lumps of a jelly-like substance before squirming as he reached for his phone on the bedside table. But it slipped out of his hand like a wet bar of soap.

He squinted as he brought his hand closer to his face before feeling the substance on his fingers, but was left lost as to what it was. So, reached for his phone again to turn on its light to almost faint after seeing a human heart on the floor. He trembled as he shone his phone around the room, falling back on his bed to gulp after the main bulb exploded.

"...Why are you doing this to me?!" he pleaded. "I just want to be left alone."

He heard a chattering below him but was now too scared to check the floor.

He just wanted out of the room.

He dropped the phone and ran to the door, gripping the handle to leave it smothered in congealed blood. But the bugs set on him before he could open it. He swung at them, confused to understand what they were, falling back onto the bed to gasp for air after they covered his face. They bit into him, releasing blood to attract more; leaving him fighting to get them off as some slipped beneath his pants to rip off his penis. His eyes bulged as his boxer shorts were painted red, his body weakening as the blood gushed down his legs.

He bellowed and whimpered, but seconds later was dead.

CHAPTER FORTY-THREE

Nini shook inside the hole as thoughts of being attacked entered her mind.

She watched the others through the night vision goggles, pleased to see their concentration on full alert as they waited for the bugs to show. Neal and Jon stood firm with their weapons raised whilst Dan hovered near a light switch.

"Are you sure they'll turn up?" Nini asked, staring at her feet. "I don't like this."

"They have to. If any are still alive." Dan replied, feeling unsure.

He checked his watch to find they had been there longer than planned, as his head spun from negative thoughts draining his confidence to leave him almost giving up. He watched Nini come close to collapsing, fearing if she did then she could be set upon, so clicked his fingers to gain her attention. She was thankful he did. But Dan became confused as to why nothing was happening.

He scanned the room through his goggles to see Jon and Neal grimace, knowing they felt the same.

"...Are you positive the lights will work?" he questioned, seeing Neal nod. "I don't want to get an electric shock."

"All sorted, chief. We fixed the mains." Neal stared at Dan. "Why don't you flick the switch?"

"It's too risky. We need those things to show up first...If I put the light on they may not turn up..."

Dan moved away from the light switch, sweating as he walked back to the hole; trying in vain to calculate all the evidence gained. But it was making no sense.

"...This has to work," he said, glaring inside it. "They have to be under here."

He felt embarrassed after realising he may have been wrong the whole time, as the clues from the library, the chat with his grandfather, and the fact he told his officers the plan made him feel sick.

CHAPTER FORTY-FOUR

Gina Lovell stared at the stockroom door like she was waiting for Grant to appear; her face drained and emotional after seeing the – '*No Entry*' – sign. She cringed, close to tears as her heart sank.

She'd heard all the warnings about staying safe, but somehow the store had drawn her to it. She reached out and touched the police tape, shaking from the thought of stepping inside the room, panicking as she let go to sob into her coat sleeve as she walked away. She grabbed the store keys off the counter before opening the main door, glancing at the stockroom again as she slowly left. She locked it to be hit in the face by a blast of wind, but she just stared at the sky, her mind too far gone to care.

She walked towards the car park unaware of how quiet it was, her face motionless as she reached her car. She heard something flapping above, getting closer to spook her, but, as she glanced at the sky, saw nothing there. She sighed as she reached inside her pocket for the car key, but the sound faded, leaving her to think it was some type of bird.

But, as she placed the key in the door, her head smashed

through the window, leaving her face a bloody mess as she screamed. She shook and cringed upon being dragged to the ground; her wounds dripping blood onto her clothes as she tried to escape. But the smell excited the queen to snap mouths as she landed nearby.

Gina wiped a hand across her forehead to stop more blood from stinging her eyes, but her vision was blurred to prevent her from seeing the queen close in. She flapped her wings and roared, scaring Gina to cower against the side of the car before a louder scream was heard by the officers inside the house.

"Move yourselves!" Dan cried out. "I think that freak is back."

"But what about the bugs?" Nini asked, slowly moving out of the hole. "Are we abandoning this?"

"No! We'll come back."

Dan raced out of the house to stop in the street, scouring the sky to hopefully catch sight of the creature as he waited for the others to catch up. He listened but no more sounds arrived.

He frantically moved from side to side in an attempt to guess the beast's direction, holding his gun tight to see the others do the same, as Gina lay in a pool of blood.

She was dead; her head almost severed from a single strike as the queen flew off again.

Neal stared at the sky after hearing a strange sound, sweating as he adjusted his goggles to see more clearly. He knew it had to be the creature but panicked because he didn't know in which direction to look. He saw the others do the same as the sound closed in, with each moving around like headless chickens as they aimed their guns at the sky.

"It's coming!" Neal yelled. "Can you see it?"

Dan saw the creature descend fast, scaring him into bumping against Jon.

"Is everyone ready," he rushed from his mouth. "We take it down. No missing this time..."

He watched everyone lock their guns, ready to fire, but the queen changed direction and flew away.

"...Fuck! It's aiming for the empty building again!" Dan shouted.

"Do we go after it?" Jon asked.

"Damn!" Dan yelled. "Nah...We need to stay put in case those bugs turn up?"

But Jon grimaced, fearing Dan made the wrong choice.

He glanced at the reinforcements, seeing their focus falter after the queen frit them before sighing as they nervously gawped at the sky.

"Send them," Jon said, pointing. "They don't seem to be doing much."

But the officers became tense as they tried to hide in the darkness.

Dan took off his goggles and moved towards them, feeling their nerves the closer he got. But he needed them to be strong.

This is their time to help save the day.

"Are you up for this?" he asked, watching them come out of hiding.

He received no replies, just nods, so felt relieved that they never ran away before leaning forward to grab the nearest officer.

"...It's okay to be scared. We're scared too. But we need your help desperately."

Dan waited for his words to sink in before smiling after seeing the officers re-focus. He hoped they wouldn't let him down.

"Where do you need us?" the officer asked, touching Dan's shoulder. "We've got this."

"Find the empty building and keep it secure. And don't let anyone in."

"And the creature?"

"If you see it destroy it." Dan checked the man's gun. "And put this on full power."

He noticed the confidence spread amongst the officers as they topped up their guns; pleased to see their determination back as they ran towards police cars to enter swiftly before driving off at speed.

"Are we heading back inside?" Jon asked, closing in.

"Yep," Dan replied, smiling. "But this time we make more noise."

"More noise?" Neal interrupted. "So they hear us?"

"Exactly! It's the only way." Dan walked back to the house before adding, "If noise made the creature act all weird then noise may attract those critters to show up."

"We don't have to sing again, do we?" Jon asked, cringing.

"No, not you. But Nini can." Dan winked at her as she entered the house before seeing her cautiously move towards the hole. "At least I can stomach your singing."

Nini smiled, but it wasn't a confident one. She was scared.

She looked at the others, frowning as she waited for at least one of them to mock her before entering the hole again to open her mouth to sing. It was a Chinese song, slow and soothing, but it wasn't bringing the bugs to the surface. She shook as she kept going; her voice trembling from the fear of not knowing when they would attack. But Jon raised a hand to stop her.

"I don't think they like Asian music," he said, sniggering. "Try something upbeat, like when we were back at the house."

But Nini burst into tears as Marek entered her mind.

She breathed deeply until the tears stopped; her voice louder upon singing something faster in English. But she struggled to stay inside the hole; coming close to jumping out as the song echoed around the room.

Dan noticed her fear, so joined in to help keep her focused before smiling at Neal for attempting to keep up the beat. But Jon was finding it awkward. He tried joining in but made the song sound terrible.

"Is it working?" Nini nervously asked.

"Nope, not yet," Dan replied. "But keep singing. It's got to work..."

But nothing was changing as everyone's voice started to croak.

"...Okay, stop," Dan said, holding up a hand. "We need to try something else."

"Like what?" Jon asked; worried he needed to do something he wouldn't normally say yes to.

"Like put on that drill and deafen' the fuckers."

Jon stared at it, smiling as he approached. But Nini jumped out of the hole to stop him from grabbing it.

"Not a wise choice. That thing will make more people come out of their homes."

"And you think the racket we just made won't?" Jon sniggered.

Nini shrugged her shoulders and sighed as Dan stared at Neal to make him feel restless.

"Why are you looking at me like that for?"

"Don't worry," Dan said smiling. "I'll keep my hand on the switch at all times. You'll be safe."

"Safe? What am I doing?"

"I need you to get inside the hole."

"Not to sing I hope...We've just tried that."

"No. Not to sing." Dan pointed at the floor. "I need you to grab the hammer and chisel and chip away at the hole...I think the drill sent some kind of vibration below ground, that's why the bugs attacked, so maybe it'll work with those tools?"

"Anything is better than singing again."

Neal reached down, picking the items up before moving slowly towards the hole, puffing out his cheeks as he bent down to strike it. But, after only three hits, he began to move strangely.

"Put your back into it," Jon said, close to laughing again.

But Neal shuddered like he was doing a crazy dance.

"Hey, what are you doing?" Dan asked. "Stop messing about..."

Neal stepped out of the hole before falling facedown, shaking uncontrollably to leave the others scared.

"...Neal, are you alright?!" Dan shouted. "Does anyone know if he suffers from fits?..."

Nini and Jon shrugged, feeling sick to see Neal's body retreat towards the hole. They were terrified by what was going on.

"...Do something!" Dan cried out, hovering his hand over the light switch. "Check to see if he's got pills in his pocket."

Jon nodded.

He reached down to grip one of Neal's legs, happy to see he'd stopped moving. But it was only momentarily as Neal pulled away again to close in on the hole.

Jon pulled with all his strength, panting for air as his face burned red, but Neal kept on moving.

"Something's pulling him!" Jon yelled, gritting his teeth after seeing Neal reach the hole. "It's too strong."

"Then pull harder!" Dan yelled, itching to turn on the light.

Nini closed in to pull on Neal's other leg but it was no use, he just kept moving, dragging her and Jon with him.

"Pull, Nini!" Jon hollered. "I'm tiring."

"I'm trying."

Dan gulped as he raced over to help; pleased that his strength was enough to help gain control to pull Neal to safety.

But he wasn't awake.

"Nini, find out what's wrong with him," Dan said, racing back to the light switch.

Jon helped her turn Neal over but the sight of bugs crawling around inside his goggles left them in shock.

They jumped back as the bugs scuttled out, leaving Neal's face dripping dark liquid to make Nini scream.

"What's up?" Dan asked, sweating after watching her crab-like crawl away from Neal's body.

She sat on the floor weeping as the bugs chewed on Neal's face, but Jon couldn't stop staring. He was glued to what they were doing; his stomach heaving after Neal's nose disappeared.

Dan switched on the light, igniting the bugs as Jon gradually rose off the floor. He heaved again before finding his focus, flipping Neal's body over to watch the insects below him burn to a crisp.

"Fuck!" he cried out, as Nini returned to her feet. "Light does kill them."

"But is it all of them?" Dan asked, feeling worried.

Jon didn't have a clue.

He checked the floor as the bulb smashed, scaring them to run into the hallway.

"It's happening again," Dan rushed from his mouth. "We need to get out of here."

Jon was the first to race for the door but was set upon in

seconds. He swiped at his clothes in a frantic attempt to stop the bugs from biting him, sweating from fear that his life was about to end. But Dan and Nini swiftly switched on their torches to wipe the bugs out.

"Thanks," Jon said, still swiping to see if any bugs were still on him. "I thought I was next."

"You were lucky," Dan replied. "But Neal wasn't."

"I can't be here anymore!" Nini cried out, swallowing hard as she reached the front door. "I just can't."

Dan felt the same as he shone his torch up the hallway walls.

"I think that was the last of them," he said, hugging Nini.

"Let's hope so," Jon replied.

CHAPTER FORTY-FIVE

They reached the edge of the front garden to find more people standing in the street; their nosiness back after not seeing the flying creature in a while. They gawped at the officers, seeing how tired they looked before waving some form of weapon in the air to show they were ready to fight.

Dan sighed after seeing a woman swinging a rolling pin stand next to a man pulling a golf trolley with a bag full of clubs, but he said nothing as they screamed obscenities towards the house. He gathered his thoughts, hoping his next words would calm the people down, but they talked amongst themselves and ignored him. He moved towards, followed by Jon and Nini, but their presence made no difference as the people were only interested in what had happened inside the house.

"We're not going back home this time," the woman with the rolling pin said as her husband hugged her. "If that thing comes back then we're ready for it."

"With that?" Jon replied, tiredly smirking. "Unless you

want to bake the thing a pie, I suggest you leave it to us and go home."

The woman glared at him as her anger boiled. She stepped towards him but was yanked away by her husband as the rest of the crowd closed in.

Jon stared at Dan, who was trying his best to usher the people away. But his silence over what happened inside the house annoyed the crowd even more.

"Calm down! Will you all just calm down!" Dan yelled, trying to catch his breath. "You need to forget about the thing in the sky and just go home. We have this covered."

He looked over at Nini to see her eyes fill with tears, hoping the crowd didn't catch on that an officer died inside.

"Have it covered?!" A man standing at the back of the crowd shouted. "We saw that thing attack, someone, in their home. It's not safe inside. We have to fight it."

His words caused more anger to brew from within the crowd, leaving Dan, Jon and Nini panicking. They knew the people were restless, tired, and eager to find the creature, but their attempts at getting them to back down were failing.

Dan saw people from the crowd split away to run down the street, leaving him to think they were going home, so needed to tread carefully with the ones left behind.

"Okay! Okay! You can stay and help."

"But Dan?" Nini questioned, feeling sick to her stomach that he would let them. "It's too dangerous."

"I think we can all agree on that." Dan looked hard at the people, noticing none were backing down. "You all know the risks."

He shrugged as Nini shook her head, not budging on his decision even though he knew it was wrong. He couldn't protect the residents and find the creature so gave them a choice to be victims or heroes.

"What can we do?" the man asked, making his way to the front. "Just tell us what you need."

"For a start, you'll need a better weapon," Dan said, staring at a wooden spoon the man was holding. "Go home, grab something sharp and then team up to patrol the street."

"But what happened to the other officer?" the man awkwardly asked. "We know that four of you went inside."

Dan's face dropped from a sudden rush of sadness and couldn't look at the man. He waited for more questions to arrive but the man just touched his shoulder and walked away, leading the others back down the street.

"You do know this could backfire on us," Jon said, not pleased to have to babysit the townsfolk as well as find the beast. "They don't have a clue how dangerous this is."

"We just need to trust them," Dan replied. "They want to do this."

———

The fleeing crowd, who Dan assumed was going home, had just climbed over the back fence of the Tanker house. Two of them were brothers aged fifteen and seventeen, whilst the third was their uncle.

"We get in and out quick," said *Alan*, the uncle. "No fuck-ups from either of you. You got it?" he said, approaching the back door.

He clipped the brothers around the ear as he broke into the house; his authority overpowering them as they entered the kitchen. But neither expected to see so much blood and death inside.

They knew about young Tommy's death but somehow weren't fazed by it, but the bodies of the fallen workmen had them fearing for their lives. They froze after the moon lit up the room until *Casey*, the seventeen-year-old ran back to the door.

"*Bradley*, grab your brother before I drag him back," snarled Alan, as he searched the pockets of the mutilated men. He glared at Casey, grunting before adding, "Stop being a wimp...You don't see young Bradley behaving like a little girl, so get back over here." He watched Casey fumble with the door handle before turning to walk back. "Good boy. We have a house to rob."

Casey sighed, now nervously regretting his decision to tag along. He only did it to stop Bradley from getting into trouble but was now caught up in something he wanted out of. He hated how easily Bradley believed everything Alan told him, and how he looked up to the uncle who had not long come out of prison. As soon as Alan hinted about robbing the house, Bradley became excited.

Casey hated his uncle for being a thief but knew he needed to stay to keep his brother safe.

"What if the killer comes back?" he whispered. "You've seen the bodies, so let's just leave."

"Boo Hoo! Casey is scared." Alan grabbed his arm, pulling him towards a body. "If you get us caught, you'll pay."

Casey squirmed upon gripping the floor to stop his face from touching a pile of intestines, listening to Alan laugh to make him want to cry. He begged Alan to let him up, but his whiny voice became annoying as he was dragged across the floor and out of the room.

Bradley watched on in shock, now worried as Alan shone the light from his phone into the living room. He stood over Neal's corpse to leave the brothers close to puking, not daunted by the grotesque sight as he walked towards the window; smiling after seeing the officers walk away from the house.

He pulled a rucksack off his shoulders before grabbing a child's piggy bank off a shelf to place inside as he left the room. But the coins rattled loudly to spook Casey into thinking someone was nearby.

"You can't take little Tommy's money box," he begged, staring at Alan. "It's too cruel."

"Stop being a sensitive, sad sap. It's not like he's goin' to need it now."

Casey looked at his brother for backup, hoping that after witnessing Alan's lack of remorse towards little Tommy, would also want to leave. But Bradley just shrugged his shoulders and said, "He's right."

Alan entered another room to place more items into the rucksack, feeling excited to have the freedom of the house.

"Come on lads. I bet there's loads of stuff we could steal from here," he said, smiling.

Bradley moved into the hallway, lighting up more bodies' with his phone before staring at the stairs to bow his head. He partly wanted to respect Tommy's death as he reached them but was too excited to know more about what happened to him to not climb them; picturing the crime scene in his mind until it made him *gulp*.

"I bet there are more dead people up there," he said, pointing at the steps.

Alan shook the rucksack in Casey's face before pushing him as he sniggered; following Bradley up the stairs to leave Casey in creepy darkness. He heard the sound of shoes touching down on each step as he followed the light from the phones, waiting for someone to speak as the others disappeared from view. But the quiet worried him.

He tried the light switch to find it not working, so released his phone; shining it towards the top of the stairs to witness Bradley sobbing into his hands.

"What's up with you? What's Alan done now?"

Bradley shivered, dropping his phone before miming - 'Go home!', but Casey thought he was messing around.

He stood on the first step but stopped after seeing something wrap around Bradley's throat, causing him to gasp for air. He saw a tongue drag Bradley along the landing, not sure if it was some type of prank, as a whimper coming from the top of the stairs spooked him to stumble back to the bottom.

"Bradley! Bradley!" he shouted, finding the courage to race to the top. "Where are you?..."

But Bradley was gone to freak him out.

He stared at the closed doors, stopping at little Tommy's room to wince after a flashback of the last time he babysat him flooded his mind. He knew he had to enter.

He opened the door, sweating to see no one inside; glancing at the dried bloodstains on the mattress before swiftly turning away. But he shivered even more after opening another door.

"...This isn't funny. You can come out now. Nice trick."

He knew what Alan was capable of because he'd played a lot of scary tricks on him growing up, but this became more real by the second. He entered the room to find it empty, but a faint groaning coming from the parents' bedroom made the hairs on the back of his neck stand up. He breathed fast as he rushed to push open the door, but again it was the same outcome. He shook his head, thinking that maybe what he'd just heard wasn't real, that the darkness was teasing him, but the groan happened again.

"...Is that you Brad?"

His nerves caused him to stall as he stared at the final door; his courage was almost gone as his knees trembled loudly. But he found the courage to open it after the groan happened again.

He walked slowly into the room to hear the sound escalate from behind the bed before rushing over to find Alan slumped on the floor; his head bleeding as he slowly sat up.

"Where's Bradley?" Casey asked, helping him up. "What did you do to him?..."

Alan stumbled, touching the blood to appear confused; stuttering his words to make no sense as he sat on the bed.

"...Did someone hit you?" Casey questioned, fearing it to be the strange creature he saw.

"Yeah...Someone hit me when I was with Bradley and threw me across the room."

"I don't think it was someone," Casey replied, anxiously tugging on Alan's arm.

"What do you mean?" Alan asked, touching his wound again.

"Just help me find my brother." Casey tugged on his arm again. "If anything happens to him then you're to blame."

He expected to be slapped around the head for his angry reply, but Alan just let it slide. He just wanted out of the room.

They heard someone sniffing inside the parents' bedroom, assuming it had to be Bradley upon racing to it, but Casey was left confused after seeing his brother shivering and crying on the bed.

"I've just checked this room and you weren't here."

He stared at Bradley, almost in tears after receiving no reply, watching him cling to the bed like he was on a raft surrounded by sharks. He wasn't attempting to get off and it worried Casey.

He closed in on Bradley to see a thick red line around his neck; his eyes transfixed onto something that scared Casey as he sat next to him. He witnessed his brother's pupils enlarge to reveal a reflection of something behind him, but, as he turned, saw nothing inside the room.

"What was it that grabbed you?" he asked, as Bradley's lips trembled. "And where is it now?"

"What you goin' on about?!" Alan snapped. "Where is what?"

Bradley flinched when Casey touched him before quickly retreating to the top of the bed. He quivered like a leaf upon humming like a crazy man, leaving Alan scratching his face in confusion.

"...What's got into him?" he asked, sighing as he dropped the rucksack. "Who the *fuck* is here with us?"

Casey glared at him as Bradley rocked from side to side.

"You need to listen to me. I saw something grab him and it wasn't someone."

"Yeah, I heard you before. So."

Casey shook his head at how dumb Alan's reaction was.

He came close to replying but the queen appeared, smacking Alan across the jaw with a wing to send him flying across the room before stabbing a leg through his head to rip it open like a watermelon. Casey leapt off the bed, screaming as he cowardly backed up against a wall, covering his face with his arms to the sound of mouths snapping at him.

————

Dan turned to the sound of more screams but became worried as they suddenly stopped.

He looked at the others upon shaking his head and checking his gun, thinking only of getting back to the house before more vigilante residents arrived.

"Call this in," he said to Nini. "We need the backup here, now."

He ran ahead to be caught up by Jon; both shaking their heads in a frantic attempt to spot the creature as Nini approached.

"Chief, I'm getting one of my bad feelings again," she said, holding her phone out so Dan could see it was still ringing out. "Something's not right. No one is picking up."

"Did you use your shoulder radio?"

"Yes, chief, but I got nothing."

Dan stared hard as Nini put the phone back to her ear; her face scrunched as they approached the house.

"Just leave it." Dan was annoyed that the call was ignored but knew the officers could be in trouble as he smiled sadly. "It looks like it's just the three of us."

They re-entered the house to place their goggles back on as a reminder of Neal's death caused them to shudder before passing the living room and aiming for the stairs. But Nini couldn't avoid looking back.

"Are you okay?" Dan asked, knowing she was freaking out inside.

"What do you think?"

Dan never replied.

He looked at the top of the stairs before slowly climbing them but saw no one around. Just open doors to leave him guessing on which room to enter.

He waited for Jon and Nini to arrive before pointing at each one, turning on his torch in *fear* of seeing more bugs as he lit up the landing. He tapped Nini on the shoulder as he pointed at young Tommy's bedroom, but she found it tough to step inside. He watched her cautiously enter; glad to see her face the demon inside her mind from the last time she was there.

He moved towards a room as Jon did the same with

another, both entering to meet up again within seconds, angry to find nothing.

"Now what?" Jon asked, gripping his gun tight. "We heard someone scream, right?"

"Yeah, but there's no sign of them now."

They saw Nini leave the room, holding her gun high as she reached another one; her concentration alert as she walked inside. But she quickly retreated, shivering to worry the others.

"You don't want to go in there," she said, choking.

Dan and Jon moved past her to see Alan's body, cringing from the mess made to his head as brain matter dripped down a wall.

"...Do you know who it was?" Nini asked.

Dan stared at the body before puffing out his cheeks, closing in to cough as he extracted a wallet from the back pocket. He opened it to find a driver's licence before shaking his head after spotting the rucksack; sighing as he handed the licence to Nini.

"We know him, or knew him," Dan said, shining light over the rucksack. "Looks like he was up to his old tricks again."

"That thing must have killed him," Jon said, quivering. "And we've missed it again."

They moved away from the room, carefully aiming for the stairs, but a thunderous crash rattled their eardrums.

"What was that?" Nini asked, rapidly pointing her gun at every room.

Dan looked at the ceiling after hearing a floorboard creak. "It's up there."

"Shit!" Nini muttered.

The noise continued, becoming frantic, leaving them trying to work out where the creature was situated as Dan

348

mimed the words – 'No talking. I think it heard us' – upon creeping along the landing.

He knew it could easily disappear again if spooked, so needed to think fast. But the ceiling cracked, forcing him to retreat. He glared at the weak spot, noticing it spread; ready to fire if the creature fell through the ceiling. He motioned to the others to prepare themselves to shoot, but, as more floorboards creaked above them, the ceiling held firm.

Dan bit his lip in frustration before moving towards the attic door, but Nini gripped his arm to whisper, "It's too dangerous."

"What other choice do I have?" Dan whispered back. "We need to destroy it..."

Nini and Jon checked their weapons, making sure they were set to maximum strength as Dan stood below the door; looking at it as a cold shiver raced over him. He breathed heavily as he focused again before moving a finger to produce an invisible drawing of him opening it, but Nini and Jon knew he was petrified. They waited, engrossed as Dan reached up to pull the door open, but he cursed after being a few inches short.

"...I can't get to the bolt," he whispered. "I need something to stand on."

He shook after another loud THUD left him regretting his decision, but Jon arrived with a chair to boost his confidence to carry on.

Dan smiled and stood on it, gripping the bolt as Jon kept the chair still, but the bolt screeched as it moved to make Dan sweat.

He closed his eyes, thinking the creature would burst through the ceiling to attack before taking a deep breath to open them again, pleased it didn't upon looking at the others. He wiped the sweat from his brow as the bolt was released, gripping the door to drop it open upon reaching for the ladder before getting off the chair to see Nini aim her gun towards the attic entrance.

Dan and Jon gathered below it, staring worryingly into the darkness to wait in silence.

"I think it may have gone again," Dan whispered, shaking his head. "But I'd better check."

He climbed the ladder to receive fearful stares from the other two before looking inside to almost slip after a shadow raced past him. It frightened him, causing what little adrenaline he had to be crushed as the others watched, itching to fire. But Dan held up a hand to show he was okay.

He adjusted his goggles as he peered inside again before nervously reaching for his torch after spotting a pile of boxes; smiling excitedly to be using the blowtorch mode upon pressing a button to release a flame.

He gulped after seeing the flame grow, realising it was the first time he'd used it before silently praying it wouldn't go out. He pointed it towards where he thought the shadow would be to hear a deafening SCREAM shake his bones. But the sight of Casey rushing towards him knocked him off balance to fall down the ladder.

Jon and Nini stared at Casey as he cried; spotting a burn on his arm to leave them cringing, as Dan slowly returned to his feet to hold his head.

But Casey wobbled like he was about to faint, seething in pain as Nini raced for the ladder. She climbed it to grab him, but a gush of blood landed on her.

She wiped her eyes and stared at him, looking shell-shocked as she choked on his blood, his stomach ripping away to reveal one of the queen's legs as his body was torn in two.

Nini squealed as the top half of Casey fell on her.

She jumped off the ladder as the body crashed to the ground, shaking upon seeing the queen swallow the legs before freaking out after the creature's dark eyes glared at her.

But Jon and Dan were slow to react after seeing Casey's face on the blood-soaked floor, their minds lost as another person screamed from inside the attic. They looked up to see the queen gone from the opening, but, after the person screamed again knew where she was.

She shrieked to rock the attic, smashing aside boxes as she tried reaching Bradley, but he moved quickly to escape, hiding behind anything he could to avoid being caught.

"Help me, please!" he screamed, ducking down as a wing passed over him. "It's hard to see up here."

"Get down!" Jon yelled, feeling anxious. "Aim for the open hatch."

"I can't. Something is stopping me."

"I can't leave him up there," Jon said to Dan, kicking the wall. "I think it's my turn to climb the ladder..."

He slowly stood on it to tremble as he climbed to the top, shining his torch inside as Dan and Nini aimed their guns at the ceiling.

"...Just follow the light," Jon whispered. But Bradley had gone quiet. "I'm over here. Do it now..."

Bradley came out of hiding covered in cobwebs.

"...Jesus, kid, you scared me," Jon said, rushing the light around the attic. "Where did it go?"

"It's still here," Bradley replied, gripping Jon's arm to move quickly towards the ladder. "It's just invisible."

Jon panicked, thinking the creature was next to him as he helped Bradley to the ladder. But he gulped after a tongue tightened around Bradley's leg to pull him away.

"Hey!," Jon yelled, nervously reaching for his gun. But Bradley's grip loosened. "Just hold on..."

The queen's other tongues wrapped around Bradley's body to make it harder for him, as Jon dropped his torch to grip his arm to pull him back.

"...Just keep your head down. I'm going to shoot it."

He aimed at the queen, hoping to get a clean shot, but the tongues pulled harder to lift Bradley into the air, leaving Jon straining to keep his grip.

"Do you want us to shoot it?!" Dan yelled up to him. "Just tell us where it is?"

"It's...too...risky," Jon replied panting, placing down his gun to grip Bradley with both hands. "You may hit the boy."

He pulled hard to leave Bradley crying from the thought of being stretched. He tried wriggling to loosen the tongues but the one on his leg squeezed harder to snap a bone, causing him to scream in agony to make Jon more nervous.

He gulped and reached for his gun again before quickly firing into a wooden beam to see it fall on the queen; the tongues letting go as Bradley dropped to the ground. But he was too petrified to move.

"Just get him out of there!" Dan hollered, aiming his weapon at the ceiling. "I'm gonna shoot the bitch."

Jon frantically pulled Bradley towards the hole, but his screams got the queen's attention again. She gripped his broken leg to snap it once more, causing him to faint as Dan fired into the ceiling. He saw the queen through the newly created hole flap her wings, as her tongue slithered away from Bradley's leg. But the smallness of the attic left her flapping against the walls, leaving them shaking before suddenly cracking.

Jon grabbed onto Bradley again as Dan moved along the landing; shouting to confuse the queen to know where he was. She crashed her head into the ceiling, snapping more beams to scare Jon as he lowered Bradley towards a still-shaking Nini, who was halfway up the ladder.

"Grab him!" he hollered. "It's not safe. The house could fall apart at any time."

She gripped Bradley quickly upon hearing the attic creak but cringed after seeing bone appear through his skin; her hands trembling to almost drop him as Dan appeared to help bring him down.

They felt the house shake more violently, becoming worried for Jon as he tried to stay on the ladder, but he kept his balance to see more of the ceiling fall on the queen.

"Nini, shoot it!" Dan shouted, checking his gun. "My weapon's not ready."

But Jon squirmed as he landed at the bottom.

He rushed Bradley into his arms before carrying him down the stairs, the sound of Nini's gun firing pleasing him as he placed Bradley down on the hallway floor. But he was still out cold.

Jon's nerves took over after seeing the queen's head appear through the attic entrance, causing him to sweat as he fired an energy blast into her face. She staggered and shrieked to creep him out, but Dan fired into her mouth to leave her whining like a wounded animal, leaving her retreating inside the attic before more shots were fired.

"Remove your gas masks!" he ordered. "It's time to end this."

He watched Nini and Jon replace their goggles with the masks before he did the same; smiling as Jon raced up the stairs to light up the attic with his torch. But, as Dan released gas pellets from his belt, he couldn't spot the queen. He sighed and climbed the ladder, hoping the others had his back as he threw the pellets inside.

"Let's see if the fucker can still breath," he said, reaching the floor to see a cloud of gas flow out of the attic.

They stood back and waited, hoping it was quick and the queen would die. But the waiting dragged on to leave them worried.

"...I threw three up there," Dan muffled, holding up three fingers. "That should've been enough."

"Do you want me to throw more in?" Jon muffled back.

"Just wait for a touch longer."

The silence above them melted their minds, as not knowing if the queen was dead or alive freaked them out. But Dan couldn't wait any longer. He nodded to Jon to see him near the ladder, but the sound of the queen thudding against the floorboards stopped him.

Dan saw her through the recent hole sway from side to side, tongues dangling like a thirsty dog as she desperately tried to shriek. She crashed through the ceiling to be blasted again before hitting the floor, shuddering as she smashed against walls to try to escape. But this time the energy blasts were too strong.

The queen crumbled after attempting a weak roar before lifting a leg to attack. But it dropped heavily to stick into a wall. Nini gulped as she waited for the queen to die, feeling more relaxed after seeing her dark eyes slowly close. But the queen rose again after shaking off the blasts.

Dan pushed Nini towards the bathroom before following along with Jon; each eager for a swift recharge after seeing the queen extract her leg from the wall.

"Shut the door!" Dan yelled. "It's not dying."

Nini did, but her heart was beating too fast.

She feared for her life as she did when the bugs attacked, sweating as she cowered inside the bath before screaming after hearing a thud against the door. Dan and Jon sat, pushing their backs up to it; hoping it was enough to stop the queen from ripping it off its hinges.

They cringed as the thudding smacked against their backs, almost in tears after seeing tiles crack one by one around the room. They knew soon the house will fall apart.

Nini lay down and placed hands over her face, silently praying that the queen would kill her quickly. She sobbed as Dan and Jon waited to be defeated, but the sound of more energy guns blasting across the landing revitalised their willingness to live.

Nini removed her hands and watched the door, feeling her heartbeat slow down before cautiously getting out of the bath to stand next to the others.

"Wait!" Dan whispered, gripping the door handle.

He heard feet shuffling around, confusing him to stall on opening the door.

But the words - "You can come out now," caused him to smile.

He opened it to see the other officers hover over the bleeding queen, as she lay exhausted and close to death.

"You still think we don't do anything for you?" one of them asked Jon.

But he was speechless; glad that the mask hid the burning redness of embarrassment on his face.

He shone his torch at the queen to see her smoking as she did the last time they fought, but he wasn't convinced she was dying.

"Shouldn't we finish it off?!" he snarled.

Dan stared at the creature to see it sluggishly move towards the corner of the landing, its wings failing to lift as it blinked rapidly at him like it knew it was defeated. He aimed his gun but a tear fell to stop him from firing.

..."What are you doing? Just kill it," Jon said, pushing Dan.

"We won," Dan replied.

Jon snarled again as he reached for his gun, but Dan stood in his way.

"...I need you to leave," he said, sadly gripping Jon's hand. "I need to do this on my own."

"Are you crazy?... It's fakin' it. It'll kill you."

"Maybe, but I need to know why it was communicating with my grandfather and why he died?"

"It's not going to talk to you, Dan, so come on, let's kill it now."

But Dan wasn't budging.

"No...I need to do this for my pops."

Nini placed a hand on his shoulder before nodding as she walked away, but Jon cursed, taking longer to move. He stared at Dan, annoyed that he didn't look back before storming past the other officers to race down the stairs.

"Fuck this shit! It's your funeral, Dan!" were the last words heard before he left the house.

He stood against a wall before looking down to see Bradley whimpering; surprised to see him awake and also have the energy to reach the outside.

"...I don't think I need to ask you how your leg is," Jon said, removing the mask. "Looks fucked."

He sighed after Bradley cried some more before opening his mouth to speak again, but a few neighbours closed in, feeling courageous to help Bradley. Jon smiled as he stood next to the door to watch the officers exit the house, but Nini wasn't following. She was just standing at the top of the stairs, watching Dan near the queen. She couldn't leave him to deal with it on his own, even if he wanted her to, so kept a hand on her gun ready to fire, hoping that whatever he was about to do next was enough to avenge Eddie's death.

Dan turned to her as he wiped his mask; glad to find the

last of the gas had leaked out of the attic. He held out a hand to let her know he wanted her to return downstairs, but Nini became stubborn to move. She pleaded with him to let her stay, almost teary-eyed again upon standing on the stairs. But Dan's focus remained on the queen.

"But Dan," Nini said, reaching step two. "This is suicide."

"Please. I need to do this on my own," Dan replied, lifting his gun towards the queen. "I'll be fine."

Nini lowered her head as she walked down the stairs before taking off her mask to throw against a wall; reaching Jon to hug him as she listened out for Dan. She hoped he was on his way down, but his gun didn't go off.

Dan shook after realising he was on his own; his confidence fading to leave him regretting letting Nini go.

He glared at the queen, wanting her to attack so he could wipe her out completely. But she wasn't trying to get up. She seemed to *fear* Dan.

She whined to make him think she was like a helpless puppy, but her attempt to grab his attention faded after he remembered what Jon told him about her faking it.

He removed the mask as he closed in, but the smell of her burnt skin left his nose sore.

He stared into her eyes, wanting her to see the pain of losing his grandfather, but she just flipped out a tongue and shrieked.

Dan felt sorrow towards her so stalled again to finish her off before noticing tears drip down her face to make him gulp. He breathed deeply as he switched his torch into blowtorch mode, but the flame frightened the queen to shock him.

He avoided her faint flapping wings upon watching her act like she knew she was about to die before taking a deep breath to lash out with the blowtorch, slicing her head clean off.

CHAPTER FORTY-SIX

Dan slowly entered the outside, dragging the queen's head along the ground to be watched by everyone there; their faces squirming after seeing green liquid drip off his clothing.

He let go of the head to see the tongue unfold like a red carpet, as the crowd became restless to rush the officers to get inside the house. But Dan just let them. He was happy it was over.

He stared at Jon and Nini before shrugging his shoulders after the reality of what happened caught him up, knowing they were drained of energy.

"Just leave them," he said, as Nini hugged him. "Let them have some fun. It's over now."

"But the house could fall at any time," Nini said, pointing towards the chimney as it collapsed.

"Fuck!" Dan hollered. "I forgot about that."

They saw the people race back outside, puffing out cheeks as the upstairs caved in; shaking their heads in anger towards Dan as they headed home. But Jon just smiled and patted him on the arm.

"Looks like the neighbours hate you now."

Dan shrugged again and smiled back.

———

He led Nini and Jon inside the hospital as the time reached *9:30 pm* but winced after checking his blood-stained uniform.

He never spoke as they neared the ward, but Jon and Nini knew it was because he was trying to find the right words to explain to Ben what had happened to Neal.

All they could do was be there for him when it happened.

Dan became nervous as he looked up to see the Ward sign, feeling itchy the closer he got to Ben. But Nini smiled and held his hand, reassuring him that everything would be fine.

They closed in to see Ben searching for Neal, pulling a face like he knew he was somewhere nearby. But Dan almost lost it.

"You okay?" Nini asked, squeezing his hand. "You've got this. He needs to know."

"I know he does."

They reached Ben as he held up his hands; smiling like he expected Neal to jump out on him. But no one was smiling back.

It worried Ben as he waited for someone to speak.

He gulped after seeing the sadness in their eyes, his heart skipping beats from the agony of not knowing the truth.

"It's a bit late for a visit," he nervously said. "Where's Neal? Is he back at the station?..."

Nini and Jon cowered behind Dan to bring tears to Ben's eyes, as their lack of eye contact gave him the answer. But he stared at them, still wanting to hear it.

"...I know there's something up, so who's goin' to tell me?"

"It's Neal," Dan softly said, standing by the bed.

But Ben pretended he didn't hear as his mind desperately searched for something positive to take the place of the sad news that was about to arrive.

He saw Dan sit in a chair before placing his hands on the bed, clasping them together as if he was praying.

"...Ben, speak to me," Dan said, feeling nervous. "You need to know what happened."

"I know what happened. He never made it," Ben snapped, releasing tears before closing his eyes. He heard the others send out words of comfort, but his heart sunk into his chest. "You can go now."

EPILOGUE

Two cocoon-like shells shook inside the spaceship, with one moving violently until a hand burst through to reveal a young girl.

She climbed out to wipe sticky liquid from her body, feeling lost and confused as to why? and how? she ended up where she was.

She stared at the other shell, touching it to see a person trying to get out; her heartbeat flickering after seeing the shell swing from side to side.

"Hey! Can you hear me?" she asked, noticing the person stop moving. "I can see you. Do you need help?"

She released more liquid before flicking it off her fingers as a flashback of her standing with her mother in the street entered her mind. She looked around to see lights on a large metal-like wall, observing them before realising she wasn't anywhere near home.

But where am I?

She shouted again as the other person moved before the shell split open to reveal a girl she recognised from school. But, as she walked closer to help the girl out of the shell choked and spat up blood. She held her stomach as pain suddenly ripped through her, as the red liquid poured from her nose; staring at the girl to plead with her to help before dropping onto the floor to scream in agony. She saw the girl climb out of the shell as more blood spilt from her mouth before shuddering as she tried to get up. But her eyes showed no signs of life as her stomach cracked open, revealing a horde of tiny insects.

The other girl smiled after seeing them devour flesh before forming into a dark shadow to hover towards her. She knelt and stared at the torn body before moving her head to one side, placing a finger into the blood to suck it off. It made her excited.

She sniffed the body, licking more blood before savagely biting into the girl's neck; shrieking as she returned to her feet to allow the insects to crawl over her. She didn't fear them.

She walked through the blood, acting fascinated by the lights that controlled the spaceship; watching them flash to please her before vanishing to appear seconds later on the ice-cold street; soaking up the wind like it was nothing as she smiled and walked home.

———

A scientist wearing a thick, thermal-lined padded coat, thick gloves and a mask walked inside the secret government building where Eddie Mckay once worked; holding a tray filled with test tubes upon nearing a large refrigeration room. He opened the door and entered, placing the tray onto a shelf before aiming for a plastic sheet; smiling as it was moved to reveal a large ice cube filled with bugs.

And next to it stood a frozen alien queen.

ABOUT THE AUTHOR

Lee lives in Bedworth, Warwickshire, England.

He writes novels that read like movies playing out on paper, taking the reader into an imaginary world that he created. He adds comedy moments in his stories to break up the horror, with silly characters who will make you laugh.

Lee wants readers to see inside their minds the stories he writes, and to live with the characters as they battle the enemy.

Lee's stories are not written to confuse, but to entertain the reader, and to make the reader smile.

———

His novel - *Clifton Falls* - was originally released as *Zombies (Morgue of the Dead)* around 2011, but he changed the name to the movie script version. He has rewritten the novel as a 2 part story, releasing Part 2 in the summer of 2022.

mybook./cliftonfalls2

Part 3 is scheduled for release in 2023.

———

Lee's other released novel is a story about "Killer Rats." Titled - *The S.T.A.R.S. PROJECT* – (Scientific testing aimed at a rat's survival)

It was released in 2018 and is also available from Amazon Worldwide.

mybook.to/thestarsproject

———

Lee also writes movie scripts, with 11 written to date. And he's also written a Sci-fi, horror TV pilot for a British Production Company.

———

To keep tabs on Lee's progress please LIKE his Facebook author page –

facebook.com/mrwritermanauthor

or check out his website –

taylorlee544.wixsite.com

Ingram Content Group UK Ltd.
Milton Keynes UK
UKHW010726070623
423023UK00001B/11

9 798223 199120